GRUMPY THE BEAR

BLUEBALL BAND OF BROTHERS

MARIKA RAY

Grumpy the Bear

Copyright © 2023 by Marika Ray

This book is a work of fiction. Names, characters, places, and incidents are products of the author's imagination or are used fictitiously. Any resemblance to actual events, locales, or persons, living or dead, is entirely coincidental.

First Edition: June 8, 2023
Cover Model: Blaze
Photographer: Wander Aguiar
Cover Artist: Jennifer Olson

Ebook ISBN: 978-1-950141-59-3
Original Paperback: 978-1-950141-60-9
Special Edition Paperback ISBN:

DESCRIPTION

He's a tattooed, blue-eyed jerk who has no business being a single dad. He's also my next-door neighbor, and after negotiations, my grumpy employer for the summer.

I don't put up with cocky males normally and I certainly won't put up with that man making noise at all hours of the day and night while he builds his glamp-ground. I offer advice, but the stubborn fool just turns his tractor on to drown me out. He returns the favor by pushing my buttons and making me so angry I can't see straight. And I really want to be able to see his gorgeous body in those well-worn jeans and backward hat.

Amidst the verbal warfare, I discover he's hiding scars from a recent accident. I also find out his light eyes heat up to a smoldering icy gray when I give as good as I get. Makes me want to see just how far I can push him and what he'll do when he boils over.

Gannon's been dealt a rough hand in life, and when I find a way under that gruff—and stupidly handsome—exterior, I find that maybe he's not Grumpy the Bear as I nicknamed him, but instead just a teddy bear.

CHAPTER ONE

annon

I NEVER THOUGHT rock bottom would feature a shit ton of dolls and a tongue that never stopped licking me.

Yet here I was in my truck, driving across farmland that looked several years deep in a drought, dancing a doll across my dashboard to entertain my daughter and fending off a puppy spinning around in a circle on the passenger seat before leaping across the console to paint his tongue across my face for the fifth time in as many minutes.

"Down, Meatball!" The little mutt just looked up at me with misplaced adoration and not one lick of sense in his head.

"Be nice, Daddy!" Elise chimed in from the child seat in the back. Thank God for five-point harnesses to keep the minx in one spot while I drove. Maybe Meatball needed one too.

A headache was brewing, but that was nothing new. Probably had one for six straight months now, one that not even the heavy-duty painkillers could take away. You see, my life had been golden for close to thirty-five years. Sure, I'd lost my mama when

I was a little boy, but my dad, while a bit on the cold, demanding side, had been decent, all things considered. I'd played football to burn up my teenage aggression and then moved up the ranks as a firefighter as an adult. I'd been told a few times I wasn't bad looking, so I enjoyed sowing my wild oats with the ladies, never once wanting to settle down. One oat went a little too wild, but that was a story for another day.

"We're almost there, E-bug." I glanced in the mirror to see her bopping her dark head of curls to the country song playing through the speakers. By five-year-old standards, my daughter was adorable. I'd taken one look at her on my doorstep six months ago and nearly had a heart attack. After the initial shock of her existence wore off, I'd fallen on my ass yet again, this time straight up in love with the girl.

The front wheel of the truck hit a pothole as I made a sharp left onto a dirt road. Meatball slid to the floorboard in a heap of trash from our fast-food lunch. Elise let out a squeal of excitement, all four of her limbs raised in the air, dancing about. The silver Airstream trailer I'd bought for a song and a whistle from a guy too old to use it any longer was waiting for us at the end of the drive. She gleamed something pretty in the dying sunlight.

"Home sweet home," I muttered, bouncing up the last bit of driveway to our new home.

I'd taken every single penny of my disability check and bought five acres of land in Blueball, California, a small town on the edge of the Pacific Ocean, tucked into the pine trees like a well-kept secret. Bain Sutter, an old friend from my high school days, had suggested the town to me when I called, looking for advice about my new business adventure. I didn't normally ask for advice, so when I finally asked, you bet your ass I listened. Dad thought I'd lost my mind and told me so every chance he got, but considering how much he helped out after my accident, I couldn't tell him to shove it. I'd swallowed down the criticism, determined as ever to make this new venture work.

"Uh-oh," Elise singsonged from her seat.

"What?" I spun around and got a mouth full of Meatball's tongue. The damn thing managed to french me yet again. Sadly, I'd gotten more action from the dog than I had a warm-blooded woman the last six months.

"Down, Meatball!"

"I have to pee, Daddy!" I'd learned that everything out of Elise's mouth was spoken at a volume that signaled an emergency. Based on how much she was wiggling, I figured I had another few minutes before she burst.

"Let's get you out, then, huh?" I clicked the seat belt and climbed out of the truck, careful to keep Meatball inside. That damn thing might run away and break Elise's heart if I wasn't careful. I got in the backseat and managed to only swear once while trying to unsnap the harness of her car seat.

"Come on. Let's check out our new bathroom." Meatball jumped in the backseat and I grabbed him under my right arm, Elise on my left. With a hip check, I got the door closed and strode toward the trailer. When I got there, I realized I'd have to put one of them down to get to the key that was in my front pocket. I looked back and forth, wondering if I trusted a five-year-old or a puppy more. It was a crapshoot, honestly.

I put Elise down in the dirt with a stern warning to stay put. My leg cramped as I stood back up, but I ignored it. I didn't have time for that shit. I had a life to build.

The key fit in the lock and the door swung open before Meatball licked me again or Elise ran off, so I considered that a win. Minor as it might be, I was chalking it up in the win column. It was a pretty desolate column so far.

"I'm ho-me!" I sang to the trailer, picking Elise back up and climbing the two metal stairs to enter.

I ducked my head automatically, then realized I didn't need to. You didn't grow up to be six feet five and not duck your head through doorways. Only took one concussion at sixteen to drive that lesson home. Thankfully, this RV had a ceiling height that would allow me to stand straight up, praise the Lord.

I turned in a circle, locating the bathroom at the south end of the trailer. I had to slide sideways to fit through the doorway, but got Elise to the bathroom in time for her to pee in the toilet and not on the floor. Meatball got the zoomies and ran up and down the aisle of the trailer, only pausing to sniff out his new home after he was panting with his little tongue hanging out.

Elise pulled her underwear up after doing her business and tried to reach the sink. I helped her, happy I'd hired a guy to come out ahead of us and hook up the water and sewer lines.

"Now what?" Elise looked up at me, then made a face with her eyes crossed and her tongue hanging out, looking surprisingly like Meatball.

I clapped my hands, the first glimmer of excitement hitting me. We were finally here. "Let's build Glamper's Paradise!"

Elise wrinkled her button nose. "Wamper dice?"

"No, Glamper's Paradise." I leaned down and swung Elise up into my arms, almost clipping her head on the ceiling. Damn. I'd have to watch that. I wasn't used to living in an RV. "I'm building a place where people can come and rent trailers on their vacations. It's like camping, but fancier."

Elise pulled the baseball cap off my head and plopped it on hers, the bill covering her eyes entirely. "What's camping?"

"Okay, that's enough questions for now. Let's find the leash for Meatball and walk around our land, huh?"

Elise put her hands out like a zombie. "Where are you, Daddy? I can't see you."

I shook my head, finding her adorable and yet so dang tiring. The energy of a five-year-old was a lot, even on my best days. And I hadn't had any best days in six months. I pulled the hat off her head and threw it on the table.

"Actually, let me make a phone call first. Can you sit at the table and play with your dolls for a second?"

I plunked her down at the Formica tabletop, impressed with the leather seats. Maybe I hadn't bought a hunk of junk like my father kept saying. I pulled out two dolls from my pocket—on day two of being a dad I learned to always carry dolls with me to stave off tantrums—and handed them to her. Her eyes lit up, and she immediately went into self-play mode. I wasn't sure she should be so good at self-play mode at her age, which made me worry about how her mother had treated her the first five years of her life. But that worry would just have to wait.

"Gannon! You made it?" Bain answered my call almost immediately.

I scratched the top of my head. "I made it alright. Trailer looks good. Haven't had a chance to walk the land yet, but I will shortly. Hey, I got another favor to ask."

"Sure, man. What's up?"

I hated asking favors or asking for advice, but hitting rock bottom had humbled me in a way I hadn't anticipated. "You got any idea who might want to be a nanny this summer? Someone good with five-year-olds?" I looked down at my precious girl, a sense of protectiveness hitting me like a freight train. Fuck mama bear. This was papa bear mode. "Preferably a female?"

"Not off the top of my head, but my wife, Lucy, would know of someone. Let me ask her. She'll have women coming by to interview by tomorrow." Bain chuckled.

"Okay, that'd be fine."

"Hey, if no one's told you yet, welcome to the area. Blueball isn't Auburn Hell, but it'll do."

I scoffed. "Blueball kind of describes my predicament, so it seems fitting."

"Fatherhood will do that. Don't worry, they get older and you can find alone time again."

I thought about my mangled leg and single status and shook off that idea. "Yeah, well, I just need to get Glamper's Paradise up and running and I'll be satisfied enough."

"Let me know when you got the first one ready. Lucy, myself, and the kids will be your first renters."

I looked down at my boots. Good friends were hard to come by. I should know. "Thanks, man."

We hung up and I texted Dad to let him know we got in safely. He answered almost immediately, and I wished he hadn't.

Dad: Glad to hear it. Better get that thing up and running or you'll run out of money.

I didn't bother answering. Panic, the kind I never even felt when entering a burning building, twisted my insides. Life had handed me some shit the last few months, and I was trying to make the best of it.

I'd purposely never gotten seriously involved with a woman because I didn't want anyone depending on me. I had a good career because I craved stability and a decent job I could have until retirement. All that blew up when that house had blown hotter than it should have. The blast was unexpected and so was the white-hot pain that lit up my right leg. My buddies had gotten me out, but not before eighty percent of my leg was covered in deep second-degree burns. I'd spent a week in the hospital, followed by some of the most painful doctor visits I tried to forget about. Even just thinking back on that time made me break out in a cold sweat. Work had given me six weeks of paid time off to recover, barely enough to wrap my head around my injury, let alone be back to full speed for the job.

It was on week five, just when I was starting to see the light at the end of the tunnel, when I heard the ominous knock on my front door.

"Daddy?"

I blinked, seeing that Elise had her arm up, the redheaded doll extended out to me. "Yeah, E-bug?"

"Play with me!"

How could I ignore those pretty blue eyes that nearly disappeared into her cheeks when she smiled?

I swung into the seat opposite her and held the doll in front of my face. Throwing my voice into a falsetto, I gave her what she needed. "Oh, hello there, Crabby. You look nice today."

Elise giggled, as I knew she would. "It's Abby, Daddy!"

"Oh, sorry," I said, still in the falsetto. "Let's be friends, Abby."

Elise made her doll jump across the table. "Okay! Let's walk the dog."

We both looked over at Meatball, who stood by the refrigerator with an innocent look on his face. He lifted his leg and peed on my new appliance, not even blinking. Savage little thing.

I knocked the underside of the tabletop scrambling out of my seat but he was already done emptying his bladder. "Jesus H. Christ, Meatball!"

Elise came up behind me. "Jesus H. Cwist, Meatball!" Her voice was almost an exact replica of mine, just a few octaves higher.

I sighed, taking a second to rub my pounding head, and then grabbed the dog. "Let's go take that walk, huh?"

"Okay, Daddy." Her sweet little hand slipped into mine, and even with everything pressing in around me, I held my shit together.

Barely.

Always for her.

CHAPTER TWO

aisley

"WELL, I think this little break is perfect. You can put your focus on dating again. How is it that all five Hellman brothers have managed to find spouses and you haven't, Paisley?"

I rolled my eyes and focused on keeping the cell phone jammed between my ear and my shoulder as I hopped from my bedroom to the bathroom. Not as easy as you'd think, especially when what I really wanted was to drop the phone and end this horrific conversation with my parents.

"I don't know, Mom. Those boys are pretty good looking." It was true. I'd even dated one of them—Ethan, the youngest one—when we were seniors in high school. He'd been such a gentleman he waited until we both turned eighteen before taking my virginity. Sadly, we grew apart quickly after high school and decided to move on as friends.

"Well, you're a beautiful girl, too. That hard hat doesn't do much for you, but you clean up well." Mom sniffed, and I heard a whole lot of judgement in that whiff of air. She and Dad had never approved of my choice of employment. Line work was a man's job, they said.

"Speaking of." I grabbed on to the lifeline with all I had. "I need to get going. The girls are coming over tonight and I'd like to shower and do my nails."

"Oh? Maybe you could go out with the girls instead? Maybe run into an eligible bachelor?"

I squeezed my eyes shut and counted to ten, the latest technique I was trying out to deal with my mother.

"Paisley?"

My eyes popped open on ten and I didn't feel any calmer. "That's a great idea, Mom. Thank you."

"You bet. I'm happy to help my girl find her future husband. I can't wait to show off my grandbabies." Mom sounded delusional. As usual.

A giggle almost escaped at the rhyme. "Okay, sounds great. Love you!"

I hung up and let the phone clank onto the countertop, staring wide-eyed at myself in the mirror. "Ugh!"

Whenever I got frustrated, I'd taken to bellowing out the most guttural sound I could manage. It helped. Slightly.

"Little break?" I asked my reflection, crossing my eyes and sticking out my tongue, behavior I would never engage in outside of my own house.

I wasn't on a break from my job as a line worker for the county. I was on job disability from slipping off the bottom rung of the pole like a total rookie. The company doctor had ordered X-rays and then diagnosed me with a high ankle sprain. I'd been ready to suit back up and get out there, but my foreman had sent me home with an order not to come back for four weeks.

Four weeks! What the hell was I supposed to do with four weeks of paid time off? Keva, Audrey, and Marlo, my three best friends, had tried to tell me that this time off was living the dream. More like nightmare. I had nothing to occupy my days on crutches and boring nights staring at the ceiling, contemplating where my life was going.

Unlike Mom's ambitions for my life, I was not aiming for a husband by thirty. I wanted to be foreman by the next decade, and that wasn't going to happen if I was away from the job for a whole month. It was hard enough convincing all the males at work that I was perfectly capable despite doing everything they could do and hiding my aching muscles under layers of an icy/hot rub I bought by the gallon. Now that I was injured? It would be doubly hard.

A car door slamming had me hopping out of the bathroom and to the window at the side of my bedroom. A truck had shown up next door overnight. I'd heard the acreage next to me had been sold, but I hadn't found out who bought it and what they intended to do with it. I was hoping for a regenerative garden run by a middle-aged woman who could become my adoptive mom friend.

Currently, a woman who was most definitely not middle aged, in cork wedges and a sundress I coveted, sashayed her way across the dirt and knocked on the door of the Airstream. The door popped open, but I couldn't see who was inside. The woman climbed the stairs with a feminine giggle I could hear all the way over here.

I rolled my eyes and let the curtain fall over the window. Great. I had a new neighbor who was probably some creep who liked to hire female companions. Snatching the nail polish off my end table, I flopped on the bed and maneuvered my booted foot onto the mattress so I could reach my toes. The polish on my pinkie toe had started to chip off, and I hated that. My fingernails were total trash from my job, but I liked to keep a nice pedicure to balance the feminine scales. When that was sufficiently touched up, I grabbed my crutches and headed for the bathroom to start my shower. Wasn't easy showering with one foot hanging out the shower curtain.

I'd just rinsed out a new Brazilian conditioner from my long hair when I heard a pounding on my front door. Smelling like I was coming off a beach vacation surrounded by coconuts and cabana boys, I wrapped a towel around me, grabbed my crutches, and headed for the door the best I could still slippery as an eel. The girls weren't supposed to be here for another hour.

I swung the door open and nearly sent myself to the ground when it clipped my right crutch and sent it pinging off into the wall. My weight shifted, but I was a strong girl. I righted myself and tucked the towel in tighter across my chest. A tall man in jeans and a T-shirt stood on my doorstep, the kind of good looking and pissed off that instantly made my ovaries take my mom's side of the argument. Maybe finding a spouse was a good idea after all.

"Hello?" the man groused from a jaw I wanted to run my tongue along just to see what his whiskers felt like.

I blinked. Wait a minute. I should be the one grousing. I was the one who was rudely pulled from their shower.

"Yes?" I snapped back, plenty of don't-give-me-no-shit in my tone. I dealt with know-it-all men every damn day on the job. *Don't try me, handsome.*

Disturbingly light gray-blue eyes stared at me from beneath the bill of a trucker hat. The man lifted his hand in the air, his fist wrapped tightly around something bright red. His muscled shoulders blocked all the sunlight from the doorway.

"These yours?" he asked, words clipped as if expending any further energy on the simple sentence was just too much for the man.

I frowned and put out my hand without thinking. He immediately let his fist go and the red ball dropped into my palm. It was as it draped onto my hand that I saw the familiar lace. My brain froze and my insides went hot, a confusing combination.

This perverted new neighbor of mine had my panties.

"What the fuck?" I snapped, closing my hand around the satin and whipping it behind my back.

He dropped my gaze, pulling his hat off his head and

scratching his thick dark hair before plopping it back on his head. He had colorful tattoos up and down both arms. "You, uh, have your laundry on the line."

He gestured to my side yard, the one that separated my land from his. I had a clothesline I kept there for drying all the clothes that couldn't be shoved in the dryer, which was surprisingly a lot. Sadly, there was no privacy fence yet. Hadn't felt the need to spend the money on one when no one lived next door. That would be changing. Like, tomorrow.

"You pervert!" I snapped, hand closing around the doorknob and sliding off because of the satin still clutched in my hand.

His icy gaze snapped up to mine in alarm. "No! It's just that Meatball—"

I swung my arm in an arc, slamming the door in his handsome face. Those softball batting lessons in high school finally came in clutch as the whole wall shook from the force. I, too, shook with rage. What kind of asshole introduces himself to the new neighbor by stealing her underwear and then giving it back to her like he wanted some sort of medal for being a knight in shining armor?

"The perverted kind, that's who," I grumbled to myself.

"No, I swear. I just found the, uh, underwear," the guy said, clearly still on my doorstep. And he'd clearly overheard me through the door.

I glared at the door. "Sure you did, buddy. How about you get off my property before I get my shotgun and make you?" I didn't actually have a shotgun, but he didn't know that.

"Whoa. Okay, yeah. I'm sorry about the, uh, underwear thing. I'll keep a better eye on Meatball."

I frowned at the door, listening as he walked away, boots crunching against the cement walkway. Who the hell was Meatball? Were there *two* guys who had moved in next door? I fetched my crutch, the one that slid to the floor, and hobbled away from the door. I saw movement out one of my living room windows and I stopped to watch as the man walked back to his

Airstream. I found myself shaking my head. The man had one fine ass in those jeans, made finer by the broad shoulders above. Too bad he had a panty-snatching problem.

As the man pulled open his door, a streak of reddish brown bolted out and across the dirt. The new neighbor hollered and ran after him, hat flying off and landing in a cloud of dust. It was kind of funny watching a grown man chase a puppy. The guy moved pretty quick for being so large, but ultimately the puppy bested him by coming full circle, and at the last second, leaping back into the trailer through the open door.

"Goddammit, Meatball!" the man hollered, stooping to pick up his hat and plunk it down on his head. He straightened and looked right at me through the window. I froze. He huffed and turned away, stalking across the dirt and back into his trailer.

Well, I found out who Meatball was, and I liked him better than my neighbor.

Glancing at the clock, I hobbled to my bedroom and sank onto the bed. My hours were still messed up from being on graveyard for over a year. I'd just catch a quick catnap before I had to get ready for the girls' night in.

***

"You look like you're doing this time-off thing right," Audrey drawled, pulling a can of ranch water out of her paper bag and tossing it to me.

The girls had had to pound on my door to wake me up. That power nap had turned into a deep slumber of blue-eyed giants and puppy dogs in a field of lavender. Currently, I had my foot propped up on the coffee table while my three best friends sat around me, sipping our canned drinks and opening a bag of tortilla chips. All of us stocked up on the handmade salsa old Mrs. Rodriguez sold at the Saturday farmer's market. No one made salsa like Mrs. Rodriquez, so we were sure to always have some on hand for lazy summer afternoons like this one. Nothing was better than chips and salsa when the pavement was hot enough to melt your skin off.

"I don't know about that," I mumbled. "I think I just got so mad at my new neighbor, I had to sleep it off."

"Oh no. Who bought the place?" Keva asked, checking her phone. She was a single mom. If her son wasn't with her, she was always checking her phone.

"Some asshole."

"Wow. That bad?" Marlo sat back in the couch and tucked her black jeans-clad legs under her. Marlo always wore black. To fit her mood.

I shrugged and swallowed my bite of tortilla chip and salsa. "He snatched a pair of my panties off the clothesline."

Keva gasped.

"How'd you find out? Did a pair just go missing? Did he confess?" Audrey asked all the questions.

"He banged on my door and handed them back."

Audrey and Keva exchanged a look while Marlo just shook her head, her shiny black hair swinging.

"Okay, but why would he bring them back if he was using them nefariously?" Audrey asked.

"And don't panty sniffers usually like them dirty, not clean?" Keva interjected.

I took another sip of my drink and grimaced. "How should I know? I don't hang out with panty thieves."

The rumble of an engine, followed by a loud enough whoop to wake the whole town, cut through our conversation. All four of us scrambled to our feet, but my three friends got to the front window faster than me on account of my crutches. The ranch water wasn't exactly helping my coordination either.

"Holy mother of asses, Batman," Keva breathed against the window.

"I swear on all things holy I will give up chocolate if he takes that shirt off," Audrey said reverently.

"Guys." I tried to push my way through, but they weren't budging. "What's happening?"

"Hey, he's got one of those new scrapers." Marlo pointed out the window. "We have a backhoe, but it's way older than that rig."

"What the hell?" I hip checked Keva and got a front-row seat to the action taking place next door.

My panty-snatching neighbor had a little girl duct-taped to the trunk of the tree in his front yard while he ground the gears on the John Deere scraper, letting out a terrible racket. The puppy I'd seen earlier ran in circles between the two with little concern for its safety.

"Dear God, he's truly insane," I whispered, not sure who to worry about more. The little girl or the dog.

When the little girl let out a cheer looking relatively unharmed and the dog took that moment to face-plant into the blade on the front of the scraper, I'd had enough. Crutches flying and ankle screaming at me, I wrenched the front door open.

I had some choice things to say to this asshole.

CHAPTER THREE

annon

THE THREE WOMEN Lucy Sutter had sent to my trailer were entirely unsuitable. The first one had felt up my biceps before licking her lips suggestively. My libido tried to rev its engine, but died a quick death when Elise toddled through the trailer without her normal sundress on.

"Daddy, I missed."

I'd spun around to find her in just a pair of underwear and a purple plastic bracelet on her wrist.

"Missed what?"

"The toolet." She grinned up at me, showing all her baby teeth, her eyes closing to slits on account of her chunky cheeks.

"Okay, go get dressed and I'll clean it up in a second."

I spun back around to see the woman grimacing. Not a good sign. Five-year-olds were known for making messes with mysterious fluids.

"How do you feel about cleaning?"

The woman snapped her painted lips back together and dug

in her purse before handing me a business card. Pretty sure the damn thing had been sprayed with perfume. Her name and phone number were the only thing printed on the fancy cardstock.

"I don't think this position is for me, but why don't you give me a call? I can show you around or simply take you out for a drink once the...little one...has a sitter."

The way she said little one told me everything I needed to know about this woman. Papa bear wasn't happy.

"Yep. Have a nice day." I swung open the door and kept the thing open to air out the place long after she'd left.

The next two had also been unsuitable. They seemed to like children just fine, but the one had a mole on the side of her cheek that had a dark hair growing from it. There was no way I could have her coming and going around here every day without making some kind of mole joke, like Austin Powers in that one horrible yet somehow funny movie. I knew my lack of a filter would be an issue.

The second one was too pretty. And way too young. That would also not be a good pairing, for obvious reasons. I was new in town and hoping to build a life here for my daughter. I had no intention of having some dad on my doorstep with a shotgun for staring at his little girl.

Speaking of shotguns and pretty girls, I had a feeling I was already on the wrong foot with my neighbor. I'd been trying to do something nice by returning the pair of underwear I'd found Meatball wearing on his head. When I saw her clothesline, I assumed they were hers. I hadn't quite anticipated how it would look when I returned them, or the names she would call me.

Anyway, that was all in the past. The present was looking mighty fine. Elise was safely out of the way and my scraper had been delivered. Given enough time free of dogs and kids, I could get the land scraped for the first couple of trailer sites.

"What the hell do you think you're doing?"

I pivoted in the seat of the scraper and peered down at my

neighbor. She looked pissed again. Or maybe she just always looked that way. At least she was dressed this time, though the cutoff jean shorts and strappy tank top didn't cover as much tanned skin as her towel had.

I lifted my hand to my ear. "What's that? I can't hear you."

"Turn it off, asshole!"

Ah, okay, we were back to name-calling. What a delight this neighbor was turning out to be. With a sigh, I turned the key and felt the engine vibrate off. When all I could hear was off-tune singing from Elise and the panting of Meatball as he ran over, I turned back to the woman.

"Can I help you?"

"You sure can, cowboy. How about you secure your dog and child before I call CPS and the ASPCA?" She took her crutches from under her arms and leaned them against my scraper.

Meatball sniffed the boot on one of her feet and started to lift his leg above the other shoe. I whistled harshly, and he put his leg down.

"Oh, well, now that sounds interesting. Should we call the FBI and the CIA while we're at it? How about CSI and ATF?" I could think of a dozen more.

Her pretty face scrunched up. "What?"

I shrugged, noticing that three other women had somehow come out of her house to pile onto her doorstep, all staring at us like we were the only entertainment in this town. "I thought we were throwing around acronyms, my bad."

The woman huffed, but one of the ladies on her doorstep snorted out a laugh before her friend elbowed her and cut her off.

"You can't duct-tape your kid to a tree." The woman crossed her arms over her chest and I had to swallow hard and look away. I kind of wished she was back in that towel that hid everything. My neighbor couldn't be much older than the girl that had come by wanting to be a nanny this summer. I definitely shouldn't be looking at her tits.

"Why not? It's like a car seat, but in a tree." Elise took that moment to pull a leaf off the nearest tree branch and put it in her mouth before spitting it out.

"That's why!" My neighbor half hopped, half hobbled on her booted foot over to the tree. Meatball followed her, ears flopping in the wind. Before I could express my displeasure, she began to rip pieces of tape off my masterpiece of a tree-seat.

"Hey!" I scrambled to get off the tractor, ignoring the pain in my leg to jog over and intercept whatever this whacko lady had in mind. "What the hell do you think you're doing?"

The woman ripped another piece of tape off, smiling at my girl before turning a frown on me. "Rescuing this little girl before she harms herself without adult supervision."

That pissed me off. "Adult supervision? I'm right here, lady. Don't get much adulter than her own daddy."

The woman's hands froze mid-rip. "This is your daughter?"

I put my hands on my hips, just about done with this woman, despite how pretty she looked with her long blonde hair and skimpy outfit that reminded me of summers at the lake without a care in the world. For having not known Elise existed until a few months ago, she was my world. And she looked like a female, little-kid spitting image of me. Same light eyes, dark hair, and spicy personality.

"Yes, this is Elise, my five-year-old daughter. So if you could kindly take yourself elsewhere, preferably not on my property, I can get back to work."

Instead of leaving immediately, like I hoped my thunderous look would convey, the woman turned to my daughter and introduced herself. "Hey, Elise. I'm Paisley Pearse. I live next door."

"I'm Elise and I live there." Elise pointed at the trailer. "And dat's my daddy!" Then she pointed at me. "He snores when he sleeps."

Paisley rolled her lips inward before nodding. "That sounds about right. Well, it's super awesome to meet you. Maybe we can play sometime? I was hoping to plant some flowers outside and maybe you can help me."

"I love fwowers!" Elise squealed.

"Me too. Especially the red ones. Oh! Or maybe purple like your bracelet." Paisley pointed to my daughter's fashion jewelry, the one piece she'd had on her when her mother deposited her on my doorstep and left without looking back.

"Okay, well, we'll have to see if we can work that into our busy schedule." I moved to stand in between Paisley and my daughter. Elise proceeded to kick me in the back.

Paisley narrowed her eyes at me, as if studying what lay beyond the surface and finding me lacking. Her assessment was not wrong.

"Listen, why don't you text me next time you have some power tools you need to use? I can watch Elise for a bit so she doesn't have to be taped to a tree." There was a hell of a lot of judgement in that last sentence.

I folded my arms across my chest. "You got a background check I can read through first?"

One of Paisley's eyebrows lifted, and I got the sense she never backed down from a challenge. "Do *you* have a background check I can read?"

I shrugged, enjoying the way she got so riled up. "Didn't expect to need one."

"Same, cowboy, same."

I pointed down to her boot where Meatball was currently seated, panting up at the woman like she was his new favorite toy. "How you gonna watch Elise with a bum foot?"

"It's a bum ankle and I can do just fine with a boot. Better than duct-taping her to a tree."

Damn. The woman just wouldn't get over that. I thought the idea had been a stroke of genius, but apparently some people couldn't see past their conventional ideas of safety seats. I fished out the cell phone from my back pocket, pulling up a new contact.

"Alright, give me your number and I'll text you."

Paisley rattled off her numbers and watched me shoot her a text before sliding the phone back in my pocket.

"You going to give me your name or should I just keep calling you cowboy?"

A grin threatened to pull on my cheek. "I kind of like cowboy. Has a nice ring to it."

She tilted her head and gave me a deadpan look.

"Okay, fine, if you insist. I'm Gannon. Gannon Hart." I stuck out my hand, and she took it, her handshake almost as firm as mine. If I wasn't mistaken, the woman had some callouses lining her palm which didn't vibe with showering and hanging out with friends in the middle of the workday. "You got working hours I should know about?"

Paisley took her hand back and put it in her shorts pocket. Her shoulders, the ones that looked like she lifted weights with the big boys, were starting to get pink out here. "I'm on temporary disability right now, on account of the bum ankle."

"Ah. Tripped over the step ladder at the library?" When Paisley lifted that eyebrow again in challenge, I guessed again. "Slipped in the flour on the floor at the bakery?"

"I slipped in pee today," Elise announced from behind me.

I grimaced, but Paisley just laughed. "I'm a line worker."

I have a pretty fuckin' good poker face, but nothing prepared me for that. This woman, the one with the long blonde hair, pretty painted toes, and breasts that would overflow my palms just perfectly, was a lineman? Line person? Line worker. Whatever the hell they called themselves these days.

"Damn. That's not an easy job." Wasn't a safe one either. I'd had plenty of friends who'd been linemen for a bit. Made good money and then gave it up before they got seriously hurt. Paisley was lucky it was just a sprained ankle.

"Hey! Hi." Her group of friends had walked over, standing in the shade of the tree and waiting for us to notice them.

The short one came forward and shook my hand. "Hi, I'm

Keva. This is Audrey." She pointed at the tall blonde with a wide smile on her face. "And this is Marlo." The dark-haired one just sent me a two-fingered wave.

"These are my best friends," Paisley supplied.

"Abby's my best fwend!" Elise piped up. I wasn't going to explain that Abby was a doll.

"Nice to meet you all. I'm Gannon."

Keva grinned and she looked like she might be a tiny bit twisted behind that girlishly round face. "So glad Paisley has a friend out here now. With her stuck at home all month, we know she'll feel safer with a big strapping man out here to protect her."

"Okay, that's enough." Paisley pushed her friends back toward her house, calling over her shoulder, "Nice to meet you, Elise!"

Then she made brief eye contact with me, her dig clear. It wasn't nice meeting me. Well, same, lady, same. Only nice thing about meeting my neighbor was watching her walk away. The woman had an ass like an athlete, all firm muscle above shapely legs.

"Nice job. Got his digits, player," one of her friends whispered to Paisley. Loudly enough I could hear her and had to duck my head to hide my smile.

I would not be using Paisley's phone number to text anything but pertinent neighbor information. A refrain I repeated to myself over and over as I fired the scraper back up and got to work. I didn't get far before Elise needed a potty break and Meatball found something else to chew on that he shouldn't. As much as I didn't want to have Paisley watch Elise, it was becoming obvious that I'd need her help if I wanted to get anything done around here.

That night, as I popped a frozen lasagna in the tiny microwave above the one-burner cooktop, I pondered how to bathe Elise in a trailer that didn't have a bathtub. There was a garden hose outside, though I had a feeling Ms. Prim and Proper next door might have something to say about me hosing off my kid. Thing was, us boys at the fire station used to do a version of that every now and again when the captain wasn't around. Hilarious as shit to see a grown man try to stay on his feet when hit by a powerful spray. Not that I intended to do anything like that with Elise.

"Oh, Daddy," Elise called from my bedroom in the back of the trailer. "Abby needs you!"

I looked up at the ceiling and prayed for patience.

"Coming, bestie!" I called back in my highest falsetto.

aisley

MY PHONE RANG, waking me from a dead sleep, and I wasn't sure what time it was. Switching from night shift to daytime was a slow process when you had nowhere to be at any given time. I answered without looking at the screen, my first mistake.

"Hey, Pais," came a familiar voice on the other end. Benny Campbell was the only coworker of mine who dared called me by a nickname. The rest had tried, but I beat their ass out on the job, earning me the use of my full name and a small ration of respect. Benny was a special case of stupid.

"Benny, what a surprise." I sat up in bed and blinked to clear my vision. My alarm clock said five thirty in the morning.

"Just got off another shift without you there and thought I'd call. Everybody misses you."

That was a lie, and I wanted to know why he even bothered speaking it out loud. "Really? Did Ken cry from missing me so much?"

Ken was the oldest lineman on our crew and he hated me on

principal. Thought the work was only for men. I'd proven I could hold my own about a hundred times, but ol' Ken liked to settle in real deep with his long-held beliefs.

"Well, now, not Ken." Benny chuckled. "But I missed you. Figured I'd take you out to dinner to catch up since you're not at work anymore."

Was I still asleep and currently stuck in a nightmare? I scrubbed a hand across my eyes. Benny was only five years older than me, but he had that creepy air of the old guy that went to clubs to perve on all the young girls. I'd rather take a job selling hair bows than date Benny. "You know there's no dating coworkers, Benny."

"Ah, but you ain't a coworker now, are you? You're off for a month!"

"Still a coworker, just taking some time off. I appreciate the offer, but I have to go." I hung up on his sputtering, feeling a twinge of guilt for practically hanging up on him. I'd told him no about five times now if my count was correct. I reassured myself that the stronger measures were warranted to make sure he understood the meaning of the word no.

I swung my legs over the bed and fumbled for my crutches. I didn't want to put the heavy boot on quite yet, so crutches would have to work while I got ready and made breakfast. I was on my second cup of coffee and perusing the official City of Blueball social calendar—such was my depth of boredom—when my phone rang again.

"Batting a thousand today," I muttered, switching over into a peppy voice to greet my mother.

"To what do I owe the pleasure, Mom?"

"I got the invitation!"

I wracked my brain and came up empty. "Invitation to what?"

Her disappointed sigh was pretty much a given in every conversation we had. "The invitation to Nikki Hellman's wedding. Remember? She and Jason got engaged and kept telling everyone they were going to have a 'small, intimate gathering.'

We all knew that was code for only the 'it crowd' would be invited."

I put my mug in the sink and hopped back to my crutches, where they were propped against the tiny island. "You and Dad are part of the 'it crowd'?" Didn't sound like a group I wanted to be part of.

"Of course we are. Everyone wants me to write about their business in the magazine, and your father has represented pretty much everyone in their divorce."

My father was a divorce attorney with so much dirt on everyone in town I think he got hush invitations that he mistook as popularity. Mom wrote a column in a gardening magazine, so I wasn't sure she had the clout she thought she had, but they lived in Hell. Everyone was a little odd there. To be honest, everyone in Blueball was a little odd, too. Maybe that was why the two towns had a silent rivalry that went back a few generations.

"It was addressed to your father and I, but your name was on it with a plus-one. So, find a date, darling!"

I winced. "Pretty sure the plus-one thing is just an option."

"Paisley." Mom's voice was firm. I could just see the face she was making with her reading glasses slid to the tip of her nose. "You're going and you're bringing a date. I already responded. Plus, you can't show up single with all those Hellman boys married."

"I'm pretty sure I can."

"Paisley."

I counted to ten. Even thought of something really horrible to help me reframe this conversation. Nothing was working. My phone vibrated in my hand and I pulled it away from my ear to check the notification. It was a text. I put the phone back to my ear.

"Fine, Mom. Let me think on it. I'll let you know."

"Oh, but I have ideas. What about—"

"Mom! I said I'll think on it. I gotta go."

"Okay, bye, love you!" she rushed to say before I hung up.

I tipped my head back and let the usual rip from the depths of my soul. "Ugghh!"

I felt marginally better. Pulling up my text messages, I saw that I had one from my new neighbor.

Grumpy Cowboy Next Door: I need help.

I snickered.

Me: Clearly. I suggest using less duct tape in your parenting.

Grumpy Cowboy Next Door: Not with that, smart-ass. I need help with Elise. You still up for watching her?

Me: Oh, shoot, I would but my background check's not in yet…

Grumpy Cowboy Next Door: I'll make an exception just this once.

Me: So gracious. I'll be over after I get dressed.

Grumpy Cowboy Next Door: Looks like your white bra is dry.

I gasped out loud in my empty kitchen. My face burned hot, and I didn't appreciate the embarrassment.

Me: Quit looking at my underwear!

Grumpy Cowboy Next Door: Quit hanging them right outside my door!

Me: It's on my property, panty thief.

Grumpy Cowboy Next Door: I'm only going to explain one more time. Meatball had your underwear, and I was being a gentleman by returning them.

Me: Pretty sure Gannon Hart and gentleman don't belong in the same sentence.

I hopped to my room and slid my foot in the boot, pulling the Velcro tight.

Grumpy Cowboy Next Door: Damn right and don't you fuckin' forget it, woman.

My jaw dropped open. The burning sensation on my cheeks had gone south. Way south. If I wasn't hallucinating, the asshole next door had me feeling some kind of way. Which couldn't be right. He was pretty to look at, but he was a jerk. Worse than the guys I worked with every day. Historically, I'd only been attracted to good guys. The kind that didn't steal my underwear or admit they weren't gentlemen, but Gannon was testing my own theories on attraction.

He was also testing my theory about never letting a man best me.

I threw on a T-shirt and slid myself into my shortest pair of jean shorts. Mr. I'm Not a Gentleman was going to get an eyeful today. Two could play this game.

***

"DADDY GETS IT EVEWYWHERE."

Elise finished her peanut butter and jelly sandwich with a minimal amount of food down the front of her purple shirt. I helped her clean off her hands with a wet paper towel and then we were off to the front yard to plant flowers. My neighbor had that annoying tractor going again. It was hard to hear one another over all that noise. Meatball ran over, happy to be away from the scary tractor.

"Boys aren't usually as clean as girls, generally speaking."

Elise scrunched up her nose and stared up at me in the hot summer sun. "How come?"

I shrugged and dabbed a bit of sunscreen on her arms before rubbing it in while she giggled and danced around. "I think they're totally capable of being clean, they just don't care."

Done with the sunscreen, Elise plopped right down in the dirt. "I like dirt!" She grabbed a handful and let it rain down next to her, coating Meatball in a sweater of soil. A good gust of wind and that dirt would be in her hair next.

"Oh boy," I muttered. I'd babysat for several kids growing up, but felt a bit rusty. I'd forgotten just how much work they were. Add in a puppy and this was straight chaos.

I handed her a trowel and told her to start digging some holes. I had a whole tray of seedlings we were going to plant. I looked around for the gloves I'd brought out earlier. I glanced up as the tractor swiveled in an arc over on Gannon's land and nearly swallowed my tongue.

The bastard had taken his shirt off. His tan skin was fully on display, showing off slabs of muscle moving and shifting as he ground the gears and manhandled the machinery. Colorful tattoos lined both arms and wound up and over his massive shoulders. The man didn't have an ounce of fat on him, as evidenced by the washboard abs.

Worn jeans, a sweaty chest, and a baseball cap had somehow become my favorite look on a man.

He happened to look up right then and caught me staring. I tried to avert my gaze, as if the hill of dirt he'd created on the front of his property was fascinating. The last thing that man needed was another female feeding his ego. By the sheer size of him, his ego had to be huge. And now I was sweating, thinking of other things of his that might be just as huge.

"Worm!" Elise yelled.

I nearly tripped turning back around to see her holding up a juicy earthworm. I'd forgotten she was there. "Just put him back in the dirt, Elise."

She put both hands on the poor little guy, splitting him in half before I got over to her. "Ooh! Two worms!"

I winced. "Okay." I gently guided her hands back down to the dirt and got her to release the worm. Sorry, *worms*, plural. "Let's get the flowers planted!"

I stood back up and cast a quick glance over my shoulder, only to confirm that my grumpy neighbor was now sporting a cocky-ass grin on his face while he scraped his land. And I couldn't have that. I might look sweet on the outside, but I was a fierce competitor on the inside.

"Let's put the seedlings right in that hole." I bent over to help Elise, making sure my ass was on display in the best way possible.

The breeze told me plenty of skin was showing and I was not too shy to admit that plenty of men over the years had told me my ass was fine indeed. The gears of the tractor ground so hard the engine sputtered off. I grinned like a loon, patting the dirt down and moving on to another seedling, making sure to arch my back and bend down nice and slow.

Gannon let loose a curse that had me swallowing back laughter. He got the engine going again but didn't seem to be moving about as much as he was before. I kept my ass-show going, bending over for each little seedling that needed to be planted. Meatball insisted on digging up one out of every three seedlings we planted, so believe me, there was a lot of bending over going on. By the time we got done, the front yard was a colorful mess and both Meatball and Elise were covered in dirt. The tractor sputtered to a stop and my ears rejoiced.

"Time to clean up."

I spun around to see Gannon wiping sweat from his face with a T-shirt, abs flexing as he walked over. My mouth went dry, and I wondered if I'd become a victim of heatstroke. The man bent over and I realized he was the one who should have been putting on the ass-show. His jeans cupped his muscled butt like a second skin. Then he stood up again and my brain short-circuited on his broad back that tapered into a fit waist. The man was unfairly gorgeous.

The blast of cold water hit me right in the face, simultaneously cooling me off and firing me right up into good and mad. Elise yelped in excitement and Meatball shot around the yard as Gannon cleaned everyone off with my hose, whether they wanted it or not. He shot me a wink as I sputtered and wiped the water from my eyes. I felt a steady drip trickling down into my boot.

This. Was. War.

***

Grumpy Cowboy Next Door: I really think you should wear more clothing around Elise. It would help her get over the naked phase she's been in.

Me: I think my clothing is perfect for the hot summer weather, but thank you for the suggestion. Maybe if her daddy wore a shirt more often…

Grumpy Cowboy Next Door: Sorry, no can do. Hot summers and all, you know?

Me: I was thinking we could run through the sprinklers tomorrow. Does Elise have a swimsuit? Mine's white with little red cherries on it. Maybe I could get her one to match me?

Grumpy Cowboy Next Door: Don't even think about it, Pearse.

Me: Hey, you started it with the hose to the face...

annon

PRETTY SURE I was living in the no-man's-land in between Hell and Blueball.

I was going to hell for thinking about Paisley in those short shorts all night. I'd gone rock hard the second I looked over at her from atop my tractor, proving that at least one body part of mine still worked like a twenty-year-old. Speaking of, she couldn't be much older than that. She'd called me a pervert the first time I met her and maybe she was right because my brain was stuck on her ass and that mouth of hers. As if the ass and her smart mouth hadn't been enough, her shirt had gotten soaked through when I turned the hose on her. Even her bra couldn't contain those tits, the spillover looking like a mighty fine place to rest my head. I was officially jealous of a bra.

Add it all up and I was breaking a sweat while I tossed and turned, despite the Airstream pumping out a steady flow of cold air from the air-conditioning vent. Sleep had evaded me once again.

"Daddy! I see light!"

Elise's happy trill had me blinking the sleep I didn't get from my eyes and hauling ass out of bed. I'd lain around enough when I was injured. I had shit to do and a life to build, for Elise's sake. And she was right. The sun was up and that meant we should be too. I pulled on jeans and the first clean shirt I could find.

I threw open the door of the bedroom in the back of the trailer and saw my daughter sitting up in her makeshift bed that was the kitchen table and bench seats during the daytime. Her hair was a wild mess around her head and Meatball had his head lying on her leg, his tongue hanging out the side of his snout as she pet him. All the mental turmoil of last night fled in an instant. These two whackos were my whole life.

"Is it a pancake day or a waffle day?"

Elise's face lit up with a smile that made me forget all about our neighbor. "Waffles for me. Pancake for Meatball!"

I sat on her bed and the damn thing let out a groan that made me wonder if I'd put on some weight in my time off from a job. I threw my hands up in the air, as was our tradition, and Elise let out an ear-piercing scream. Meatball jumped to his feet and began to bark his head off, as if that little ten-pounder could save Elise from a big guy like me. I dove those hands down dramatically and began to tickle anyone I could find. The dog snapped at me, but Elise just giggled wildly, squirming around until she'd slid out of bed and ran to the bathroom like I'd wanted her to.

"You cwazy, Daddy!" she sang, right before slamming the bathroom door.

Meatball gave me one last bark as I stood up. I growled at him and he whined, sitting his skinny ass down. "That's what I thought. Who's the alpha here?" His paw came up and tapped my thigh. Damn thing might actually be smarter than I thought. "Come on, boy. Let's let you go out too."

I opened the trailer door and let him do his business while I pulled the frozen waffles out and got them toasting. Elise came out of the bathroom with one arm out of her pajama shirt and stuck to her side. I'd quit asking what happened in the bathroom. It was probably better I didn't know. She sat down to eat once I put the table and benches back together. Meatball eventually came back in and ate his dog food—not pancakes—and I texted my neighbor, requesting help again.

I ate my waffle leaning against the counter, not even pretending to act like I wasn't low-key giddy waiting to see what smart-ass thing she'd write back.

> Pain-in-the-ass neighbor: Just have to head to town for a swimsuit for Elise and then I'll be over.

I groaned out loud and Elise copied me with a mouthful of waffle.

> Me: I thought we talked about this.

> Pain-in-the-ass neighbor: No, you threatened, and I ignored the ridiculous threat. It's summer. Kids run through sprinklers.

I wracked my brain but came up empty with that childhood memory. Couldn't see my dad letting me waste water like that, but maybe it was a normal kid thing to do on summer vacation.

> Me: Fine.

> Pain-in-the-ass neighbor: Oh, gosh. No need to thank me! Seeing your daughter's eyes light up is thanks enough. Xoxo

I scoffed and shoved the phone in my back pocket, trying not to smile. What was it about this annoying woman that clawed at me? I wanted her sass just so I could get all riled and pissed off. I wanted to stare at her ass while berating myself for even looking at her that way. She had me twisted up real good.

"Uh-oh!" Elise shouted.

I looked down and saw Meatball taking a crap right there on the floor by my bare foot. I hopped out of the firing range, the reminder of the responsibilities in my life like a hose to the face. I didn't have time to rage-flirt with my too-young-for-me neighbor. I had a business to build and a child to raise all by myself.

I cleaned up after Meatball and got Elise dressed without thinking about Paisley one time. I promised myself I'd stick to staring at my land and not glance over at her house while she and Elise ran through sprinklers. Surely I was mature enough to handle that. Even when Paisley showed up at the trailer all fresh and glowing with a bag full of activities for the day, I kept my eyes on Elise and handed her over.

"Any chance we can make this a regular thing?" I asked the window in the door above Paisley's head.

"Uh, sure. I mean, I have three and a half weeks left."

I nodded, scraping a hand across my cheek. I needed to find my razor one of these days and shave. "Great. Can't pay you much, but it sure would help."

Paisley went up on her tiptoes on her good foot, Elise on her hip. Her new elevation put her directly in my line of sight. Fuck, she was beautiful. I could have spent my morning just figuring out the exact color of her hazel eyes.

"We'll work it out," she said softly.

And I decided right then and there I preferred her stinging comebacks to the soft voice that made me want to pull her into my arms and vow to protect her from the world. I went from being single a few months ago to having to care for Elise, Meatball, and now this new business venture. I was fresh out of arms.

"Just get that background check to me," I snapped.

Paisley rolled those pretty eyes and dropped back down to her feet to step out of the trailer. "You either trust me or you don't, cowboy," she tossed over her shoulder.

I found myself watching her ass walk all the way back to her property, tearing up the ground like she commanded nature itself. When I realized what I was doing, I squeezed my eyes shut and turned around, reminding myself of my promise. No looking. Just working.

It was a refrain that repeated in my head all day long, even when I heard the shrieks of laughter from my daughter and I knew they were going through the sprinklers. My jeans got tight just thinking about what Paisley must look like in a swimsuit. Bet her tits would bounce as she ran. I could have turned around and found out, but I was a more mature man than that. Okay, definitely not mature, but desperate. I only had one shot at getting this business up and running and staring at my young neighbor was not going to get me there.

The sun was waning by the time I shut the tractor down for the day. I'd gotten a shit ton of work done. I should be able to get the first two trailers in place in the next two weeks if I kept this pace. A bit of infrastructure in the form of sidewalks and entertainment and I'd be ready to rent them out.

Another engine rumbling had me looking over toward Paisley's house for the first time that day. A minivan pulled up to the curb. I slid from the tractor and winced as my leg made it be known that it did not like being in one position all day. My stomach also let out a racket that skipping lunch was not ideal.

Bain Sutter got out of the minivan, looking older than when I'd known him years ago, but definitely happier, even if we both had a bit of silver threaded through our hair. A tall blonde got out of the passenger side with a broad smile, and three kids climbed out too.

"Mind if we take a look at the place?" Bain came over and we shook hands before slapping backs.

"Been too long, man." I waved a hand over my shoulder. "My place is your place."

"Hey, Lucy!"

My neighbor's voice was like nails on a chalkboard except the opposite. It flowed so pleasantly I couldn't stop the full-body shiver of pleasure.

I turned to see Elise toddling out the door of her house, Meatball following. I came over and hoisted Elise up in my arms and introduced her to my old friend. Apparently Paisley and Lucy already knew each other based on the enthusiastic hugs, so I didn't bother introducing them.

"Oh my gosh, you must be the cutest thing I've ever seen!" Lucy pulled Elise from my arms and danced her around as only an experienced mother could. "Why don't you two go grab some food and we'll babysit? Roxy's been looking to get into babysitting, so this would be a perfect time to help her figure it out. Do you mind?"

Lucy turned her expectant face on me, and as much as I wanted to snatch my kid back and refuse dinner with my neighbor, I owed Bain and Lucy big-time for all their help.

"Uh, yeah, sure." I pulled the hat off my head and scratched, feeling all kinds of awkward. "I have to get cleaned up first."

I shot a glance at Paisley and she smirked. "Please do. I can smell you from here."

Lucy let out a peal of laughter. "Oh dear. They sound just like us all those years ago, don't they?" She laid her head on Bain's shoulder and he smiled fondly down at her.

"Okay, well." I felt super uncomfortable, so I excused myself to take man's quickest shower in my trailer. I grumbled the whole time, wondering how to get out of this, but not seeing a way out without being a serious asshole to someone. And while I'd normally choose that route, I was new here in town and didn't want to start off on the wrong foot for Elise's sake. Or, I could just remind myself constantly that Paisley was just my neighbor and getting some food was just being neighborly. Right?

By the time I came out of the trailer, showered and dressed in clean clothes, Paisley was also outside with a little sundress on that had me gritting my teeth. Seriously? A dress? Fuck me. Her long legs were bare, her pretty toes tucked into a strappy sandal on one foot and the other in a boot.

"Why don't you guys hit up that BBQ place that's only open on Fridays and Saturdays?" Lucy looked excited about that prospect. "Their brisket is chef's kiss."

I didn't know why the hell chefs were kissing anything, but I could use a beer right now. "Okay. Be back in a few." I started walking to my truck, purposely ignoring Paisley. This wasn't a date, and I didn't need to be guiding her to my truck or opening doors. I waited until she'd climbed in, slamming the door and looking around my vehicle.

"Not bad," she muttered.

I cranked the engine. "Not bad? It's a year-old F-150 crew cab." I fuckin' loved this truck.

Paisley shrugged and my gaze zeroed in on her bare shoulders sporting tan skin. The dress only had two tiny straps that were holding it up. "Yeah, not bad. I mean, it's no F-250 like mine."

My jaw dropped. "You have an F-250?"

She looked over at me, smirking so hard I visualized smacking a woman for the first time in my life. "Size doesn't matter, does it?" she asked innocently.

With a growl, I pulled out of the lot, following her one-word directions to this BBQ place. Silence filled the cab in between, neither of us taking the bait. I could smell the place before I saw it. I pulled into the parking lot, taking the last available parking space.

"Ready to eat, neighbor?" I asked, opening my door and climbing out. I waited by the hood, even though it killed me to watch her struggle to get out with her foot in a boot.

Not a date, not a date, not a date.

We stood in line, a good two feet between us as we studied the handwritten menu board like our lives depended on it. Paisley waved and said hello to multiple people, never introducing me, which was fine. Totally fine. This wasn't a date. We finally ordered, and I paid.

"Since you watched my kid and all," I grumbled as an explanation, taking the change and dumping a few of the ones in the tip jar.

"I see an open picnic bench." Paisley pointed and then limped in that direction. I followed, careful not to check out her ass, though I did see several other men not being as careful. I didn't blame them. Her ass was a sight to see. Same with her smile. And her tits. She was the whole package and I could see why men were staring.

We sat down and the whole damn table leaned in my direction. I poured beer into the two plastic cups they'd given us when I bought a pitcher to share. I handed one to Paisley and sipped my own, studying everyone around us. A band was playing at the far end of the covered yard. A small dance floor was empty currently, but based on the number of pitchers of beers that were being sold, I had a feeling it might get full soon.

"God, this stuff is terrible." Paisley made a face and set her beer down.

"I didn't want to say anything, but I hope the BBQ is better than their beer."

"Yeah, I mean you wouldn't want to be an asshole. That's not your style," Paisley said with a smirk.

I folded my arms across my chest. "Anyone ever told you that you have a smart mouth?"

"Every single day of my life. Just ask my mom."

A server plunked two baskets down in front of us and left without a word. The aroma coming from the baskets was enough to take my attention off the woman across from me, so you know it was out-of-this-world good.

We struck a silent truce, both of us digging into our barbecue until we'd cleaned our basket. A pile of dirty napkins was towering between us. I groaned, rubbing my belly.

"Shit, that was good."

Paisley let out her own groan, and it had me forgetting how full I was. "Right?"

I stood up so fast, Paisley almost fell off her bench as the whole picnic table tipped in her direction. Instead of making sure she was okay, I grabbed our baskets and headed for the trash cans, needing to get away from her to let my instant erection settle down. My leg was not happy from all the work today, and try as I might, I couldn't hide the limp I'd worked so hard to get rid of over the last few months.

"Seriously?" Paisley snapped as I eventually came back to our table.

"Huh?" Shit. Had she caught sight of what was happening in my pants?

"You're making fun of my limp?" Anger and hurt splashed across her face in equal measure.

I opened my mouth to defend myself, but the band cranked the volume and started in on a new number that had the entire crowd hollering and getting to their feet.

CHAPTER SIX

aisley

I STOOD up from the picnic table, my entire body trembling with anger. This guy already had me on edge. Knowing he lived right next door was aggravation enough, but add in how sweet he was with Elise, and then the construction porn all damn day long in dirty jeans, shirtless torso, and backward hat, and I was having a hard time reminding myself why I didn't like this man. Then he opened his mouth, and I remembered real quick. Now the bastard had taken it up a notch, making fun of my limp from an injury that poked at my theory of complete competence on the job.

What an asshole.

"Take me home," I shouted over the music.

The people at the table next to us rushed to the dance floor, and I had to lurch to the side to get out of the stampede. Gannon was suddenly there, his big body acting like a wall, putting me between his heat and our table. The delicious smell of barbecue and something else that was all man flooded my brain. Why did he have to smell so good?

"Paisley." His deep voice was mostly just a rumble against my chest. "Look at me."

I schooled my features into a resolute scowl and lifted my head. I hadn't looked at him much since we left the house, but seeing his eyes clear as day without the baseball hat covering half his face was like a two-by-four to the heart. The anger that had flared hot and bright faded a bit.

"I was not making fun of your limp. I have an old injury that was aggravated by the work I did today."

I studied him for a beat, seeing nothing but guarded honesty in his eyes. My breath whooshed out of my lungs. "I don't know why I believe you, but I do."

He must have heard me over the music because he tipped his head down in acknowledgement. I opened my mouth to attempt an apology for yelling at him, but Muriel Gayle, the owner of Gin/Tan/Laundry, crashed into us, a smile on her face that hinted at the chaos residing in her head. She wasn't that much older than me but was already tanned like a leather hide and usually had a flask of gin in her hand. I never saw her in dirty clothes either, so she clearly used all three businesses she ran out of the same shop in town.

"Come on, you two! It's the 'Watermelon Crawl'!" She yanked my arm and my plastic boot slid in the dirt. Damn thing had zero traction.

Gannon grabbed my other hand and pulled me upright while we trailed Muriel. Callouses and heat. That was the only thing my brain latched on to as he held my hand. We found ourselves on the tiny dance floor, a wave of line dancers pushing in our direction. It was either dance or get run over.

"Come on, cowboy." I shrugged and immediately stepped right into the line dance, having done this one so many times growing up, I'd lost count. Except this time I had to hop more than usual to spare my injured ankle. Thankfully, I wasn't a quitter. I'd prove you didn't need two functioning feet to line dance, dammit.

Gannon grimaced and swiveled his head, looking for the exits. The next slide to the right had me crashing into him. I snaked a finger through his belt loop and took him with me when we slid left.

"Don't tell me you've never done the watermelon crawl!" I added some twang to my voice that made him roll his eyes.

"Jesus H. Christ," he spat under his breath. He watched me try to hop forward when it should have been more of a slide and decided he'd seen enough. "I had just enough of that shit beer."

I leaned toward him, trying to hear his whining over the loud music thumping through the speakers. "What?"

He grit his teeth, making that square jaw look even more impressive, and picked me up by the waist. I gasped at the elevation change, my hands coming to his massive shoulders to steady myself.

"Put your feet on mine," he barked.

My hands were sending a thousand messages to my brain, mostly about the exact breadth and hardness of Gannon Hart's muscles. "What?"

"Just do it, Pearse!" Gannon lowered me and I found my feet on top of his. I was also plastered to his body, heat pumping off of him like a furnace.

He slid left, in perfect time with the line dancers, and I went with him, just backward. He kept moving, his movements a little smaller than the rest, probably because he had the weight of a whole person on his feet, but the bastard knew every move.

I smacked his beefy shoulder. "You sneak. You know this dance perfectly."

Gannon flicked a glance at me instead of furiously studying the people to our left. "Never said I didn't."

And then his hands tightened on my waist, pulling my hips fully into his just in time for the hip swivel that was positively filthy. My eyes nearly rolled back in my head, and given just a few more of those hip swivels, I could have orgasmed right there in front of the whole town. It wasn't because of his hips, though they were quite impressive. It was the hard erection wedged between us that was currently testing the binding capabilities of his zipper.

Heat, the kind you can't hide, flooded my cheeks. All the other blood in my body headed south to where we were pressed against each other. Just as suddenly as he'd pulled us together, Gannon let me loose, sliding right back into the dance as if we hadn't just done a little bump and grind on the dance floor.

I stared at Gannon as he studiously ignored me, going through the motions of the dance with a preciseness that surprised me. He might not like me, but his body certainly did. That realization, combined with the cheap beer and too much sunshine today, went straight to my head. A giggle bubbled up and out, surprising both of us. Then there were more and I couldn't contain any of it. The more I laughed, the harder Gannon frowned, which just made me laugh harder.

"Watermelon Crawl" bled into another song and then another. Gannon never broke rhythm and knew all the steps. Muriel cheered for him as she danced nearby, giving him an appreciative once-over that made my stomach lurch. I ignored her and clung to Gannon's hard body. Soon I was laughing my ass off again, making it the most enjoyable evening I'd had in a while.

The band took a break, and I stepped off Gannon's feet. For not having done any work, I was the one breathless. "Alright, cowboy. You win this one. You're full of surprises."

Gannon broke the heavy frown to toss me a smirk so full of ego I wanted to snatch back my compliment. But he grabbed my hand and pulled me off the dance floor, slowing down immediately so I could hobble behind him at a reasonable pace in my boot.

The truck ride home was completely silent.

· · ·

***

Grumpy Cowboy Next Door: Thanks for watching Elise today. I'll cover the weekends.

Me: Sounds good, but if you need help, text me.

Grumpy Cowboy Next Door: Know where I can buy a tether ball set?

Me: You can't string up Elise to a tether ball pole.

Grumpy Cowboy Next Door: Wasn't planning to, but that might work now that you mention it...

Me: Don't make me call CPS.

Grumpy Cowboy Next Door: Here we go again with the acronyms...TTYL

Me: LOL

Grumpy Cowboy Next Door: STFU

Me: Rude!

Grumpy Cowboy Next Door: I win. That wasn't an acronym.

Me: Good night, cowboy.

Grumpy Cowboy Next Door: 'Night, Pearse.

***

"I WAS SLEEPING, MOM," I groaned into the phone, blinking at the clock on my nightstand. It was Saturday, and the sun was barely up. I hadn't gotten to sleep until after midnight due to my sleep schedule being all messed up still. Definitely not because I was reliving the hotter-than-hot hip grinding of a certain grumpy neighbor.

"If you would have answered my call last night, I could have let you sleep in. I want to have lunch with you today so we can catch up. Noon at Grass?"

My brain tried to remember what I had going on, as if I had anything going on these days. The next twenty-three days of time off loomed in front of me, a wasteland of inactivity. At least the salads at Grass were tasty and Mom always paid for my meal. "Yeah, sure."

"Your enthusiasm is overwhelming," Mom said dryly.

I rolled my eyes and stuck my tongue out at the ceiling. "You caught me dead asleep, Mom."

"Look at it this way. You now have time to get up and do something nice with your hair. Who knows, you might meet Mr. Right today."

I sucked in a slow breath, counting to ten and then going on to twenty. "Okay. See you soon."

Sadly, the irritation of my mother and her not-so-subtle matchmaking made it so that I couldn't drift back to sleep. With a grunt, I threw back the covers and got up. I took a quick shower and put my hair up. A cotton sundress in pale pink high-lighted the tan I'd been getting from being outside with Elise the last few days. A single sandal and my boot and I was good to go. I left early, wandering around the shops on Main Street in Blue-ball with a cup of coffee in my hand.

My best friends texted that they wanted to get together that afternoon and I agreed. Maybe some time with them would keep my brain off my neighbor or the inquisition of my mother as to who I would be bringing as my date to the Hellman wedding. I wasn't so naïve as to think she just wanted to randomly have lunch with me. There was an agenda, and my dating life was topic number one.

A few minutes before noon, I walked over to Grass, seeing their adorable outside dining area with bistro tables and hanging baskets of flowers. I told the host at the front that I was meeting my mother. She showed me to a table outside in the corner and I perused the menu while I waited. A shadow over the table had me looking up into the baby face of a guy I knew.

"Josh?"

"Hey, Paisley." He leaned down to give me a hug. I'd gone to prom with him my junior year when he'd been a senior. We'd had a good time, but it was obvious he liked me and I didn't feel the same way about him. I'd let him down gently and we'd remained friendly, though I hadn't seen him in a couple years since he moved away to college, and to my knowledge, hadn't moved back once he graduated.

"What are you doing here?"

Josh pulled out the chair across from me and sat down. A sixth sense of sorts told me something was off. He smiled and leaned over the table, just a little too close for my comfort. I leaned back in my chair but kept a smile on my face.

"I just moved back here, actually. I saw your mom yesterday at the grocery store and she told me that you'd been talking about me. I was pleasantly surprised that you wanted to have lunch."

My mouth opened, but no sound came out. Wow. She'd gone too far this time. Way, way too far. I cleared my throat and envisioned several ways of killing my mother. Okay, not really, but I was incredibly angry at her.

"Oh, Josh, I'm so sorry, but I think you're a victim of my

mom's overzealous attempts at matchmaking. I had no idea you were back in town."

The smile on his face fell as the realization sunk in. This was so awkward. Nope, changed my mind. I was going to kill her, after all.

"Oh." He sat back and laughed, but I could tell it was forced. "Damn. She's good."

I nodded. "She really is. Painfully good. Can we still be friends?"

Josh winced. "Sure, but do you mind if we skip lunch?"

I heaved out a breath. "Yes, please."

Josh stood and so did I. He tugged on the collar of his polo shirt. "Nice seeing you, Pais."

It was a lie, but we exchanged an awkward hug anyway and then left, going our separate ways out on the sidewalk. I pulled out my phone and left an all-caps text message for my conniving mother.

> Me: I'M NOT SPEAKING TO YOU.

> Mom: Oh, come on. Joshy is a nice boy.

I cringed. That was the exact problem. Josh was a boy. And I wanted a man. A mental image of Gannon filled my brain. No, wait. No, I didn't. I wanted to be a foreman at my job.

> Me: You went too far. Don't ever do that to me again or I won't be able to trust you.

> Mom: Oh, Paisley. I'm sorry, but you're being very dramatic about this. You haven't dated anyone in so long! At this rate, you won't get married until I'm long dead!

I rolled my eyes and nearly ran into a sign post as I texted and walked back to my truck. Dramatic? Setting me up on a blind date and lying to me about it? So wrong.

> Me: Well, quit your matchmaking. I already
> have a date.

I didn't know why I sent that. I was just so done with having her interfere in my life.

> Mom: That's so great! Who is it?

I paused right by my truck. Yeah, that was a damn good question, wasn't it?

> Me: I'm not telling you. That's your punishment
> for lying.

> Mom: Paisley Marie Pearse!

> Me: Don't middle name me! You lied, you get
> the punishment. See you at the wedding,
> Mom.

I threw my phone into the truck. Shit. Now I'd actually have to find a date for the wedding, but surely someone I chose would be better than anyone my mother picked for me. Grabbing the handle on the truck, I hefted myself into the driver's seat and wracked my brain for a suitable male. Literally anyone would do. My stomach let out a growl, and I tipped my head back.

"Ugghh!" I hadn't even gotten a salad out of this debacle.

> Me: HELP. I need a date to Nikki Hellman's
> wedding.

> Audrey: Yay! You're coming? That'll help me
> feel less awkward as one of the bridesmaids.

Marlo: Surely you don't need to bring a date to a wedding? Like, it's not a law or something.

Me: It is to my mother.

Keva: I'd let you take me, but I'd have to find a babysitter and I'd probably have food smashed in my hair. Going stag would be better than bringing me.

Me: Absolutely not true, my love. You are a goddess and I'd be honored to have you by my side, but I'm pretty sure my mother wants a male date for me.

Audrey: What do YOU want?

Me: Definitely a male. One who's hot, but sweet. Accomplished, but not arrogant. A perfect gentleman to my parents, but filthy in bed. Too much to ask?

Keva: Definitely too much.

Audrey: That's like asking for a unicorn, I'm afraid.

Marlo: If they exist, I call dibs.

I put the truck in gear and headed home. Maybe I could just pull out my old yearbook, close my eyes, flip the pages, and put my finger down. Kind of like spin the bottle but without the kissing. That might be the only way I'd find a date for the wedding.

I pulled into my driveway to see Gannon in a pair of gray sweatpants plastered to his sculpted body, no shirt, and a garden hose in his hand while he tried to shoot water at Elise and Meatball. Elise had lost her shorts somewhere and her hair was soaking wet, but she held two water balloons high in the air with a maniacal look in her eyes. Despite the way my day had gone so far, I found myself grinning. I slid out of the truck and approached their property cautiously.

Gannon flicked his gaze my way, his perusal of my entire body from boot to head making my skin heat far faster than the midday sun overhead. Elise saw his attention shift and looked my way.

"Paisey! Come help!" And then she was tossing me one of the water balloons, horribly off target.

annon

I WATCHED as the water balloon flew through the air in slow motion, hitting the ground a foot in front of Paisley's wild grab. The balloon broke instantly, water splashing up onto her dress and soaking her legs. She let out a yelp that had me biting my lip to keep from laughing. Her head came up, and she was spitting fire out of those pretty eyes, finger extended as she pointed at me.

"Don't you dare laugh."

Meatball barked at me, like he understood the situation and was defending Paisley. I shook my head as laughter bubbled up in my chest and threatened to burst like that flimsy water balloon.

"Wouldn't dream of it," I managed to mumble.

"Sowwy!" Elise cried. She ran over and handed her other prized balloon to Paisley. "Here. You thwow it."

I'd literally done nothing to deserve a kid with a big heart like that, but now that I knew she existed, wild animals couldn't have taken my daughter away from me. We'd had a hell of a day walking around the hardware store getting the supplies I needed to start building out some of the entertainment my future glampers would enjoy. Elise had knocked over a display of PVC pipes that had rolled at least eight aisles down and gotten a rhododendron flower petal in her mouth before I snatched it out and explained that just because it was pink didn't mean it would taste like sugar. I'd lost my cool when she ran the shopping cart into the side of my truck, but I made up for it by filling some water balloons and playing in the water with her this afternoon. Paisley had been right. Jumping sprinklers in the summer was fuckin' fun.

"Why, thank you, Elise." Paisley took the water balloon and eyed me with something not-so-neighborly in her eyes. "Who do you think I should soak?"

"Daddy!" Elise threw her hands in the air with her mighty roar. Meatball jumped around and barked his fuckin' head off. The little traitors.

Paisley cocked her arm back in an obvious threat. Frankly, I wasn't worried. I was fifteen feet away and seeing Paisley in that little pink sundress didn't exactly make me think she had much aim. When the balloon smacked me in the face and doused my head with lukewarm water, I could admit I was damn wrong.

I wiped the water out of my eyes, ignoring the sting. And the hit to my pride. "Jesus."

Paisley smiled smugly while Elise cheered. "Played softball all four years of high school."

Because of course she did. The woman had muscle for days. Put her in tight pants and she'd look like a collegiate softball player. I was starting to think I shouldn't underestimate this new neighbor of mine. Instead, I got even.

Lightning fast, I grabbed the hose and squeezed the lever, shooting water right at her torso because as much as I wanted to get her in the face, even I knew that crossed a line with a lady. Paisley sputtered back and put her hands out to shield herself.

Oh, lookie there. Her sundress got almost see-through when wet.

"I get the bawoons!" Elise ran off to the bucket I put by the trailer, Meatball hot on her heels.

The bucket was filled to the brim with water balloons just waiting to get thrown. As my gaze was diverted, Paisley advanced on me, charging through the stream of water and letting out a shriek at the last second. I dropped the hose right as she barreled into me. All those curves that were on display in her soaking wet sundress took me down to the ground. I'd like to think I would have stayed on my feet with a little warning, but as it was, the second I felt her body slam into mine, I lost the breath in my lungs.

It was the same feeling I'd had when she'd been pressed up against me last night. I hadn't meant to grind my erection against her during that stupid line dance, but somehow I'd lost all oxygen to the brain and done something stupid I couldn't take back. My dick knew the feeling of her body now and he wanted more.

I barely kept my head from smacking the ground, but at least Paisley had a human cushion. My leg felt like someone had stabbed me with a hot poker and then went numb. Paisley's long legs straddled my torso, and she grabbed the abandoned hose, holding it like a gun in my face.

"Say you're sorry, cowboy!"

I stared up at her, the good sense knocked clean out of me. Not by the tackle that would have made my old football coach proud, but by the sight of Paisley above me. Her long blonde hair was soaking wet, and yet she looked like some kind of ethereal mermaid, her eyes sparkling and her chest heaving. Her dress clung to her curves and told me she finally wore that white bra I'd seen out on her clothesline. And if that wasn't enough to make a man permanently mute, the heat of her was sitting directly on the one part of me that still had life left in him.

I knew the second Paisley felt it. Her eyes went wide and her tongue slipped out to lick her bottom lip. She shifted her hips and we both let out a soft groan. The grin slipped from her face, replaced with a look so desperate and needy I forgot all about my daughter just a few feet away. Then a blur of reddish brown hit my field of vision and the wrong tongue was having its way with my face. Paisley's laughter hit my ears, along with Elise's happy shriek.

"Jesus, Meatball!" I pushed away the mutt and wiped my mouth.

Paisley rolled to the side and off of me, trying to pull her dress down over her legs while also getting it to unstick from her skin. Elise barreled into Paisley and loaded her lap up with a pile of balloons.

"Am I interrupting something?" a feminine voice asked from the curb somewhere by Paisley's house.

I rolled, needing to hide the erection that felt like a giant volcano about to explode in my sweatpants. Paisley's cheeks went red, but she was smiling. Facedown in the dirt that had become a bit muddy from the water balloons, I lifted my head.

"Oh, hey." I gave a little wave, knowing I looked awkward as shit facedown on the ground for no apparent reason. "Marlo? No. Keva?"

The short girl I'd met the other day smiled, though it was lined with a knowing smirk that I couldn't really call out considering my dick was currently drilling a hole better than a post hole auger.

"Hey, neighbor man. Should I be concerned that my bestie is all muddy on the ground when she should be resting her injured ankle?"

I shook my head and willed away the erection that just wouldn't quit. I had a backup situation. That had to be it. It'd been six long months since I'd used the damn thing and now it was malfunctioning.

"She started it."

Yes, I had the maturity of a five-year-old. Probably why Elise and I got along so well.

Paisley gasped and finally used that hose, shooting me right in the face and blowing my hat right off my head. I sputtered and spat, realizing belatedly that nearly drowning had done wonders for my erection. It also made me respect the woman a bit more for having the balls to take the shot. I pushed off the ground and stood, offering a hand to Paisley.

"Truce, slugger?"

She looked up at me with suspicion, but she was the one with the hose and a pile of water balloons in her lap.

"You know, you could make it up to her."

I twisted my neck to see what the hell Keva was talking about. "Huh?"

She walked over, careful to avoid the muddy parts. She still hadn't lost that knowing grin, the one that spelled trouble for me. "You clearly owe her an apology and the best way to apologize is to offer to do something nice for the other person, right?"

I frowned, arm still extended. "Yeah. I'm gonna help her up."

Keva shook her head and patted my arm. "I think you owe her a little more than that, don't you?"

I frowned harder. "No, I really don't."

Keva brushed away my words. "She needs a date for a wedding in two weeks. You should take her."

Pretty sure I broke out in hives just hearing that word. Paisley also must have had an allergic reaction because she scrambled to her feet—without my gentlemanly help—and rounded on her friend.

"No. Absolutely not."

My jaw snapped shut. Hold up. What was so wrong about going with me? We'd had a nice time last night, right? Besides, if she was so keyed up not to go with me, I kind of felt like I had to push the envelope a little. Just to see her squirm.

Keva put her hands on her hips. "You know your parents are going to make you take someone."

Fuck that. Paisley shouldn't just take any ol' guy to this wedding. Guys were mostly assholes. She didn't want to deal with one of those just because of her parents.

"Hold on there, Pearse. I'm actually very good with parents."

Keva and Paisley both snorted, a lack of faith in me I did not appreciate.

"What? I'm serious. Parents love me."

Paisley put her hand up, her head still shaking. "Please. How many of your girlfriends' parents have you even met?"

Well, now that was a very specific question. "I'm not sure. I haven't kept track."

"It's zero," Paisley deadpanned.

Keva was looking past Paisley and I. "Should we be worried that Elise is sitting on the tractor with the dog?"

I didn't even look over. "She's fine. I taught her how to drive it this morning."

Paisley's eyes lit up like the Fourth of July. "She's five!"

I shook my head. This woman was killing me with her lack of faith. "Relax. I didn't leave the keys in it."

She huffed and still looked pissed.

"Hey, you need a date to get your parents off your back. You're helping me with Elise. The least I can do is be your date for the evening. I'll be so nice to everyone, just you wait."

"You know, he has a point," Keva interjected. "You can introduce him to everyone since he's new in town, and it'll get your parents to calm down. At least for a little while. And he's not bad looking."

It was that last part that had me smiling like a pig stuck in mud.

Paisley rolled her eyes, but dropped her shoulders. "Fine."

I shot her a wink. "There's that enthusiasm I love to hear when I ask a girl out."

"This isn't a date."

"It kind of is," Keva muttered from the side.

I pointed to her friend.

"Fuck off, cowboy."

"Right back atcha, slugger."

We just stood there, glaring at each other. I couldn't help myself. She was hot even when she was pissed off and muddy.

Keva clapped her hands and broke the stand-off. "Okay, well, this has been fun, but we need to get Paisley all cleaned up. We have a girls' afternoon planned. And boys aren't allowed." She put her arm around Paisley and steered her toward her house.

Without a backward glance, the two left me in the mud with a shrieking five-year-old and barking puppy that had somehow found a stick that looked a lot like a broken irrigation pipe. I rounded up my mess of a family and headed inside to get cleaned up.

I tried not to look out my window and monitor what was happening next door. Paisley was none of my concern. I'd only offered to be her date to help her out, just like she was helping me out with Elise. I absolutely could not, would not, get another erection over my daughter's new nanny, for shit's sake. Sure, she was ridiculously attractive with her little dresses and smart mouth, but I had no business getting involved with someone at this stage of my life. Especially when that someone was at least ten years younger than me.

Yet as I fell asleep that night, all I could focus on was the feel of her strong body tackling me. The way I knew instinctively that I couldn't hurt her, even with her foot in a boot. Those strong muscles were like a siren call to a big guy like me. Her hips had ground down on my erection, I was sure of it.

As if her body wanted me as badly as my body wanted her.

***

Me: FYI, don't wear white.

Pain-in-the-ass neighbor: Are you seriously giving me wedding fashion advice?

Me: Hey, I told you I'd be a good date.

Pain-in-the-ass neighbor: No, you said you were good with parents, which we established was a lie.

Me: Not a lie exactly. I'm sure I'd be wonderful with parents if I ever met them.

Pain-in-the-ass neighbor: Well, buckle up, cowboy. You're about to meet mine.

Me: Should I be scared?

Pain-in-the-ass neighbor: If we're giving each other wedding fashion advice, you might want to wear a jockstrap with a cup.

CHAPTER EIGHT

aisley

WHAT'S a girl to do with all the thoughts swirling in her head that kept her up all night? I had a theory that if people just did more manual labor, we'd solve all the road rage incidents and the ill-advised self-cutting of bangs. Nothing like a good sweat out in the sun to evaporate all the negative thoughts and put simple survival top of mind.

Currently, I was clinging to my ten-foot ladder, attempting to power wash the eaves of my house. If I could get the job done, I'd be one step closer to convincing my foreman that I was ready to come back to work. I'd miss seeing little Elise every day, but avoiding her hot dad was a more pressing matter.

What was wrong with me? I'd tackled a grown man, straddled his massive body, and dry humped him right in the front yard. I guessed it wasn't really dry humping since we were soaking wet, but you get my point. I'd lost my damn mind.

My boot slipped off the rung, but my grip with my left hand saved the day. I got my booted foot back on the rung and kept right on spraying. My mother would be horrified that I was doing yet another "man's job" but that was part of the appeal. The more she told me what I couldn't do, the more I wanted to prove to her that I could.

"What the actual fuck are you doing?"

Gannon's sharp voice had my boot sliding again. I gritted my teeth and held on for dear life, getting my boot situated again before looking down at six feet, five inches of pissed-off man. At least this time he wore jeans and a T-shirt instead of gray sweatpants.

"Sorry, can't hear you!" I shouted over the noise of the pressure washer. I could hear him just fine, but two could play this game.

I cleaned off another two feet of eaves when the spray trickled down to a drip and the compressor turned off. Rage, the kind that pops up when one is denying inconvenient feelings and spends most of one's night staring at the ceiling instead of sleeping, swelled up in my chest. I dropped the hose line and made my way down the ladder, working up a good tirade in my head. Gannon stood there waiting for me with his arms crossed over his chest. I stood toe to boot with him.

"What the hell do you think you're doing?"

He leaned in closer and I could smell maple syrup, along with that scent that was uniquely Gannon. "Stopping you from hurting yourself further, dumbass."

My mouth gaped open. "Did you just call me a dumbass?"

He scrunched up one side of his face. "If the name fits..."

Every encounter with every hardheaded male out on the job coalesced into a film of red rage over my vision. "I'm on my property, doing maintenance on my own house, and you think you can come over here and tell me what to do? You. The guy who runs a goddamn tractor all day long every day, making the whole neighborhood sound like a construction site. Really?"

Gannon leaned down, his jaw irritatingly hot with the two-day scruff. A little vein on the side of his forehead was pumping out a rhythm that matched the anger coursing through my veins. "I'm not annoyed by the noise, Pearse. I'm trying to keep you from killing yourself. You have a boot on, for Christ's sake. You can't be climbing ladders."

"Says who?" My chest may have bumped into his crossed arms. I was not afraid to tackle his ass again if need be.

His gaze flickered down to said chest before coming back to my face. "Says me."

I reached up and pulled on the neckline of his shirt and tried to peer downward. He lurched back, but I was a woman on a mission. I grabbed his belt and yanked him left and then right.

"What the fuck are you doing?" He tried slapping my hands away.

"I'm looking for your badge. Got the fucking safety police on my ass, apparently."

He stilled, giving me a deadpan expression. "Very funny, Pearse."

I schooled my features with an innocent expression. "I don't come over there telling you what to do with your property. Don't come over here telling me what to do with mine. Simple, really."

"Oh, so you didn't come over and tell me I couldn't duct-tape Elise to my own tree?"

I threw my hands out. This man was insane. Hot, but insane. "That was clearly unsafe!"

Gannon threw his hands out, mimicking me. "So is this!"

I tapped the toe of my boot on the grass. We were at an impasse. Gannon just stared at me, those light blue eyes assessing and hard. When it was clear I wasn't going to cry uncle, he sighed.

"Just let me finish the job for you."

I rolled my eyes. "You were just limping the other night, and you told me you have an injury, too."

"Old injury, Pearse. There's the difference."

I narrowed my eyes, irritated with myself for feeling like I was about to let him have his way. "Fine, but you're a stubborn mule."

"Takes one to know one," he shot back.

I spun on my boot and went back inside my house. If he thought I'd be babysitting his daughter so that he could do the job I was fully capable of doing, he'd lost his goddamn mind. I sat on my couch and stewed. The compressor kicked on again outside. There was an idea percolating in my head, but I wasn't sure if I wanted to go through with it. It would require torturing myself in the process. I picked up a celebrity gossip magazine one of the girls left from yesterday but couldn't find anything to hold my attention.

A giggle and a yip came from the front of my house. I hopped up and marched over to throw open the door. Elise nearly rolled into my house. She had sheets of construction paper all over my front step, half of which had dirty paw prints on them. Meatball sat on his haunches looking up at me, tail sweeping some of the papers off into the flowers we'd planted last week. Elise waved.

"We're colowing!" She held up a sheet of paper with a whole rainbow of colors on it.

"I see that. You okay out here?" The early morning sun cast the front stoop in shadows so at least she wouldn't get sunburned.

"I good," Elise said, already back to coloring. Her little pink tongue was sticking out the side of her mouth while she concentrated. So was Meatball's, but his wasn't from concentration.

"Okay, well, I'll be out back if you need anything."

Elise nodded but kept right on coloring. I turned and decided to move forward with my stupid plan. Heading for my bedroom, I dug in my drawer for my skimpiest bathing suit, the fire-engine-red one I'd worn to Mexico when me and the girls had gone on a quick trip after high school graduation. Honestly, I wasn't sure if I even still fit in it, but the back of the suit was barely a string, so it would be perfect for my plan.

Grinning like the devil, I put that sucker on and barely got all the necessary bits covered and tucked in before I pranced out the back door with my towel and suntan oil. I laid the towel out on my grass in the full sun. Out of the corner of my eye, I saw Gannon still on the backside of my house, but his back to me. I lay down on my stomach and tilted my head in the opposite direction.

I didn't have to wait long. The ladder clanged rather dangerously, and then I heard a not-so-muffled *fuck*. The compressor turned off, but not before water sprayed across the yard, misting my backside. It actually felt lovely since the sun was already quite warm. I grinned, imagining him darting angry, lustful looks in my direction. As much as we irritated each other, I knew he liked my body. There was no explaining away that impressive erection from yesterday.

"Seriously, Pearse?"

I lifted my head, blinking innocently. "Something wrong?"

Gannon adjusted the front of his jeans, then pulled his hat off to run his hands through his hair before plunking it back on his head. He looked like he was in pain and I almost—almost—felt bad about my part in this. "Why are you like this?"

I rolled over and popped the top off the bottle of oil, beginning to rub it into my arms and legs. "Hey, you wanted to finish the job, so I figured I had time to sunbathe. Just worry about getting those eaves clean."

He swore under his breath. "Please don't tell me what to do."

"Same, cowboy, same."

The next thing I knew, something hit me in the face. I looked down at my lap after securing the bottle of oil. It was his T-shirt. I looked up to see him shirtless and oh so fucking hot with those ridiculous muscles and colorful tattoos snaking up his arms while he stood in the sunshine. His cocky grin completed the look.

"You looked like you were getting burned," he said impishly before picking up the hose and getting back to work.

I flipped him off, but he didn't see. Still felt good to do it. I counted to ten, and just when I felt like I had a handle on my frustration, I flipped back over on my stomach and lay down again, this time with his shirt as a pillow. I may or may not have inhaled deeply, letting his scent soak into my brain.

"Paisey?"

Elise's voice woke me up. I'd somehow drifted into a nap despite the racket of the compressor. Gannon was nowhere to be seen, but the compressor was still going. He must be around the front of the house. Elise held out a sheet of that construction paper.

"Is this for me?" I sat up and made sure my boobs had stayed in my tiny swimsuit top.

"It's us!" Elise said, immediately sitting down on my lap and pointing out the stick figures she'd drawn.

Her character was taller than us all, but mine had a huge smile and yellow hair. Meatball was a round red blob with a disproportionately large tail. And then there was Gannon, next to my character. A shadow fell across us and I shielded my eyes to see Gannon over my shoulder, peering down at the picture.

"What the hell?" he grumbled.

I looked back down. Elise had drawn Gannon with three red devil horns on his head.

I burst out laughing and Elise joined in, not knowing what I was laughing about. "She...got it...right!"

"You like it?" Elise said over her giggles.

I hugged her to me. "I love it!"

Gannon turned and walked away, mumbling under his breath about women. I watched him walk away, smiling so hard my cheeks hurt. Hopefully, he'd think twice before coming on my property and trying to tell me what I could and couldn't do.

***

Me: Children are so perceptive, don't you think?

Grumpy Cowboy Next Door: Hardy har, Pearse. And I wouldn't know. I'm still figuring this fatherhood thing out.

Me: Learn quicker, cowboy. She's already five.

Grumpy Cowboy Next Door: I didn't know she existed until five months ago, so hold up with the judgement, neighbor.

Me: WHAT?

Grumpy Cowboy Next Door: It's a long story.

Me: I got nothing but time the next three weeks…

Grumpy Cowboy Next Door: Maybe if you're real, real nice to me, I'll tell you the story.

Me: Which means I'll never hear the story.

Grumpy Cowboy Next Door: Probably not. I like you feisty though.

CHAPTER NINE

 annon

"WHAT'S the ratio of kids to sitters? And do you have a fire extinguisher?"

The woman behind the counter of the gym daycare gave me a patient smile that seemed genuine. She had a baby with sticky hands on her hip and a toddler clinging to her leg. I needed to find a regular gym in my new town, but the only one I could find was called Alpha Bros & Hoes. Not exactly a ringing endorsement, but I was desperate.

"We have three ladies on duty at all times with no more than twenty kids. And yes, we have a fire extinguisher, a first aid kit, and a PA system that can alert you immediately anywhere in the gym if we need you."

I nodded, looking down at Elise where she patiently held my hand and waved her doll in the air, lost in her world of imagination. "Okay. I won't be long. And she's got a doll, but I'm not sure how she is with other kids yet, so if you could watch her closely."

The woman nodded. "Me and little Elise are going to be just fine. I'm Faith, by the way." She came around the counter and crouched down to eye level with Elise. "Hey, Miss Elise, are you ready to have fun with us today?"

Elise looked up at me, as if checking it was okay. I gave her a nod and an encouraging smile. She let go of my hand and ran to Faith, who immediately got her involved in the activity play place on the far wall. I watched her for a few minutes, just to make sure she wouldn't cry. When I finally made myself walk out of the gym daycare, it might have been me that felt a little emotional. What was I going to do when she started school in the fall?

I had a ton of work to do on my glamping ground today, so I needed to push some weights around and get the hell out of here. Paisley and I had agreed she'd come over around nine to watch Elise, which gave me about an hour to get this workout in. I'd lost some strength during my injury—especially in the lower body, hence the gray sweatpants to cover up—so I needed to get some of that back, even if building my new business was my top priority behind Elise. Besides, if I didn't keep working out, I'd have an early heart attack and leave Elise with no one. Funny how becoming a parent changed my focus of working out for health, not vanity.

A skinny guy with tall socks and a gallon jug of water next to him was in the back corner pushing weights on a bench press. I set my water bottle and phone down on the bench next to him and began to stretch out my arms.

"Little...help."

I looked over to see the bar hovering dangerously close to the guy's neck. I jumped behind him and helped him push the bar up and re-rack it. He sat up, his face bright red.

"Thanks, man."

I nodded. "No problem. Might drop down a plate or two. Getting more full-range reps in builds more muscle."

He eyed my chest and apparently I still had it going on at

thirty-six years of age because he gave me a respectful head nod and proceeded to take a plate off each side of his bar.

I was halfway through my sets when I heard a commotion. I racked my bar and sat up. A few guys had joined my skinny friend, and they were whispering louder than Meatball snored, all looking over at the free weights area. Following their gaze, I saw a pretty blonde seated on a bench, pressing thirty-pound dumbbells overhead. My heart skipped a beat.

Paisley.

She had her long blonde hair in a high ponytail wearing a blue sports bra with matching tight shorts. One foot was in a pair of white tennis shoes and the other was in her black boot. She had a sheen of sweat on her skin, making a few wayward hairs stick to her neck. The weight she was pressing was more than enough to garner respect from even the guys.

She looked fuckin' delicious.

I shook my head and ignored her, getting back to my next set. She was hot alright, but not for me. I needed to find something else to stare at, even if she had her entire ass hanging out like she did yesterday in that goddamn swimsuit. I'd nearly fallen off that fucking ladder when I caught sight of her. She had the firm muscles of a track athlete with the curves of a porn star, a lethal combination.

I growled and put more weight on the bar. The guys next to me kept whispering like a bunch of schoolgirls instead of working out. I tried to ignore them, too, knowing they were lusting after my neighbor. None of my goddamn business.

"Dang, she's strong."

"She lifts, like, double the weight you use, bro."

"She can lift me if she wants. It's kind of hot."

"Fuck, yeah, it's hot. Bet she's only on top."

I growled again, and they ignored me. What douchebags, talking about a woman minding her own business in the gym.

"She can ride my dick anytime she wants. She might squeeze the life out of me with those thighs, but what a way to go."

I slammed the bar down on the rack and scowled at the young guys. They barely peeled their eyes away from Paisley's ass as she did some bent-over rows, but when they saw my face, they jumped into action, removing the weight plates and choosing a different machine. Wise decision.

No one was going to be lusting over Paisley on my watch, not even me. And they sure as hell weren't going to be talking about her like that in front of me. I shook my head and took a drink of water. Elise would one day be Paisley's age. Would she have to face asshats like these three? Had men always been this gross? I had a feeling they had, me included, but being a dad of a little girl had opened my eyes.

I heard a soft grunt behind me and cast a quick glance over my shoulder. Paisley was lifting another weight over her head, this one heavier than before, but I could see she was struggling. The weight shook, then stalled out halfway up. Without thinking, I strode over and put my hand on her wrist, assisting just enough that she could lift it all the way overhead and not conk herself in the temple.

Her gaze found mine in the mirror, surprise written all over her face. Her cheeks went pink and she let me help her lower the weight until she had it in her lap.

"Hey," she breathed, placing the weight on the floor and straightening up again.

"Hey back." I came around to her side, eyeing the forty-pound dumbbell. Didn't seem smart to lift that kind of weight without a spotter. "That's a lot of weight."

Paisley straightened her back and stood, hands on hips. I would not look at her boobs in that sports bra, no matter how much it squished them together and begged me to bury my head between them.

"Maybe for you, cowboy."

My eyebrow winged up. "Are you challenging me, Pearse?"

She shrugged. "If you're scared, say you're scared."

Game. Fucking. On.

"Step back and let me teach you a thing or two."

She snorted, but stepped back. I picked up the dumbbell and did a few overhead presses on each side. Fucker was heavy, and I hadn't warmed up my shoulders. Add in being almost forty, with joints that felt every single one of those years, and it wasn't as easy as I thought it would be, but I got the job done.

I stood and smiled at her as she bit her lip. "Your turn, champ." As she pushed past me to sit, I smacked her on the ass without thinking it through. I would have done the same to any of the guys in the fire station. Hell, I had done it many times. But not to a female. And definitely not to the ass that had kept me up later than I wanted last night.

Paisley hissed, but not for the reason I thought. She put her hand to her ass and held it there, biting her lip to the point I thought it might bleed. She rubbed her ass cheek and let out a whimper. My shock at my actions turned into stabbing guilt.

"Did I hurt you?" I took a step closer to her, trying to gauge what was going on by her facial expression.

Her cheeks—the ones on her face—turned bright red. Paisley finally looked up at me and I had a front-row seat to those hazel eyes. There was a ring of moss green in the center and a ring of brown on the outside.

"I, uh, might have gotten a little sunburned yesterday," she said sheepishly.

I pictured her gorgeous ass bright red and tossed my head back to laugh. She joined me and pretty soon we were causing a different kind of scene. When I could collect myself, I teased her some more.

"I gave you my shirt to cover up."

She shrugged, wiping her eyes. "I know, but I needed my ass out to piss you off."

I stilled, eyes heating, remembering how much that ass affected me. Desire hit me like a punch to the gut. "Believe me. Your ass doesn't piss me off."

Her laughter faded, and we just stared at each other for a

long moment, caught in some ridiculous attraction I couldn't seem to break free from. I imagined what it would be like if she were mine. If I could pull her hair out of that ponytail and kiss the hell out of her. If I could mark her ass and every other body part as mine so every fucking nut job in this gym knew that they'd have to get through me to get to her.

"Hey, Paisley!" A voice to my left broke the stare-down.

"Hi, Joey," Paisley answered, giving the beefy guy a hug and breaking the moment.

I didn't like the intruder immediately, though I appreciated the interruption. I shouldn't be thinking things about Paisley like that, anyway. The guy in the polo shirt with the Gym Bros and Hoes logo on the breast looked like he lived in a gym. He looked to be about Paisley's age, too. Was that the kind of guy she preferred? The ones with a neck wider than their skull?

"Gannon?" Paisley's voice broke me out of my inspection of this guy.

"Huh?"

Paisley widened her eyes. "I was saying, this is Joey Caruso. He owns the gym."

I stuck my hand out to shake his. "Sorry. Gannon Hart."

"Nice to meet you, buddy. I can tell a big guy like you lifts. Have you checked out our new squat racks? State of the art, my friend."

I nodded along. "Yeah, I'll hit those next."

"Good, good. Don't want to miss leg day, do we?" Joey chuckled, not knowing that being able to even use my leg was an accomplishment for me. "Well, I'll leave you to it." He walked off to say hello to some other gym members, and I begrudgingly felt like maybe he was a good guy after all.

"Okay, well, that's it for me today." Paisley bent to grab the weights, but I beat her to it, re-racking them before turning back to her.

"Going home already, Pearse? You're gonna get weak in your time off." I meant it as a joke. The woman was clearly strong as an ox, but the hardening of Paisley's jaw told me she didn't find the same humor in it.

"I'm not weak, asshole."

I held my hands up. Whoa. That lit her ass on fire more than all the sunburns in the world. "I was joking. You're anything but weak. In fact, you push harder than most men I know."

And I respected the hell out of her for it. I used to be the same way with my body and my career before I fucked up my leg and it was all taken from me.

Paisley sighed and looked around the gym before answering. "Sorry. It's just I have to prove myself over and over again on the job. I work with all men and it gets exhausting defending myself."

I nodded, seeing things from her perspective. We used to have one female firefighter, and she dealt with the same shit. She was good too, but she had to work harder than everyone else to prove it. Sad thing was, all that hard work would be for nothing if Paisley got seriously injured like I did.

"Just have a backup plan, Pearse. Never know when you might need it."

Paisley folded her arms across her chest and I had to clench every muscle in my body to refrain my eyeballs from drifting south. "Thanks for the warning, but I can handle myself. I learned a long time ago that the only one who believes in me would be myself." She brushed past me, obviously butthurt over something I said. "I'll be by at nine for Elise."

I spun around and opened my mouth to try to set things right, but I wasn't sure what I'd done wrong. Didn't matter because Paisley's long legs had eaten up the ground and gotten her halfway across the gym before I even had a fully formed thought in my brain. I hung my head for a second, realizing I'd just poked the beast. Paisley didn't back down, and she didn't let things go. She'd probably be spitting fire when she came by later this morning.

With a sigh, I got back to my workout, humbled when I had

to use half the weight I used to use when I got to the leg exer-
cises. By the time Elise and I headed home, my whole body was
a quivering mess.

***

Me: Sorry about this morning.

Me: I obviously put my foot in my mouth, which
I happen to do frequently.

Me: You can hit me in the face with a water
balloon if that would make you feel better.

Me: I'm not exactly good at reading women but
I'm going to take this silence as you needing
space. Again, I'm sorry I said something that
pissed you off.

Me: And now I'm done. 'Night.

CHAPTER TEN

aisley

I COUNTED to ten approximately fifty-five thousand times this week. The eye rolls alone were giving me a headache, but still I persisted with my silent treatment where Gannon was concerned. I simply didn't trust myself around him. He was far too good looking to be anything but the devil in disguise. Then he opened his mouth and confirmed it. But then I'd see him with Elise and my heart would send out an SOS to my ovaries and things got all twisted up inside.

Silence was best.

It was Friday night and I'd handed Elise off to Gannon while he stood there and stared at me with those light blue eyes that seemed to want to burrow into my soul, and now the girls were over for our "wine and bitch" session. I'd rather wine and bitch with my girls than be wined and dined by some asshole man who would only piss me off.

"Have a backup plan? What's that even mean?" Keva asked,

shoving three kalamata olives in her mouth, one after the other. No one else ate those nasty things, but I always kept some in my refrigerator for her. She'd started craving them when she was pregnant and the craving never left.

I shrugged and took another sip of the white wine Marlo brought over. Truth be told, I'd rather have a shot of whiskey, but I always started with wine, otherwise I'd be facedown on the couch before we'd gotten to the bitch portion of the night. "Who knows? That guy has a lot of shit that comes out of his mouth."

"Mmm. But what a mouth it is," Audrey growled.

I rolled my eyes. "He's pretty to look at, I'll give you that. And fun to spar with, but I'm sick to death of men underestimating me."

Keva patted my knee. "I know, hun. I get it. You deal with it every day at work, but have you considered that maybe he didn't mean it like that?"

"I explained my work situation to him and he said the whole backup thing afterward. He thinks this ankle injury is just the tip of the iceberg. I can't keep up with the big boys and need to start thinking of a backup plan. How else could he have meant it?"

Marlo grimaced. "This is why I only deal with dead men."

Now everyone was grimacing. Marlo was a mortician, following in the footsteps of her father, who owned the cemetery in town. It was an unusual occupation for a young woman, but Marlo was unusual. It actually fit her perfectly.

"Okay, so…" Audrey steered the conversation to less creepy waters. "I have my dress fitting tomorrow for Nikki's wedding. I think she's trying to set me up with a date."

"Don't remind me," I whined, leaning my head on Keva's shoulder and thinking about being with Gannon for four-ish straight hours at a wedding. Maybe we could leave right when they cut the cake.

Keva jostled my head, laughing. "You're both going to have a great time with your dates. Weddings have great food, free drinks, and dancing. How can you go wrong?"

I loved Keva, I really did, but her constant positivity could get on my nerves when I just wanted to bitch, as the name for the evening suggested.

"Yeah, maybe you'll make a love connection," Marlo said in her deadpan voice, waggling her dark eyebrows.

I snorted. A love connection with Gannon? Hard pass.

Although, as I sipped my wine and listened to the girls talk about their week, I couldn't get my brain to let go of how good it felt to be pressed up against him as we danced. How, even though his words pissed me off, his actions had always been to protect me. As much as I fervently believed I did not need protection, it was nice to have someone look out for me. Not that I'd ever admit that out loud.

Thankfully, the rest of the evening passed with more wine—I switched to whiskey around midnight—plenty of bitching, and finally sleep with the three of us crammed on the couch after Keva slipped out to go home to her son and relieve the babysitter. The room was spinning by the time I closed my eyes and gave in to sleep. I'd had more alcohol than I usually did, probably to keep pace with my increase in bitching about my neighbor.

Someone began pounding against the inside of my skull at some point while we slept. I moaned and snuggled into the blanket harder, hoping it would stop. It did not, in fact, stop. It increased in pace and volume. With a growl, I tossed off the blanket and sat up, waiting for the room to stop spinning. The girls didn't seem bothered at all, sleeping away while I was slowing being tortured. I pressed a hand to my skull and stood, holding on to furniture as I made my way to the front door. I swung it open, seeing no one on my doorstep, but the pounding got louder.

My eyes needed a few blinks to focus, but when they did, I

scanned the yard before swinging over to Gannon's land. I wasn't sure if I was still drunk, but there was a Sasquatch digging a hole in his yard. I blinked a few more times, but he didn't vaporize. Without a single care for my safety or current condition, I marched over there in one bare foot and the other in my boot.

"Hey!" I whisper-shouted when I got within fifteen feet of the furry fellow.

His head lifted and that infernal pounding finally stopped. I would have sighed in relief, but instead I wanted to hiss. Gannon. The Sasquatch was my grumpy neighbor.

"Seriously?" I threw my hands out. "Do you know what time it is, cowboy?"

He leaned on his shovel and swept his gaze up and down my body. It was then I realized I was wearing tiny cotton shorts with a camisole that didn't do much to wrangle in the girls. "Wine and Bitch" night had rules, one of which was that we showed in pajamas for maximum comfortability.

I crossed my arms across my chest and hoped the moonlight wasn't bright enough to expose the fact that my nipples had gone rock hard at the sight of the surly man. It wasn't my fault. He was dressed in gray sweatpants again, a T-shirt that hugged all those bunched muscles, and a backward baseball hat. Even his hastily thrown-on cowboy boots were hot. Name one woman who wouldn't find that hot.

"Oh, so you do have vocal cords," Gannon drawled, not looking at all contrite for making a racket in the middle of the night.

"I do," I snapped. "Got ears too, and they're ringing from all your goddamn shoveling."

His eyebrow winged up, and he tossed aside the shovel. I winced when it hit the dirt with a thud. He walked closer, stopping directly in front of me, so close I had to tilt my aching head back to keep my angry gaze locked with his. He leaned his head down and sniffed.

I reared back. "What the—"

"You been drinking, Pearse?"

I pushed his chest, but he didn't even so much as move back an inch. My nipples strained to close the distance. "I do believe that's allowed."

He leaned even closer, and I shivered despite the heat that pulsed between us every single time. "You old enough?"

I rolled my eyes, and the headache pounded once and then receded. "Twenty-six, last I checked."

He gave his head a shake, but stayed so close I could measure how long each whisker of his five o'clock shadow had gotten. "Still too young," he whispered, as if he wasn't even talking to me.

What were we talking about again? "Too young for what?"

His gaze flickered down to my lips. "Too young for what I want to do."

I had a sudden, desperate need to know what he wanted to do to me. I leaned closer, but his eyes shuttered and he stepped back. I wasn't sure if it was the whiskey or Gannon, but I swayed on my feet so much he put a hand on my arm to hold me steady.

"I told you to have a backup plan, not because I don't believe in you." Gannon felt me flinch and deepened his grip on my arm to hold me in place. "I meant it as a warning from an old guy like me who had his whole career taken from him."

I frowned, really wishing my brain wasn't addled with whiskey at the moment. I had a feeling I needed to concentrate on what Gannon was saying because he wouldn't utter it twice. Didn't look like he wanted to utter it now, but he did. He unloaded.

"I wanted to be a firefighter my whole life. I was living my dream life, and I was damn good at the job. Gave everything to it. And it took everything from me one night about six months ago. Second-degree burns on most of my leg. Spent a lot of time at home, feeling sorry for myself while everything hurt so bad I thought I'd lose my mind. Instead, I lost my job. My identity." His head hung by the time he finished.

My heart thudded in my chest. Gannon had lived through what I only feared in my head. I'd thought about what would happen if I got severely injured on the job. I usually pushed aside that thought and hustled on. But Gannon. Shit, he'd lived it.

"I'm so sorry," I breathed, feeling like the surrounding darkness held his secret safe. And I would too.

Gannon's head snapped up, eyes cold as ice. He let go of my arm and I felt the loss of his heat. "I don't need pity. I just wanted to explain why I gave you that warning. You obviously were mad about it."

"Is that why you limp sometimes?" He'd told me he had an injury, but I never would have guessed to this extent. He hid it well.

He shrugged, but wouldn't elaborate. I wanted to pull up the leg of his sweatpants and see for myself that he told the truth, but I knew it without the visual. A man like Gannon would never confess to a weakness if it wasn't true. He was gruff and downright unfriendly most of the time, but he was just an injured man trying to be a good dad.

"Shit," I mumbled, dropping my head. I felt it as sure as an ice pick to the brain.

I'd developed a sudden soft spot for this annoying man.

"What?" Gannon rumbled.

I lifted my head and bit back a smile. "Now I can't yell at you for waking me up."

He let out a soft snort. "I'm sure you'll find another reason to yell at me."

"Probably will, cowboy."

He stilled, eyeing me warily. Then he stuck his hand out. "Friends?"

I took it, ignoring the way my whole body wanted to sink into his just from the touch of his palm against mine. "Friends." I tugged on his hand. "Only if you stop the shoveling."

Gannon's lips tugged up on one side. "Deal."

"'Night, cowboy."

"'Night, Pearse."

And then we finally let go of each other and I spun around to walk back to my house. Gannon didn't move from the spot until I'd closed the door and tracked his movements through my window. As he went into his trailer, I sighed and went to bed. I stared up at the ceiling and tried to examine what had changed and what the hell was I going to do with this pulsating soft spot in my heart that seemed to pump out the sound of Gannon's name?

Marlo was the first one to wake the next morning, puttering in the kitchen to start coffee and see if I had enough ingredients to make pancakes, which I did. I stumbled into the kitchen and slurped down my first cup of coffee before turning to her.

"Morning."

She flashed a brief smile. "Any day above ground is a good one."

I loved Marlo. She was the dark cloud we all needed to balance out our endless quest for happiness.

"What's the difference between God and an electrician?" I poured another cup of coffee, doctoring it with plenty of sugar and cream.

"I'm on the edge of my seat here, Pais." Marlo cracked some eggs into the bowl on the counter.

"God doesn't think he's an electrician."

Marlo groaned.

Audrey slid into the kitchen, her ponytail hanging off the side of her head. "Please tell me you have coffee."

I held the pot high in the air and danced around her grabby hands as best I could in my boot while Marlo yelled at us to cut the crap. When Audrey looked like she might actually cry from lack of caffeine, I stopped and poured her a cup. Apparently, she'd had a lot of wine last night too.

"Ladies, I'm feeling like doing something stupid," I

announced as we sat in the living room with plates loaded down with pancakes and syrup.

"Didn't we do that last night?" Audrey grumbled.

I ignored her hungover statement. "I'm going to ask Gannon on a real date."

Marlo froze with a bite of pancake half to her mouth, the syrup dripping onto her plate. Audrey swallowed her huge bite and looked like she'd made a miraculous recovery from last's nights excess.

"Really?" she squealed.

I nodded, putting my plate down and grabbing my phone. "I know we have the wedding and all that in two weeks, but I feel like I need to go out with him before that."

Marlo still looked stunned. "Why? I thought you didn't like him?"

I thumbed out a text to Roxy, Lucy's oldest daughter, to see if she was available to babysit tonight. "I don't."

Marlo shook her head, dark hair flying. "I'm lost."

Audrey was smiling ear to ear. "I get it. You don't like him, but you do. He's like a mosquito bite that you just have to scratch. You know it'll make it worse, but you can't help yourself."

I grinned at her, loving her analogy. "Exactly. If I scratch it, maybe that'll end the itch."

Marlo went back to eating her pancake. "Y'all are fucking weird."

"Just wait 'til you feel the itch for the first time, my friend," Audrey said.

"I'll get some itch cream, like a normal person."

We all burst out laughing and ate pancakes until we were stuffed.

***

Me: What sport did you play in high school?

Grumpy Cowboy Next Door: Come on, you can't tell?

Me: Must you answer a question with a question?

Grumpy Cowboy Next Door: I don't know, must I?

Grumpy Cowboy Next Door: Mostly football and some track.

Me: How are you with a baseball bat?

Grumpy Cowboy Next Door: I can fuck up a piñata with one…

Me: I don't have a piñata, but I do have a reservation at the batting cages tonight. Want to go?

Grumpy Cowboy Next Door: Are you asking me on a date, Pearse?

Me: If that's what you want to call it, sure. But it's just batting cages. And maybe beach volleyball if the court is available.

Grumpy Cowboy Next Door: How you gonna do that with your ankle?

Me: Let me worry about that.

Grumpy Cowboy Next Door: I have Elise.

Me: Roxy is available to babysit.

Grumpy Cowboy Next Door: Well, then I guess you've thought of everything. I feel so special.

Me: Better start stretching, old man. Would hate for you to cramp up and look like a chump.

CHAPTER ELEVEN

annon

THE BAT VIBRATED in my hands, the ball flying up over my head instead of out into the netting. I ducked as it clanked around overhead before coming down. I shot Paisley a death glare as her laugh rang out between the stalls. She was watching me, leaning against her own bat—yes, a bat she brought from home like some weirdo with their own personalized bowling ball—as she watched me struggle. The woman could hit like a major league slugger. Even with a boot on her foot.

"I feel like I got conned."

The ball machine let out another warning beep and I flinched, making sure I was out of the way of the next ball that flew toward me. It hit the backstop with a healthy whack.

"You still got ten more balls, cowboy," she drawled.

I shrugged, irritated that she'd bested me. "I'm just saving my energy to kick your ass on the volleyball court."

Another ball whizzed past me and I enjoyed the breeze.

"Ahh, I see. Big volleyball player, huh?"

I walked out of the stall and hit the stop button. The ball machine let out a buzzing noise before it quit shooting out balls, as if announcing to the whole sports center that I'd failed. Pulling the helmet off my head, I threw it on the bench in the viewing area and crammed my own baseball hat back on. I wiggled the bat back and forth in the air.

"Think I got a faulty bat," I muttered, biting back a grin.

Paisley snorted, as I knew she would. "Pretty sure it was the batter, not the bat."

I feigned offense. "I've never had a date complain about my batting skills before."

Paisley swung her bat up and rested it on her shoulder. I could just picture her in her high school team uniform, one badass softball player who drove all the teenage boys wild with her sunshiny good looks.

"And I've never laughed so hard on a date before, so I guess we're just experiencing some firsts here tonight, cowboy." She stopped right in front of me, cuter than she should be in cutoff denim shorts and a cotton tank top. Two gold necklaces on her chest and matching earrings twinkled in the overhead lights. Still, they were no match for her eyes.

I frowned. "Your dates don't make you laugh? That seems like a travesty."

Paisley's smile dimmed. "I have friends that make me laugh, which is good enough. I'm more about looking for a man who doesn't tell me what to do because he thinks he's superior to me." She lifted an eyebrow.

Considering she still held a bat on her shoulder, I answered carefully. "Then what are you doing out with me, 'cause I'm pretty sure I tell you what to do all the time."

She spun on her heel and I had to lurch back to avoid a bat to the side of my head. She walked out of the batting cage area and I followed. Mostly because her ass had me wiping my chin for drool. She stopped where I was supposed to drop off my rented bat, but it took me a few seconds to get my head out of the gutter and let go of the bat.

The lighting was softer out here on the soft dirt path leading us back to the area with the two sand volleyball courts. It was quiet tonight. Not many people were out with their families on a Sunday night. They were getting ready for another week of work, after-school soccer, homework, and arguments over what to make for dinner. I'd missed out on that big happy family as a child and Elise was missing out on it, too. Life was funny that way, recycling the old and making you feel like there was nothing you could do to change things.

Made me wonder what the hell I was doing out here on a date with my next-door neighbor, who was currently my kid's nanny and entirely too young for me.

"What are we doing, Pearse?" I asked quietly.

She came to a stop and turned to me, so close I could have pushed back that lock of soft hair that had fallen across her forehead and threatened to block her left eye. She looked up at me and I tried to understand why she'd asked me here. Was it pity? We'd been at each other's throats for two weeks. I'd just told her about my injury and suddenly she was asking me out?

"Is it so horrible to be on a date with me?" she asked with a grin that didn't match her eyes.

"I'm too old for you," I said as gently as I could.

She pursed her lips. "I'm twenty-six. How old are you?"

"Thirty-six. Ten years is a lot. You should be looking for a guy without baggage."

"And that's not you?"

I huffed and looked out over the sand courts, unwilling to directly call Elise baggage, but that's essentially what I was getting at. Paisley was old enough to babysit, but not to be a stand-in mom to a five-year-old. That wasn't fair to Paisley. "You're my daughter's nanny."

"Only for two more weeks, then I'm just your neighbor." Paisley lifted her chin.

God, she was stubborn. And beautiful. And so fuckin' hot I wanted to toss all these rules out of my head and take what I wanted. What we both wanted. "We don't even get along."

Paisley shook her head slowly, her hand coming up to land directly in the middle of my chest. The gleam in her eyes was enough to have my knees trembling. "You keep telling me all the reasons this won't work. If you're scared, just say you're scared."

I leaned closer, my jaw clenched so tight I felt a headache coming on. I had been pushing Paisley away ever since I moved in. She taunted me in a swimsuit, in these tiny shorts, that ridiculous excuse for pajamas. Then she egged me on with her smart mouth. A man was only able to keep pushing away for so long. Eventually, his control snapped, and I was right about there.

"I ain't fuckin' scared, Pearse." My hands dove into her hair, skimming right past her jaw to get tangled in those strands. I tightened them into fists, pulling hard enough to make her whimper, but her eyes heated and she swayed so close her breasts were brushing against my chest. The baseball bat fell to the ground and rolled. "*You* should be scared."

And then my mouth was finally on hers, swallowing any protest she might have given. Stifling any further bullshit she'd say to egg me on further. If she wanted me out of control, then congratulations. She fucking won.

Paisley's mouth opened on a gasp and I took full advantage, my tongue sweeping in to taste her. To silence her. Fuck, it felt like heaven pressing her up against my body and controlling this kiss. She tasted like I knew she would, hot, spicy, and something uniquely happy that could only be her. Her hands gripped my forearms, like she didn't know if she wanted to push me away or hold me to her. I was out of my mind already, and getting my hands and mouth on her only made things flame further out of control.

I pushed her while keeping my mouth sealed on hers. She thudded against the wood shed behind her, the blessed pathway lights not able to shine down on us here. I could have felt guilty for handling her so roughly, but I knew Paisley could take it. And good God, did it feel amazing to have her pressed so tightly against me I was leaving a Gannon-size impression on her soft skin.

Paisley moaned, a sound I swallowed, and lifted her leg to wrap it around my hip. I was already as hard as that fuckin' baseball bat of hers, so I let her feel it. I ground against her heat lewdly, forgetting we were in public. She shook in my arms, her mouth coming away from me as she gulped for air.

"You fuckin' like that, beautiful? You want me to make you come right here?" My mouth trailed the side of her neck, tasting and biting and licking my way down.

"Yes!" Paisley squeezed her eyes tight and rocked her hips against me, finding that friction she needed.

"Then you better open your eyes."

I swept a hand up her torso and cupped her breast, nearly blowing my load right there, just feeling the weight of her in my palm. I pinched her nipple, just hard enough that her eyes opened, blazing hot and pissed off.

"There you go. Eyes on me and I'll give you what you want."

I thrust my hips and watched her eyes lose the fire and get blanketed by raw desire. "Ah, so you do like me telling you what to do, don't you, beautiful?"

"Shut up, cowboy," she breathed, her hips matching my thrusts.

I grinned and focused on not losing my shit in my pants like a preteen boy discovering girls for the first time. I tweaked her nipple a second time and Paisley whimpered. Tweaked it a third time right as I thrust into her heat, hard, and she stuttered in a breath before shattering right in front of me. Her delicate moans didn't match the way she gripped my shoulders like a steel vise.

It was the best fuckin' show I'd ever seen.

Paisley's cheeks went pink and her hair was wild around her face from tossing her head back and forth. I couldn't imagine what it would look like spread across my pillow. Her skin took on a healthy sheen and her leg trembled where she kept it hooked over my hip.

I was breathing just as hard as her, probably from trying to keep myself from tossing her over my shoulder—boot and all—and rutting against her in the backseat of my truck. I could give her all the orgasms she wanted, but there'd be no rutting. No sex. That was my line in the sand.

I was not the man for Paisley Pearse, and until she got that through her beautiful skull, I'd hold the line.

Paisley finally fluttered her eyes open, and a grin grew on her face, inch by inch. "I needed that."

I lifted an eyebrow. "Glad to be of service."

Her gaze dropped down to the front of my jeans where my dick was currently battling the confines of clothing and losing.

"Just give me a second."

Paisley giggled, looking back up. "I was wrong. The batter is not the problem."

I bit back a smile. "Told you."

Paisley dropped her leg and pulled her hands from my shoulders. She straightened her hair and her shirt. "I, ah, wasn't planning on that happening tonight."

I stepped back and adjusted the front of my jeans. "Neither was I. And it doesn't have to happen again. Don't worry."

Paisley's head snapped back up. "Why not?"

I scrubbed my hand across my face. "For all the reasons I mentioned earlier."

"You can't deny there's chemistry here." Paisley crossed her arms across her chest and I begged my eyeballs not to take in the breasts I'd just had my hands on.

"'Course there is. But doesn't mean we have to act on it. This was a bad idea. No dating, Pearse."

She rolled her eyes. "Always telling me what to do."

"Yup." She might as well know who she was dealing with. I

would not be a man to just roll over and let her do something I thought was stupid.

She tapped her foot in the dirt, trying to figure out the puzzle that was Gannon Hart. "Alright. No dating. How about neighbors with benefits?"

"That's not a thing."

"It could be a thing."

I narrowed my eyes and studied her right back. Fuck, she was temptation in human form. "Fine. But no sex. No dating. Just… scratching the itch." This was a terrible idea, and yet I was agreeing to it.

"Yes!" Paisley clapped her hands together. "That's exactly it. But why no sex?"

"Because when you finally find a guy who can give you the white picket fences, the babies, and everything else you want and deserve, we'll still be neighbors. I don't want it to be awkward."

"It's not going to be awkward that you made me orgasm outside the batting cages?"

I shrugged. "It's all I can offer. Take it or leave it."

Paisley paused, studying me. "I'll take it."

I took her hand in mine and we walked to my truck. There wasn't much conversation on the way home, but it was companionable. My dick had certain things on his mind, but I had to think about everything that had happened here before he could get what he wanted. I needed to sort through this arrangement without Paisley distracting me. If someone could get hurt, I wouldn't allow this to continue.

I dropped her off at her house and waited until she'd gone inside. I'd wanted to kiss her goodnight, but that felt exactly like a date. I paid Roxy and played cards with the girls until Bain came by to pick up his daughter. Long after I got Elise to bed and Meatball to quit running around like a possessed dog, I lay in bed and tried to talk myself out of this arrangement with Paisley. And maybe I was only thinking with my dick, but I didn't want out. I wanted in.

. . .

***

Me: Too bad we didn't get to play volleyball. I totally would have kicked your ass.

Pain-in-the-ass neighbor: In your dreams, cowboy.

Me: You most definitely will be starring in my dreams tonight.

CHAPTER TWELVE

aisley

I WASN'T TOO sure what we'd agreed to on our date Sunday night, but every day this week, Gannon had found a stolen minute or two to push me up against his trailer and kiss the hell out of me. Or find a reason to push me back into the bathroom at my house and kiss me stupid until Elise inevitably broke us up. It was heaven. It was torture.

"More balloons!" Elise tipped over the package of water balloons, letting them rain down on her head. They were unfilled, thank God.

The little girl had developed an obsession with water balloon fights, and frankly, I had too. Mostly because somehow her daddy always got involved, and the fight ended with him tackling me or me tackling him, Elise and Meatball dancing around us, screaming and barking their heads off. It was chaotic and fun and I wasn't sure if the midday summer sun or Gannon's thick body against me was hotter.

"Not right now, E-bug." Gannon's deep voice surprised me.

All morning he'd been on the other side of his property, clearing a section of land and stealing my daily construction porn visual.

I shot him a smile, but he simply skimmed his gaze over my standard summer outfit of short shorts and tank top. The way he looked at me was obscene. Every intention he had going on in that brain of his was telegraphed onto his face. I licked my lips and wished for just a second alone with him. I opened my mouth to offer some excuse for him to come inside, but he beat me to it, pulling me into his arms and lifting me off the ground.

Elise clapped her hands while I let out a yelp. "What are you doing?"

Gannon shook his head. "Carrying you inside to ice that ankle. You haven't been doing it, have you?"

I bit my lip. I didn't have time to ice my ankle. Besides, it was feeling better every day. In fact, I'd been tempted to email my boss about coming back early. Only thinking about my days with Elise and Gannon had stopped me from hitting send.

Gannon growled. "I knew it. Elise, keep an eye out for strangers."

"Aye, aye, Captain Kangawoo!"

Gannon lifted an eyebrow.

"I had her watch a couple episodes of *Captain Kangaroo* on YouTube. Did you know it was the longest-running children's show of all time?"

"I had no idea," he deadpanned, looking far less enthused than one should over an oddly addictive show.

He carried me into my house and placed me on the couch with a grunt. He let go and marched to my kitchen. I could hear him rummaging through my freezer. I took my boot off and put my foot on the coffee table. When Gannon came back, he had an ice pack in his hand and a gleam in his eye that made me rub my thighs together in anticipation.

He plunked the ice on my ankle and sat next to me, instantly leaning over to kiss me like he hadn't already sneaked a kiss first thing this morning. His tongue traced my lip before diving in and stealing my breath. I let him deepen the kiss, pulling on his T-shirt to get closer to him, yet still he didn't touch me. He held his hands out to the side.

"I want to touch you, but I'm dirty."

I grinned against his lips. "I like you dirty."

He growled and his hands almost dove into my hair, but voices outside had us both lifting our heads. Alarm stole through my chest. Gannon shot to his feet, and I wasn't far behind, but I had the annoying boot to deal with. He was out the door and I came outside just a few moments later to see both of my parents talking to Elise with Gannon standing a mere inch away from his little girl.

"Well, aren't you the cutest thing?" Mom crouched down and gave Elise the kind of smile she hadn't given me in ages. Dad stood on my driveway and tugged at the collar of his polo shirt.

"Mom? Dad?"

My parents looked over at me, Mom standing again. "Oh good. You do still live here. When I saw this cutie, I thought I'd gotten the wrong house."

I tried for a smile, but was honestly too shocked. Mom and Dad never stopped by unannounced. Especially Dad. Wasn't he supposed to be at work?

I came forward and gave them both a stiff hug. "That cutie is Elise, and this is her daddy, Gannon Hart. They're my new neighbors."

Mom nodded hello while Dad reached out to shake Gannon's hand. I rubbed my aching head. Gannon still looked ready to rip someone's head off for speaking to Elise, but at least he shook Dad's hand.

"What were you two doing inside?" Mom asked brightly.

I refused to let my cheeks answer that question. "Gannon was making me ice my ankle, as I tend to forget."

Mom eyed Gannon again, like she was reconsidering him. I did not like the light I saw in her eyes. "Oh, well, isn't that very considerate? Thank you, Gannon. Our Paisley tends to run full steam ahead and forget the little things."

And there it was. The first criticism of the day. If it was a good day, I'd only rack up a few. If it wasn't, well, I'd be pulling out the whiskey again tonight to forget all the ways in which I'd failed to live up to their expectations no matter how hard I pushed myself.

"I find her drive admirable." Gannon's rumbly voice offering me praise had me standing up taller. Might be the first time I'd heard him compliment me. Except when he was calling me beautiful while dry humping me to an orgasm at the batting cages. I'd be in my nursing home without a clue where my dentures were and still remember that.

My parents blinked, as if they weren't sure what to say. "So, what brings you out here today? Aren't you supposed to be at work, Dad?"

"Why don't we take this inside?" Dad was already working up a sweat out here in the sun. He was used to an air-conditioned office.

I glanced over at Gannon. "Actually, I'm babysitting Elise. Do you mind if I bring her in?"

"It's fine, Pearse. I can take her." Gannon had already picked her up and held her on his hip. She dropped her head onto his shoulder. My insides went soft and squishy. The same must have happened for Mom, because she put her hands on her heart and whimpered.

"Oh, no, we can't have that. Why don't you both come on in? I'd love to get to know you better." Mom had wedding bells ringing in her head, I could just tell.

With a solid count to ten, I turned around and led the group into my house. The ice pack was on the floor and my gaze couldn't help but stray to the couch where Gannon had been kissing me only moments before. I sat down and put the ice back on my ankle. Mom sat next to me and Dad took the club chair. Gannon took the floor with Elise, keeping her busy with the doll he always kept in his back pocket.

"Well, you know Patrick got a raise," Dad began.

"Actually, I didn't know that. With the time difference and my night shifts, we don't get to talk much." I looked over at Gannon. "Patrick is my older brother."

"He's an executive in Germany," Mom interjected proudly. They'd always been proud of Patrick, trotting out his successes like a game plan for me to follow.

Gannon's gaze flicked over to me, a question deep in those eyes.

"Anyway, with your brother doing so well, I feel like it's time for me to take a step back in my career. I'm not retired, but I'm downshifting. Taking more days off, working fewer hours. Basically, letting my other partners take on more of the load."

"That's great, Dad." I wasn't actually sure if it was great. I'd never heard him talk about retiring. Or hobbies, for that matter. What was he retiring in order to do instead?

Dad settled further into the chair, looking like he'd be even more at home with a cigar in his other hand. He didn't dare with Mom around. "I'd feel more comfortable retiring completely if you were squared away, too."

A thousand angry bees kicked into gear in my head. "Squared away?"

Gannon's head lifted from where he'd been keeping Elise quiet. A line formed between his eyes. He wasn't looking at me any longer. He was glaring at my dad.

Dad shrugged. "You know, a better job with security."

"I'm very secure in my job." I sat forward, too much energy buzzing through me to sit still. How many times did I need to explain this to them? "I know I didn't go to college, but I'm making great money in a career that can last my whole lifetime. That's a lot of security."

"Oh, Paisley, come on, sweetheart. How long can you actually work that job? What will you do when you're married? Kids?

How can you work nights and weekends without it becoming too much?"

My fingertips tingled with adrenaline. That's how angry I was and how badly I was trying to contain it. "I have a lot of time off, too. That will work great with a family."

"Remember Christmas?" Mom added, turning to Gannon. "She missed everything last year!"

I stood up, the ice slipping off my foot. "Our foreman was out sick. They called me up to fix those power lines after the lightning strike. I ran the whole crew and got everything fixed in record time. I'm good at my job, Mom. I'll be foreman before I'm thirty, an unheard-of accomplishment for a woman in this line of work. Why can't you be proud of that?"

Dad stood up, too. "Honey, we are proud of you, but this job isn't realistic as a long-term career. It's fine for your twenties, but you need a plan for when you're older. Once you have a family."

Gannon interrupted. "I'm sure there are desk jobs in this line of work too, right, Paisley?"

I opened my mouth and closed it. I didn't want a desk job, but I could see the lifeline for what it was. "Yes. Yes there are."

Dad glared at me and I glared right back. This was one argument I was not going to back down from.

Mom clapped her hands. "So, Paisley. What dress are you wearing to the wedding?"

I couldn't care less about a fucking dress at the moment, but she also was trying to clear the air, which I appreciated. I'd already forgotten to count to ten when dealing with my parents, and if I wasn't careful, I'd say something I'd regret later. All I wanted was for them to feel the same way about me and my accomplishments as they did for my brother's.

"I'm not sure, Mom. Maybe we can go shopping for something new?"

Mom looked practically giddy. "I'd love that! But who's your mystery date?"

My gaze flicked to Gannon. "You just met him."

Mom's mouth opened and then she pasted on a smile. "Oh, I see. That's lovely, then."

Dad turned his glare on Gannon. I felt the need to jump in to save him from Dad's ruthless questioning. He tended to forget that not everyone was a witness on the stand.

"He owns the property next to me and is opening a new business. Isn't that great? Former firefighter turned business mogul."

Gannon pulled Elise onto his lap and let her use his hands in her imaginary scenario with the doll. "I wouldn't use the term mogul," he grunted.

"Well, that's...great," Dad was able to spit out.

"And I'm glad to hear you're dialing back the work, Dad." I put a hand on his shoulder, the closest I could come to giving him a hug.

"We hate to leave so quickly, but we have lunch reservations here in town." Mom smiled impishly. "Don't tell anyone from Hell."

I rolled my eyes. "That rivalry thing is silly. Enjoy your lunch."

I walked them out, then came back inside to throw myself onto the couch. "Ughhhh!"

Elise giggled and then copied me, her own "ugh" way cuter than mine. Gannon waited until I'd collected myself enough to sit upright.

"They always like that?"

"Sadly, yes."

He shook his head, frowning harder than he had before. "It's not right, you know. The way they talk to you."

"Oh, I know. It's always been that way, though. Patrick can do no wrong, but because I've chosen an unconventional path, I'm no better than my dad's brother."

"What's wrong with him?"

I lifted an eyebrow. "He's an electrician."

Gannon scoffed. "That's your dear old dad's idea of failure?"

I sighed and came over to sit on the floor with him and Elise. "In John Pearse's eyes, yes."

"Sadly, I understand trouble in the dad department. I know exactly what you need." Gannon shot me a smile that soothed every one of my ruffled feathers like magic.

I ran my hand through Elise's curls. I already loved this little stick of dynamite, but I wouldn't have minded another minute alone with her daddy. "Oh yeah?"

"Ice cream for lunch!" Gannon announced. Elise cheered, and I laughed.

"What's an electrician's favorite ice cream flavor?"

Gannon's mouth pulled to the side.

"Shock-o-late."

Gannon only grunted, but I didn't miss the way he was fighting a smile. Elise headbutted him with the doll in her hands.

"Abby wants some too!"

"Sorry, Abby, you've been a bad girl."

Elise gasped. "Daddy! Say you sorry."

Gannon smiled at me and rolled his eyes before looking back at the doll. "Sorry."

"No, Daddy. Say it the wight way."

Gannon's gaze flickered up again, but this time he looked sheepish.

"Sorry, Abby," he said in the highest falsetto voice I'd ever heard.

I fell backward, sprawled out on my living room floor in a fit of laughter. I never would have expected to fall for a six-foot-five man who talked to dolls in that high-pitched voice, and yet here I was, head over boot for my grumpy next-door neighbor. Gannon started a tickle fest to shut me up and eventually all three of us sat on the floor eating our bowls of ice cream and playing dolls like it was the most normal thing in the world.

CHAPTER THIRTEEN

annon

"I WEAR ONE TOO!" Elise dive-bombed the clothes I had stacked half-assed on the dresser in the corner of the bedroom. I didn't have that much stuff, but I still hadn't found the time to put it away in the trailer properly. She came up for air with a pair of underwear on her shoulder and a baseball cap of mine held high. I pulled the underwear off her and tossed it back on the stack.

"Let me tighten it." I snapped the hat as tight as it would go, and still it sat so low on her head, it was pushing her ears down. Somehow she made it look adorable, so I went with it.

We were on our way to the town softball game. Paisley had invited us, saying that we needed to meet the rest of the town instead of being a hermit here on my property. I quite liked being a hermit. After all the stress and adrenaline of the job and then my injury, I felt like I was due some extended downtime. But then I'd thought of Paisley with a baseball bat in her hand and her ass in those shorts she always wore and I couldn't stay home. What if some jackass made a move on her?

Not that I had any claim over her. We'd specifically said we couldn't date or have sex. Although the more we snuck in our make-out sessions every second Elise wasn't watching, the more I wondered why the hell I'd drawn that line in the sand. Going to bed with a painful erection every night was making me rethink the neighbors-with-benefits plan we'd recklessly put together. I was still firm on the no-dating thing, but why was sex off the table again?

As I got Elise out of the five-point harness that was more adult-proof than childproof, I heard a wolf whistle from somewhere behind me.

"There's that two-steppin' heartthrob!"

I turned with Elise in my arms to see the woman who had dragged Paisley and me onto the dance floor at the barbecue place. Her thick curly hair was tied up at the top of her head and looked like it might be straining her neck muscles to keep it there. Her tan was impressive, set off nicely by the white baseball shirt she was wearing. She'd torn the sleeves off and added something glittery to her number, but the glove tucked under her arm told me she was ready to play ball.

"Hey," I answered lamely.

She smiled. "It's Muriel. I own Gin/Tan/Laundry in town."

"You mean gym, tan, laundry?"

She laughed. "Hell no. Won't catch me in a gym. But you'll always catch me with gin." She pulled out a flask from her back pocket and offered it to me.

Wow. Blueball was interesting. "No, I'm good, thanks. On dad duty tonight." I leaned my head toward Elise, who was studying Muriel as much as I was.

Muriel shrugged. "Suit yourself. Any chance you play?"

I shook my head, scanning the people parking and walking onto the field. "Nah. Paisley took me to the batting cages, but I mostly struck out." I didn't mention that I hadn't struck out in the only way that mattered. Muriel nodded. "Yeah, I get it. Too bad though. All those muscles and no batting skills."

I had to lock my jaw to keep from disputing that statement. It wasn't in my nature to back down from an obvious naysayer about my abilities, but I was here to watch and meet people, not prove how bad I was at softball.

Muriel moved on, putting her flask in her back pocket to start warming up. As I moved to the metal stands, I saw Bain's tall head. He waved me over. He was there with Roxy, who instantly latched on to Elise and had her playing in the grass in a matter of seconds.

"Not playing?" I asked the man, grateful to know at least one person here.

"Nah. Sprained my wrist last week when some of the goats in the yoga class decided to make a run for it and Lucy called me in a panic."

I shook my head at his small-town stories of craziness while scanning the field until my gaze locked on to the prettiest girl there. Her long blonde hair was up in a ponytail thread through the back of a blue baseball cap. She was wearing the same white jersey Muriel had had on, but wore it entirely different. Where Muriel had pizazz, Paisley had curves.

And I was officially staring.

I cleared my throat and tried to focus on Bain. "Isn't there some weird rivalry between Blueball and Hell?"

Bain scoffed. "Supposedly, but Lucy has been trying to make friends over here. Says the rivalry is just some stupid legend and should be put to rest. We'd do better to unite the towns and pool resources. Blueball has been a bit resistant, though."

The ump pulled on his headgear and hollered, "Play Blueball!"

The crowd cheered at his corny saying and the first player came up to bat. Paisley was out in left field, looking like she was ready to rip someone's head off despite her foot still being in a boot. The woman was competitive as shit, which made sense given the pressure I'd heard her parents put on her.

"How you getting along with your neighbor?" Bain said,

staring right at Paisley. When he turned to me, he had a grin on his face.

I schooled my features into indifference. "Good. Paisley's a nice kid."

Bain scoffed. "Hardly a kid. She's old enough her mom has enlisted the help of my wife to find her a husband."

I coughed, nearly swallowing my tongue. "A husband?"

"I hear you're going with her as her date to Nikki's wedding?"

"Whoa, buddy. I'm only going to get her mother off her ass about it."

Bain swiveled back to watch the game, but the last look he shot me told me he didn't believe a damn word I said. Shit. See? This was why I had to put limits on this thing with Paisley. We were attracted to each other, but this was one itch I couldn't scratch. At least not all the way. As much as it killed me, maybe it was better to leave sex out of it. It would be just one last thing that kept us wrapped up in each other when she should be looking elsewhere. I definitely wasn't the forever she and her mama wanted.

I saw Joey, from the gym, walk up to bat. He hit a home run that saw the ball sailing past the fences. I also saw two old men in the outfield with Paisley that looked ready to keel over at any second. Not sure what they were still doing playing softball, but hey, I guessed getting activity was important even at that age. There were a whole lot of other people I didn't recognize. Maybe Paisley was right. I needed to be less of a hermit and actually meet the people I was now living near.

Paisley's team won by a single run due to a line drive by Paisley in the bottom of the eighth. It was clear she was the athlete everyone looked to for help in clutch situations. Some asshole lifted her onto his shoulders in celebration, her thighs around his head. I was about to storm over there and demand he put her down. He looked like a jackass who'd get his hands all over her skin and accidentally drop her because he was only thinking of himself. She didn't need to jack up her other ankle.

Thankfully, she took care of the matter herself, sliding down and stepping away from the asshole before I could make a scene.

"We normally get ice cream after."

"Huh?" Bain was talking to me and I was plotting murder in my head.

"I was asking if you'd like us to take Elise to get ice cream. We can drop her off at your place after." Bain was barely holding back a shit-eating grin, and as much as I didn't care for it, the chance to get Paisley alone for a few minutes was all the incentive I needed.

"You sure?"

"Lucy's mom's got the other two. Let us take her. We won't be outnumbered for once." Lucy slid up to Bain, and he wrapped his arm around her, his face softening as he whispered something in her ear. They smiled at each other and it did something to me. They looked at each other like they were in their own little world. Just the two of them and they didn't care about anything else. It looked nice.

Sadly, that wasn't the life for me. I'd never had that with Elise's mom and didn't plan on having it with anyone else either. I was damaged goods. An injured single dad trying to build a business so he could keep dolls in his daughter's hands.

"Hey!" Paisley came up to our group, and though her gaze swung to me first, she hugged Bain and Lucy before me. She was all warm, soft curves with a steel core I wanted to dig deep enough to find.

"We're taking Elise to get ice cream," Bain stated.

Elise must have heard him because she and Roxy came running over with excited smiles. The four of them left, mostly because the girls were tugging the adults toward the parking lot, in a hurry for their sugar high.

"So, uh, Lucy drove me here." Paisley bit her lip.

Bain, you generous motherfucker. "Did she now?" I leaned in closer, seeing a few strands of hair sticking to her neck. I wanted to lick her and see how she tasted. But not here. "How about I give you a lift home?"

Paisley smiled up at me and I was pretty sure I'd agree to just about anything right then. "Only if we can stop by the lake on the way. You haven't been there yet, right?"

"Don't believe I have." I put my hand on her back, shooting a look over at the asshole who had put her on his shoulders. He was watching us, which made me grin. *That's right, asshole. She's going home with me.*

"You and Benny know each other?" Paisley was watching this interaction.

I wiped the territorial grin off my face and filed that name away. "Nah."

Paisley looked over her shoulder. "Then why—"

"So, tell me about this lake," I interrupted.

Thankfully, that got Paisley's attention. She told me all about the lake that was included in the parcel of the land to the north of mine. She wasn't sure who owned it, but everyone in town came to the lake regularly and used it without incident. When I finally parked the truck where she instructed me to go and gazed out over the placid water, the tall trees gently swaying in the evening breeze, I could see why everyone came here. It was gorgeous. And quiet. And secluded.

"Pearse." I wanted to tell her how well she'd done at the game, but she wasn't interested in compliments.

"Shut up and kiss me, cowboy."

Paisley twisted in her seat and reached for me. Before I could process the mechanics of making out in bucket seats with a girl in a boot and me with a bum leg, she was crawling over my lap and settling in between me and the steering wheel. She pulled her hat off her head and then slammed it back down backward, looking even more adorable. Her mouth came down on mine and my whole body hummed with satisfaction. A pretty girl was always amazing, but one who boldly took what she wanted? Fucking irresistible.

Her tongue demanded entrance, and I gave it to her, letting her set the pace just because I knew she liked the feeling of control. I'd take it from her as soon as I couldn't stand it any longer, but I could be a nice guy for a little while.

"Paisley?" I whispered against her lips the first second she let us come up for air.

"Hmm?" She knocked my hat off and was now running her fingers through my hair, her short nails raking deliciously across my scalp. Goose bumps rose all over my body.

"I could kiss you all night long, but with this level of privacy, I really need that pussy. Unzip your shorts."

Paisley inhaled sharply, but her hands left my hair and complied with my not-so-nice-guy request. The second the zipper was down and the tan skin of her lower belly was exposed, I dove in, shoving aside the flimsy excuse for underwear she seemed to favor. She was hot. Wet. So slippery already. A single finger found its way into her heat and she tossed her head back with a soft moan.

I could break glass with this erection, but I needed her to fall apart for me again before I dealt with it. My other hand shoved up her baseball shirt and found her breast, burrowing inside the tight sports bra and cupping her bare breast. I rolled her nipple between my fingers and gave her a second finger.

"That's right, baby. Ride my hand like a greedy girl."

Paisley ground down, her fingers biting into my shoulders, eyes squeezed shut. Her cheeks were pink and even more of that hair had escaped her hat and was sticking to her neck. I leaned in and swiped my tongue up her neck, wishing it was her pussy instead.

"Gannon," Paisley moaned, using my name for possibly the first time.

I grinned like an idiot, insanely pleased about hearing my name said with that much breath behind it. I circled her clit with my thumb, curling my fingers inside her body. Her whole body began to quake, and she moved her hips quicker over my lap. Her breaths came faster and then she was gasping as her head fell forward and her pussy milked my fingers.

I was surrounded by Paisley, her head on my shoulder, her scent filling up my truck, her boob in my hand, and her pussy dripping on my fingers. And I still wanted more. I stayed still and enjoyed having her draped across me until she lifted her head. I swiped my thumb across her clit one last time. She lurched and squealed.

"Gannon!"

I grinned like the fool I was for her. "Yeah, baby?"

She gave me a warning look that was ruined by the satisfaction in her sleepy eyes. She climbed off my lap, but I pulled her to me, swiping my fingers across her lips and making them shine with her own release. Then I kissed her with zero finesse to finally get a taste of this woman, and I was not disappointed. My erection was officially painful.

Paisley broke away and grinned at me. "I could kiss you all night long, but with all this privacy, I really need your dick in my mouth."

I nearly shot my load right there, but with a fist to my mouth and closing my eyes against the look of Paisley all messed up from my hands and mouth, I was able to hold it back. My eyes sprang open when I felt her hands tug at my zipper. She got it down and had my dick out before I could suck in enough oxygen to object. Once I did get oxygen, I had no intention of objecting.

Her tongue darted out to swipe across the tip. My hips lifted on their own, seeking more of her mouth. She obliged, taking the whole head of me in her mouth, tongue swirling and cheeks hollowing out as she came back up. Each dip downward took a bit more of me into her hot little mouth. She felt better than anything I'd ever experienced before. Her hand stayed fisted on the base of me, her head bobbing up and down as she attacked me with the single-minded attention she did everything.

"Fuck, baby. I can't—"

Paisley grinned up at me, my dick stuffed in her mouth, and I knew it was just a matter of seconds before I made a mess. I gripped the steering wheel with one fist and held on to her ponytail with the other. She slid me to the back of her throat, her face buried in my lap and her throat convulsing as I made her gag. I pulled on her ponytail, not wanting to hurt her, but she refused to budge, sliding back up a second later and then taking me all the way down again.

"Paisley. Fuck." I slammed my eyes shut and tried to hold out, but it was useless.

She used her other hand to grab my balls, not so gently I might add, but apparently that did it for me. I felt the tingle turn into a firestorm, making its way up my body and through my balls. I was spilling into her mouth, one jerk at a time, and still she didn't move away. The little hellion was swallowing me down, her talented mouth sucking me dry.

I flopped back against the seat, completely spent and unable to move. I knew I should be wiping her mouth or apologizing for nearly drowning her, but I couldn't find the strength to do anything but thank my lucky stars for advising me to move to Blueball.

CHAPTER FOURTEEN

aisley

"Don't we need to go pick up Elise?"

Gannon hadn't opened his eyes yet. The smugness I'd felt at making my grumpy neighbor lose control started to bleed into worry. Maybe I'd killed the guy. I poked him in the shoulder and he stirred, blinking his eyes against the bright moonlight filtering into the truck.

"Elise who?" he grumbled.

I laughed under my breath. "Maybe you're right."

Gannon swung his head my way, finally tucking his dick back in his jeans, movements slow as molasses. "Say that again for me."

I bit back the smile that always wanted to unleash on my face when he was around. Somehow, Gannon's incessant teasing had started to become humorous. "Maybe you are too old for me. For a second there, I thought I gave you a heart attack, old man."

That did it. Fire lit up his blue eyes. He sat up straight and jammed his hat back on his head. He swung his head my way and pinned me with a lusty stare that made me shift on the leather seat. "How many orgasms does it take to shut that mouth, Pearse?"

"I guess you'll just have to experiment and see."

Gannon growled, but started the truck. He muttered under his breath about something being a pain in the ass, but it couldn't possibly have been about me. Nope. Not when I'd just given him a blow job to remember. It would be one I remembered too. I had experience in this arena and yet I'd never wanted to ride the bull just because I'd gotten a taste. It was usually something I did as an orgasm payback or as a precursor of things to come—no pun intended—rather than as an act that brought me immense pleasure. Sucking Gannon's cock was almost as fun as verbally sparring with him.

As the familiar town came into view, I couldn't help but wonder why Gannon had chosen Blueball. I chose it because it was close to where I'd grown up, but wasn't my hometown. I had freedom to be who I wanted to be but could still go home when I felt lonely. Blueball was quirky and fun and full of people I didn't mind seeing for the rest of my life. But what would draw in a guy like Gannon?

He parked along the street, the ice cream shop in view. Roxy and Elise came out the door holding hands. Elise had chocolate all over her face and down her shirt, like she'd bathed in it instead of eaten it. Bain came out the glass door with his arm slung over Lucy's shoulders. A pang of something hit me, but I wasn't sure what it was. Maybe it was nostalgia for the days my brother and I would visit the ice cream shop. Or perhaps it was that feeling deep in my gut that I was living in the town I was supposed to. Where kids felt safe to walk on the sidewalk at night and couples canoodled instead of racing home to their television shows and devices that kept us connected but further apart than ever.

"Come on, Pearse."

I blinked out of my thoughts and got out of the truck. Elise let go of Roxy and ran over to me. She held out her sticky hands, and I heard Gannon start to bark at her not to touch, but it was fine by me. I swung her up into the air and then held her to me, sticky ice cream remnants and all. Elise squealed and held me tightly around the neck.

"Did you save some for me?"

"Uh...no?" She smiled and her eyes disappeared into those precious cheeks. I poked her in the belly and she let go of me to grab her stomach and giggle.

"You ready for bed?"

Gannon scoffed and Lucy gave me a guilty look. Elise quit giggling long enough to twist her hat backward, just like mine. She was high on sugar and little-kid energy. She might never go to bed ever again. Good thing she wasn't my kid. Gannon would have to attempt to put her down.

She threw her arm in the air and tried a deep voice on for size. "Play Blueball!"

I rolled my lips in and tried not to encourage her. She really was the cutest thing ever. I think I even liked her more than her dad. Gannon said the thank-yous and goodbyes to the Sutters and I got Elise strapped into her car seat in the back of the truck cab. We were finally on our way home while Elise tried to tell us everything that had happened at the ice cream shop. Most of it was fragmented thoughts of a child, and put together, none of it made sense.

We pulled onto our street and I sighed. "I'll miss this little thing when I go back to work."

Gannon shot a look at me before focusing on the road. "Believe me, we're going to miss you, too."

I rolled my head against the seat back. "We? As in you too, cowboy?"

He rolled his eyes and took the turn into his gravel driveway instead of mine. "Never said I was sane."

"Daddy?" Elise called from the backseat. "Can Abby sleep with you tonight?"

Gannon threw the truck in park and twisted in his seat. "Sure, but why?"

"'Cause I have Meatball. You need Abby."

Gannon smiled at his daughter and I wanted to take his picture. Every single grumpy thing about him faded away when he looked at Elise like that. He just looked like a dad who would do anything for his kid.

And I should really, really not be looking at him right now.

Those kinds of looks and those kinds of thoughts would only get me in trouble. Because while Gannon was busy pushing me away and drawing lines in the sand and telling me all the reasons we couldn't date, I was finding all sorts of reasons to do the opposite.

We climbed out of the truck, and as I turned to head to my place, Gannon hefted Elise into his arms and stepped in front of me. "Stay a bit. I just need to get Elise down, but I want you to stay."

So typical of Gannon, ordering instead of asking, and yet I already knew my answer. "Sure." And when he gifted me a coveted genuine smile, I knew I'd given the right answer.

While Gannon got Elise ready for bed inside, I sat in one of the two camp chairs outside the trailer and tilted my head back to stare up at the stars. One of the reasons I'd chosen my house and the acre of land surrounding it was because I never wanted to live in a place where the stars were blotted out by too much light from us humans. I needed to be able to look up at those stars and know I could still reach for them. And if I failed, it didn't really matter. I was just one human in this great big universe.

"Due to inflation, I'll give you a buck fifty for your thoughts," Gannon drawled in the loudest whisper I'd ever heard. He stepped off the last metal step of his trailer and took the seat next to me.

"I was just wondering what all you're doing on this property. I'll still be able to see the stars, right?"

Gannon pulled his lips to the side. "I'm making a glamp-ground, not growing a spotlight farm."

"A glamp-ground. Tell me about it, please?"

Gannon wouldn't hold my gaze, but he opened his mouth to answer. I'd had my doubts he would, so I took what I could get. "I want a place where people can come and relax and get off their damn phones. A place that's safe, old fashioned, and fun. A place they want to return to every year with their families. I want Glamper's Paradise to be the one vacation they all look back on with fond memories."

I tried to lean closer. Gannon might be Grumpy the Bear most of the time, but this bear looked like he could use a hug. "What place is your fondest vacation memory?"

Gannon shrugged. "Didn't ever take family vacations, Pearse." He stood suddenly and dusted off his hands. "Want to see what I'm building on the far end?"

I had a thousand more questions pop into my head, all of which would be invasive and probably make Gannon run for the hills. Like, where was his family growing up and where were they now? Did he have friends? Former wives or girlfriends? Gannon didn't mention anyone but Elise. It was like he was an island all to himself. I stuffed all of that down and focused on his current enthusiasm.

"Sure. Is it okay to leave Elise?"

He held up a walkie-talkie that had been clipped to the back of his jeans. "That's what these babies are for. Taught Elise how to use them from day one."

I couldn't help but shake my head. "You taught your five-year-old to use a walkie-talkie?"

Gannon tugged me toward the golf cart that had been delivered a few days ago. "Of course, Pearse. Don't you use them in your line of work?"

"Well, sure, but I'm not five."

"Can never be too careful, no matter your age." He pushed

on the gas pedal and we shot off, zooming silently over the land he'd cleared with that horrible-sounding scraper.

"Now, I built it over here with you in mind." Gannon stopped the golf cart and climbed out, staring at a wood platform next to a huge oak tree.

"Um, thanks?" I tilted my head to the side. Nope. Still didn't know what it was. "What is it?"

Gannon hopped onto the platform and spread his arms wide. "This is a dance floor and over there is going to be a small stage. What's better than camping and hanging around a fire pit?"

I pursed my lips. His silence meant this wasn't a rhetorical question. "Sex around the fire pit?"

The look he shot me was full of heat, just like an actual fire pit. "Pearse. Focus."

"Oh, I'm focused." I took in the sight of him, lit up and excited, his light eyes twinkling in the moonlight. The way his jeans hugged his tree trunk thighs. The shift of cotton as his shirt tried to keep up with his flexing muscles. He was a fine sight indeed.

"Everyone loves live music around a campfire. And beer, I suppose, but being at the barbecue place with you made me think about doing something like that here."

I nodded, spinning in a circle and checking out the surroundings. It really was beautiful. Tall trees giving off shadows, twinkling stars above. Add some string lights and a country band, and this place would be both romantic and quaint.

"I like it."

Gannon came up behind me and wrapped his arms around my waist, nuzzling into my neck. "Knew you would," he murmured against my skin.

I leaned my head back against his chest and let him kiss his way along my neck. The stars were my only witness as I let myself melt into him. For just one quick second, I wanted to pretend that this was a real hug from someone who loved me. I knew if I didn't move away quickly, I'd be tempted to tackle him right here on this platform and force him to throw out the stupid no-sex rule.

"You play an instrument, cowboy?" My question came out breathy, and I wasn't happy about it. This man was turning me inside out.

His lips lifted from my neck. "A little guitar."

I spun in his arms and shoved him back. I hated the way my body felt cold without his pressed against me, but the space was needed if I was to keep my head.

"Play something for me!"

Gannon's head dropped. "Jesus H. Christ."

I poked him repeatedly in the stomach until he lifted his head and snatched my hands away from him. "Come on. Just play one song. Please?"

"You're annoying," he mumbled.

"You're bullshitting. That's it." I snapped my fingers and started to walk back to the golf cart. "You can't actually play the guitar."

"Yes, I can," he snapped, following after me and rocking the cart with the force of him sitting behind the wheel.

I smiled smugly and let him drive us back to his trailer. He stormed away from me, and for a second, I wasn't sure if he would come back out of the trailer. When he finally did, it was with a worn guitar in his hands. I sat down and put my hands under my thighs to keep from reaching for him.

He moved the other chair so that he was sitting across from me, just a few feet of dirt separating us. Gannon settled the guitar on his knee and strummed a few chords before launching into a song I recognized.

"Morgan Wallen?" I asked, pretty sure it was "Somebody's Problem."

Gannon looked up at me and nodded once. He kept playing, and I stared at his hands moving across those strings so sure of themselves. I couldn't remember all the lyrics, but I remembered enough to wonder if he'd chosen this song on purpose.

When he strummed out the last note, I clapped quietly. "That was amazing."

"Told you I could play." Gannon put the guitar on the ground next to him.

I shrugged. "Now you just need to sing."

"Nope. I don't sing."

I couldn't take it any longer. I stood up and fell into his lap, earning myself a grunt as he put his hands on my hips. Gannon was unfairly handsome already. Add in guitar skills and he was too hot to keep my hands off him.

I pulled the hat off his head so I could see his eyes. I needed to see them when I asked this question, even though it wasn't the question I wanted to ask. What I really wanted to say was that I needed more than just a physical release from him every now and again. I wanted to date this man for real. Instead, I settled for what wouldn't send him running.

"You're not playing fair, cowboy."

He frowned. "What do you mean?"

I shrugged, not at all upset when that movement made my boobs press against his chest. "You can't just play a song for a girl and not put out. It just isn't done."

Understanding dawned. "You need more of those orgasms, Pearse?"

I tilted my head and went for what I wanted. "I need sex, cowboy. Sweaty, physical, blow-my-mind sex. I don't want to walk straight tomorrow."

Gannon groaned, dropping his head to my shoulder.

CHAPTER FIFTEEN

annon

INSTEAD OF PAISLEY WALKING FUNNY, it was me. Somehow, I'd stood up from that rickety chair and mumbled an excuse to turn in for the night. I saw the disappointment bloom on her face. Hell, I saw the edge of hurt rimming her eyes and it fucking gutted me. Which was exactly why I couldn't take her up on her offer. I was already in too deep. So I spent the week walking around my property with a permanent hard-on that turned painful, reminding me constantly of the name of this damn town.

And Paisley? That woman had gone so cold not even a polar bear could stand her. She babysat Elise all week and turned her limited smiles on her, leaving me desperate for eye contact that she just wouldn't give. It was a week from hell, honestly. It could have been the unrelenting heat and the manual labor, but I had a feeling it had a lot more to do with Paisley. I was losing my goddamn mind.

It was after the third straight day of Paisley pretending I didn't exist that I got a text from dear old Dad.

> Dad: Got the place up and running yet? Heard they got a desk job open down at that steel factory you'd drive by to get to your station.

The bastard was expecting me to fail and need to come crawling back to my old life, tail tucked under my ass. Was it too much to ask that one person believe in me? My mind instantly went to Paisley, talking me up to her parents, but quickly pushed it away. She was only trying to save face in front of the people who didn't think much of her in this fucked-up cycle of parental bullshit and baggage. She didn't actually believe in me, did she? I chucked the phone on my bed and let out a roar.

"Daddy?" Elise's wobbly little voice coming from the plastic tub I'd put in the shower basin to act as a tub reminded me that I couldn't do that anymore. Whatever frustrations I had, I needed to bottle them up. Five-year-olds didn't need to be worried about finances or their fathers losing their minds over hot neighbors and shitty father figures.

"I make a good lion, don't I, E-bug?" I hollered back. Her giggle soothed a little bit of the beast inside.

"You scared Abby."

I hung my head and rubbed the back of my neck. I was coming to find out that Elise seemed to use Abby as her voice. Whatever Abby wanted or felt was usually what Elise wanted or felt and was too scared to ask for.

"Tell Abby I'm super sorry and I'll never scare her with my lion roar again," I said, coming into the bathroom and locking eyes with my daughter. She seemed to think on that apology seriously. She looked down at her soaked doll, the two of them communicating. When she looked back at me, her big cheesy smile was back on her face.

My phone rang and I nearly let out another growl. The vision of my daughter happily playing in the bath was just enough to have me swallowing it down. I looked at the screen, surprised to see Lucy's number pop up.

"Hey, Lucy," I answered.

"Hi, Gannon. I've got a proposition for you." Lucy rattled on at a pace a brain almost couldn't keep up with. "I have Roxy and two of her friends coming over to our house to babysit Saturday night, so all of us adults can go to the wedding. All the littles are planning to spend the night as Bain's on shift the next day, so we'll be leaving the wedding early. I wanted to make sure you knew you can bring Elise over. We even rented a bounce house and bought out the pizza place in town for dinner delivery."

My brain was spinning. At this point, I wasn't even sure if Paisley would want to go to the wedding with me. But a free night? No kids. No responsibilities? Fuck. It made me want to agree and then go crawling over to Paisley's house to beg for forgiveness. If my cock was what she wanted, I could get over myself long enough to make it good for her, right?

"Gannon?" Lucy's voice brought me back.

"Hey, sorry. Yeah, that sounds good. Count Elise in and thank you very much. Let me know what things cost and I'll chip in."

"Oh, don't worry about that. I was going to do it anyway for our two youngest." Lucy's voice dropped to a whisper, but it was loud, like she pressed the phone up to her mouth. "Maybe you and a certain date of yours can use the night off wisely."

Visions of a naked Paisley, all spread out for me with not a single walkie-talkie nearby or a mad rush to get back home to my daughter, made me squeeze my eyes shut.

"I like your brain, Lucy," I managed to say around a throat almost closed shut with this forbidden desire.

Lucy laughed. "That's why I'm Hell's best matchmaker. Although it looks like I'm branching out into Blueball now, too."

And then she hung up, sounding quite pleased with herself. I let the phone drop to the bed and tried to breathe. Was I actually going to go through with this? I'd been pushing Paisley away for a myriad of reasons, none of which was the central truth.

Telling her the real reason I was pushing her away would take baring my insecurities, and I wasn't sure I was ready for that yet.

The whole time I got Elise out of the tub and ready for bed, I wrestled with this dilemma. Tucking Elise into her tiny bed, she grabbed my face and held me still.

"Tell Paisey you're sowwy."

I frowned while inhaling the little-girl scent of her. "Why do I need to say sorry?"

Elise let go of my face just to poke me in the nose, slip off the slope, and jab me in the eye. I blinked away the pain. "She stuck her tongue out at you. Said you hurt her feelers. Dat's not nice, Daddy."

My chest felt like an open wound and Elise had just poured salt in it. "I definitely should not have hurt her feelers. I'll go say sorry right now if you promise to go right to sleep."

Elise yelped and slammed her eyes shut. I bit back a grin at her antics. I poked her in the side and she let out a giggle followed by a snore so loud Meatball yipped from his doggie bed. I leaned over and kissed her forehead.

"Love you, E-bug."

"Love you too, Daddy," she whispered back, eyes still closed.

I stood and stared down at her, wondering how the worst day of my life had turned into the best thing that's ever happened to me. I looked out the window at the light on in Paisley's house and wondered if this pain-in-the-ass neighbor might be the same way.

I slipped out the door and walked over to Paisley's house, rolling some apologies through my head and determining they all sucked. This woman could eviscerate me with a single sentence and all I had was *sorry, I fucked up*. Sucking in a deep breath, I knocked on her door and stepped back. There was loud fumbling, and then the door swung open.

Paisley stood there with a paint roller in one hand, a wrap on one ankle, and a smear of lemon-yellow paint across her cheek. "Can I help you?"

Ouch. A greeting as friendly as you'd give the neighborhood vacuum salesman. "What the hell are you doing?"

Yep, I was leading this apology off with accusations. Never said I was a smart guy. Paisley frowned—as any sane woman would—and moved to shut the door. I stuck my whole leg in her house and the door bounced off my shoulder. I stood up straight and tried again.

"Sorry. Let me start over. Can we talk?"

Paisley narrowed her eyes at me, looking adorable with paint splatters in her hair and the glow of sweat on her forehead. I didn't let myself look down at her boobs spilling out of her tank top or the length of her shorts. I needed a few brain cells left to communicate properly.

"I'm busy painting. Maybe some other time."

I took the roller out of her hands and walked around her to set it down in the pan in her kitchen. She had half the walls of the kitchen painted a peppy yellow. It would look good when she was done. It would look just like her: sunny and happy. Except right now. She was most definitely not happy based on the frown, the arms crossed over her chest, and the boot tapping on the floor, as if to count down the seconds until I left.

"If you needed to paint, you should have asked me for help. Pretty sure going up and down a step stool is not in your physical therapy plan." The woman had more balls than most of the men in the county. There was literally nothing Paisley wouldn't attempt if she got it in her head to get it done. She was amazing, but her work ethic also worried me. Like now, when she was injured and should have been resting.

"That's between my therapist and me, thank you very much. What do you need?"

I came closer, putting my life on the line. I didn't have flowery words or eloquent speeches. All I had was the bald truth.

"I didn't want to sleep with you because I haven't slept with anyone since the fire."

Paisley dropped her arms, but the frown was still in place. I'd take any progress I could. I stepped closer, needing to see that ring of green in her eyes. I'd missed sinking into those eyes all week while she ignored me.

"My leg is messed up."

"I know. That's why you limp."

I nodded and swallowed. I didn't know why this was so hard. It just was. "Yes, but there are scars. Deep ones. Mottled skin. Disfigured, really. No one but the therapist and the doctor have seen it."

Paisley lost the frown, her eyes finally softening. "That's why you wear jeans and sweatpants when it's almost triple digits out there."

Her hand came up and rested on my chest, probably feeling how my heart was beating out a rapid-fire pulse. Confessing insecurities was not for the faint of heart.

"It's not because I skipped leg day," I said lamely, trying to make a joke to lighten the mood.

"I don't care about that, Gannon."

I grabbed her hips, my hands unable to stay still at my sides any longer. She felt like heaven under my palms, warm, supple, and so fucking mine it scared me.

I lifted a single eyebrow. "Says the girl who requires perfection in everything she does."

Her mouth opened and then she snapped it shut. Her hand gripped my shirt, and she pulled me closer. "Those are my standards for me, not you. Besides, having a scar doesn't have anything to do with perfection."

"Says the girl who's a walking example of perfection. Paisley, you gotta see yourself in the mirror, right? You're fucking gorgeous. Perfection of the female form with a brain that rivals any scientist and a work ethic that makes me feel like a couch potato. How can I show my faults to a woman like that?"

Paisley's eyes filled, and I felt like an absolute idiot. How had

I messed up this apology so badly that she was now crying? I let go of her hips to cup her face.

"Please don't cry. I meant to come over here to apologize and explain myself, not make you more upset. I can't take a whole week of you ignoring me. I know it's selfish, but I realized I've come to rely on our daily interactions. Our texts at night. Seeing your smile first thing in the morning. You're my catnip, baby."

Paisley dropped her head to my chest, and I held her tight. We stayed that way for long minutes, time slipping by as we just melted into the feeling of each other. When she finally lifted her head, it was with a grin on her face and a yellow streak now imprinted on my shirt.

"You know what they say..."

I had no idea what she was talking about. I grunted.

Her grin amped up. "Save a fuse, blow a lineman."

I shook my head and groaned at the lame joke. "You better not blow a lineman, woman."

Paisley sobered up quickly. "So, does this mean sex is now on the table?"

I rubbed my thumb across her streak of yellow paint, feeling like this was always the inevitable destination for us. The moment I'd met this spark plug, we were on our way to right here.

"On the table, in the bed, in the backseat of a truck, or in a tree. Wherever you want, baby."

Paisley's eyes danced, but her nose wrinkled. "In a tree?"

I shrugged, feeling lighthearted for the first time all week. "Hey, I can make a tree-seat with duct tape, I can make a tree-sex-swing."

Paisley laughed, which was my intention. "I prefer inside, thank you very much. No bark rash for me."

I leaned down and plucked a kiss from her lips. My dick pressed against her belly, thinking it was finally time for him to come out and play. "How about Saturday? I've got a babysitter lined up all night."

Paisley's smile could have lit the city. "I'm in."

I leaned down and kissed her again. "No, baby. *I'm* gonna be in."

***

Me: Any chance it's Saturday yet?

Pain-in-the-ass neighbor: You just left my house and I'm pretty sure it's Wednesday.

Me: So...why are we waiting for Saturday again?

Pain-in-the-ass neighbor: I don't know, cowboy. You're the one putting rules on all this. Got any sex rules I should know about?

Me: Hmm...pretty sure I don't, except for the 2:1 ratio.

Pain-in-the-ass neighbor: What the hell is that?

Me: Two orgasms for you, for every one for me. Minimum. I'm shooting for 3:1 though. Just so you're prepared.

Pain-in-the-ass neighbor: I like that rule...

Me: Figured you would, but if I'm being honest, it's been awhile for me. I might not be able to hold out like I normally could. Fair warning.

Pain-in-the-ass neighbor: You already making excuses, cowboy?

Me: Quit wearing those short jean shorts you've been wearing and we won't have a problem.

Pain-in-the-ass neighbor: Okay.

Me: Fuck me. You're wearing a swimsuit tomorrow, aren't you?

Pain-in-the-ass neighbor: You know me so well…

CHAPTER SIXTEEN

*P*aisley

I HAD ATTENDED many weddings for the Hellman family—all five of the boys had gotten married and now their mother was tying the knot—but I'd never had my heart pounding like this as I got ready for one. All previous dates felt like pathetic freshman-year dates with fumbling in the dark and being ditched later to spend the evening with his boys. This...this thing with Gannon was on another level entirely. This felt like something important. Something precious. Maybe even something that would lead to a wedding of my own.

"Whoa there, Pearse," I muttered to my reflection, tucking a flyaway hair behind my ear. "Just a date, not a marriage proposal."

The girls had been over earlier to help me get ready. Marlo and Keva weren't attending the wedding, but they'd been all too happy to help Audrey and me curl our hair and expertly apply makeup. They were all exceptionally giddy, making me even more nervous about something that should just be a lot of fun. It was me and my head making it into something it wasn't. I had a tendency to take something simple and make it bigger and better just because I thought I could.

Then again, sex with Gannon wasn't something simple.

I had a feeling it would rock my world and shift my priorities in ways I had yet to experience. The knock on my front door had me lurching backward from the mirror, nearly tipping over in my heels. I straightened up, insanely glad no one saw that wobble, and headed for the door. I wasn't wearing an ankle brace, and while my physical therapist had warned against heels, I refused to wear flats to a wedding.

I pulled open my door and nearly bobbled again. Gannon blocked the late afternoon sunlight in a suit he had no business wearing. He looked like a professional soccer player or a football star, leaving the locker room all showered and changed and testing the boundaries of a suit with his bulging muscles. The matching coat and pants, the light blue collared shirt open at the throat, and the brown shoes that matched the belt...it was a powerful combination.

"You can't wear that."

It was out before I could snatch it back. Gannon's smile faltered, and he looked down at himself.

"It's the only suit I got," he grumbled.

I let go of the doorknob and waved him in. "Sorry. Yeah. No. It's great."

He stepped inside, smelling like cologne mixed with soap and play dough. Clearly, he'd been playing with Elise earlier. He leaned down and dusted his lips across my cheek. "Spit it out, Pearse."

I blushed furiously. Smoothing a hand down his shirtfront —and not at all feeling up his chest and abs, promise—I figured I owed him full honesty after his confession a few nights ago.

"It's just that you look insanely hot in a suit, and I really don't want to wait until after the wedding."

Gannon growled, leaning in closer to sniff my neck like an animal. "Wait to do what, exactly?"

My eyes fluttered shut and desire wound its way through my core and between my legs. I loved when he teased me. Wanting Gannon became a living, pulsing thing in my body. "To drop to my knees, take you out of those pants, and get my mouth on your cock again."

Gannon stiffened and then dropped his forehead to my shoulder, groaning. "Now we can't leave."

I frowned, but he just grabbed my hand and pressed it against the huge erection straining the front of his suit pants.

"Ah."

"Yeah."

"How about I get you an ice-cold glass of water?"

He lifted his head and his eyes were practically sparkling without a hat to cover them. "How about you put on this corsage while I think about grandmas and football stats?"

He held out a clear container I hadn't even noticed he was holding. Apparently I'd been eye-fucking him too hard to notice the sweet gesture I didn't know he was capable of. He popped open the box and held out the flowers, white roses and light blue carnations that would go perfectly with my dress. I slipped it onto my wrist and tried not to let this man slip any further into my heart.

"How did you know what color?" I gaped at the beautiful flowers before looking back at a smug Gannon.

"I saw your mom at the grocery store, and I asked her over the apples."

Oh shit. I felt it. The exact moment Gannon slid right into my heart and made himself at home. I had zero defenses to stop this from happening. All that weight pushing in the gym and I let this grumpy neighbor just waltz right in.

I blinked up at him, not ready to expose my feelings quite yet. "We have time for a quick blow job, right?"

Gannon squeezed his eyes shut and put his hand over them

like a human blindfold. "Jesus. How about you quit saying things like that or we'll never get out of here?"

I smiled impishly. "I will if you will."

He did not, in fact, stick to this arrangement, waiting until we were milling about before the wedding and about to greet my parents to tell me exactly what body parts of mine he was going to attack first tonight. Right as Nikki walked down the aisle to her future husband, I whispered in Gannon's ear that I wasn't wearing panties. As Nikki and Jason promised to love each other forever, Gannon's hand slid higher on my thigh than was appropriate for being out in public. When we stood up to clap for the happy couple as they came back down the aisle as husband and wife, I made sure to rub my ass across the front of Gannon's pants. And so it went, the two of us trying to one-up each other all night long until the dancing started and we were both a sweating, pulsating mess of desire.

"How much fuckin' longer do we need to say?" Gannon ground out from between clenched teeth.

He held me to his body, swaying us to the music, looking hotter than any man here with his suit jacket off and his sleeves rolled up his thick forearms. I loved the peek of tattoos, knowing exactly what they looked like below the shirt. I could feel how badly he wanted me, his erection pinned between us. I was also glad I hadn't worn panties, as they would have been completely ruined by now.

"There you two are!" My mother's voice was like a bucket of ice water dumped on our heads.

We both turned in their direction, but Gannon kept me tightly tucked against him. My father's eyebrows were drawn together as he observed how closely we were dancing, but I wasn't fifteen any longer, so I didn't shove Gannon back. Besides, my father catching sight of the tented front of Gannon's pants would be worse.

"They're going to do the bouquet toss soon, so you might want to get to the front of the dance floor, honey." Mom winked at me, and I wanted to find a hole in the ground and dive in.

"I'm good, Mom," I answered weakly.

"Are you though?" Dad asked. "You're going back to work next week and didn't use this time off to find a new career. Maybe you should be looking for a husband instead."

I felt Gannon stiffen against me and not in the way I'd hoped he would tonight. "I think maybe we should let Paisley live her life as she sees fit."

Dad turned his stony gaze on my date. "Perhaps you shouldn't butt into a family matter."

"Perhaps you shouldn't talk so negatively to your daughter when she has a great career and her own house at twenty-six. She's hardly a failure."

I sucked in a breath and took control of the situation before Gannon and my father came to blows. "Okay, thanks, Mom. I better get over there." Then I gave Gannon a mighty yank and somehow the mountain of a man let me pull him away from my parents.

I dropped my forehead to his chest. "Please tell me that didn't happen."

Gannon was vibrating. I looked up and saw his face looking like a storm cloud.

"Gannon. It's okay. That's just how they are."

When he finally looked at me, his eyes were ice cold. "I know they're your parents, so I'm trying to keep my mouth shut, but I gotta tell you, Pearse. That shit's wrong."

I nodded, wanting to get back to the vibe from before. "I know it is, but it's just how they are. You don't have to defend me. It'll go in one ear and out the other."

The song changed, and we kept dancing, me clinging to the man who'd gone absolutely stiff with anger and Gannon staring out over my head. My brain scrambled to think of things to say to smooth the situation. When the last line of the song rang through, the crowd assembled on the dance floor, he leaned down and whispered in my ear.

"It's okay to need someone else, Pearse. Everyone needs someone, and I'm happy to be that person for you."

My heart fell a little bit harder, and I had to keep myself from rubbing my cheek against his chest just to get a little closer. It was those glimpses of a sweet man behind the frowns that turned me inside out. I turned my cheek so his scruff scraped my skin.

"And who is your someone, Gannon?"

He stiffened again and stood up straight, pulling me from the dance floor, my hand in his. We stopped at our table and he grabbed his suit jacket.

"Grab your things."

Great. He was back to giving orders and shutting me out. This was not how I planned this evening going. I gripped the back of my chair and stood my ground, thankful our whole table was out on the dance floor and not listening to us squabble.

"No."

He finally met my gaze. "No?"

"No. I'm not going anywhere until you acknowledge that you need someone too." I poked him in the chest. "And that someone is me."

"Pearse," he muttered. "Just let us get out of here, okay?"

I folded my arms across my chest and watched his gaze drop to my breasts. I couldn't do this if it was just about the sex. I was already in deeper than that and I needed to know he was, too. "No. Not until you say you need me too."

Gannon looked out across the grassy area where my friends and family milled about, all dressed in their finest clothes. He placed his jacket back on the chair with an ease that was polar opposite to the tightness of his entire body. Then his hands were bracketing my jaw, and he was so close I could feel his breath puff across my face.

"I need you so fucking bad I'm about to get in a fistfight with your dad right before tossing you over my shoulder and marching out of here so I can sink into your heat and pound away my frustration because I know of any woman on earth, you can take it. Satisfied now, woman?"

My belly did a sudden and complete melt, pooling heat between my legs and making me feel dizzy. "Get me out of here, Gannon."

His grin was downright lecherous. "Now you're talking."

It may have been the shortest drive home ever and probably the most dangerous, but we made it back to my place in one piece. Gannon already had my dress up around my waist and one hand teasing me mercilessly before he put the truck in park. He climbed out and came around to my side. He didn't wait for me to exit. He just reached in and plucked me off the seat and into his arms. He kicked his foot out and shut the door, hustling up to my house like I weighed nothing.

"In a hurry?" I teased, watching him fumble with the front door key I'd handed him.

"Open that smart mouth and I'll take you right here on the front lawn where all the neighbors can see."

I barely had neighbors, but still. I squeezed my legs together, insanely turned on by a scenario I'd never actually do, yet oddly wished for suddenly. I made the motion of zipping my lips and Gannon popped my door open, letting it go so that it banged against the wall before slamming shut.

He put me down, letting me slide down the front of his body before he stepped back. He threw his coat to the side, and it landed on the floor, forgotten. "You better start stripping."

The last sputter of any possible defense for my heart came through and demanded attention. I put a finger on his chest and he stilled his hands as he struggled with the buttons down his shirt.

"We do this, we're dating. You get that, right? This isn't just spectacular fucking. I want follow-through, Gannon."

His eyes lost some of the frenzied heat, but I'd never felt

more connected to another human being. He wanted me, yes, but he also took my feelings seriously, which, honestly, was the only answer I needed.

"I'm all in, Paisley, and my follow-through is epic."

I found myself smiling. "I'll hold you to that."

"You better. Now take off that fuckin' gorgeous dress so I don't have to destroy it."

CHAPTER SEVENTEEN

annon

Paisley backed away from me, her hands reaching behind her and pushing her tits out, straining against the silky dress she'd been torturing me with all evening. This woman was a badass in every way, and yet she rocked a dress and heels like some sort of supermodel. The sound of her zipper brought my gaze back up to her face, where her cheeks were already flushed and her bottom lip was caught by her teeth. The dress suddenly sprang free from her body. Paisley gave a slight shake to her shoulders and the whole thing cascaded to the floor to pool at her feet.

I groaned, jamming my fist against my mouth. She'd already told me she wasn't wearing panties, which I verified in the truck, but she also wasn't wearing a bra. Two flesh-colored sticker things were covering her nipples, but other than that, she was finally fucking naked.

"Take off the heels." My own voice surprised me. I sounded like I'd come off a long job in the middle of a forest fire and had inhaled more than my fair share of smoke. I had plans for Paisley and they didn't include her injuring herself more than she already had.

She narrowed her eyes like she was going to argue, but then thought better of it, leaning down to pull one shoe, then the other off her feet. When she was standing there in just her pasties and a sexy grin, I physically hurt from not touching her.

"You better fuckin' run, Pearse."

Her eyes widened, and when I lunged for her, she must have decided I meant it because she turned and ran, her gorgeous athletic body kicking into gear. I ran after her despite my leg barking at me. This was too much fun to care about an old injury. She shrieked as I gained on her, sliding around the doorway into the hall that led to her bedroom. I got to her right as she crossed the threshold into her bedroom. She tried to slam the door on me, but I held it with my right arm and grabbed her around the waist with my left.

Her shrieks turned into hysterical laughter as I picked her up with one arm and essentially tossed her onto her bed. She bounced and settled enough to push her long hair out of her face. I advanced on her, feeling like a lion sinking his teeth into his prey. The buttons on my shirt finally gave, and I tossed the material aside.

"You've still got a lot of clothing on, cowboy." Paisley challenged me, eyeing me from the bed, propped up on her elbows.

"Spread your legs for me, baby. Give me a little show while I get undressed." I nudged her leg, and after a second, she pulled her knee up and let it fall outward.

If I'd been feeling self-conscious about showing her my mangled leg, all that doubt fled the second I saw her pink flesh glistening between her legs. This woman, for whatever reason, wanted me and spending time worrying about my leg was time I wasn't spending feasting on her perfect body. I popped the button, slid down the zipper, and stepped out of the pants, pulling my socks and shoes along with them. My cock was already hard and ready to go. Any glimpse of Paisley, dressed or not, was enough to leave me in this condition.

Paisley sat up and reached for my hips, sitting on the edge of the bed and pulling me into her. Her hand cupped my balls and her tongue flicked across the tip of me. I nearly choked on my own spit. And if that wasn't enough to have me performing poorly when it really counted, Paisley pushed me back and dropped to her knees, her hands releasing me to stroke up my injured leg. Instead of being appalled by the pink mottled skin, she kissed her way up from my ankle all the way to my hip bone.

She could have done a lot of things that would make me lose my mind, but her being gentle and sweet with that particular part of me was making me lose a different body part. I swallowed hard around the lump in my throat.

"Paisley," I murmured, not trusting myself to say anything else.

She looked up at me, big hazel eyes shining up with trust and the kind of heat that made me confident that my leg hadn't grossed her out.

"Come here, baby." I hauled her up by her armpits because I couldn't wait any longer, tossing her onto the bed again.

"You like throwing me around?" she asked, that sunshine smile still in place. While I loved that smile, I wanted to see her come apart instead.

I crawled over her, memorizing the feel of her breasts against my chest, the drag of my dick up her leg. "Fuck yeah, I do. I love that you're strong. I know I don't have to treat you like you're fragile."

Paisley wrapped her arms around my neck. "That's the exact right thing to say to me."

If smug was a noun, I was it. I reached between us and ripped off one of those stickers blocking me from seeing her entirely. Paisley yelped, and I leaned down to pull her nipple into my mouth, laving it with my tongue to stop the sting. Pulling my head up, I got my fingers on the other one, making sure she was ready this time. She gave a quick nod, and I ripped that one off too, my tongue right there to soothe the pain. Her tits filled my palms and overflowed. I wouldn't say I was a boob man, but Paisley might have me changing my tune. Paisley hitched her leg over my hip and ground against my length.

"You're a greedy girl, huh?"

Paisley's breaths were coming faster and there was no way in hell I was letting her come until I was inside her and could feel her pulsing around me. I pulled my hips away from her and she instantly stuck her bottom lip out.

"Condom," I barked, trying to remember where I'd left my pants.

"Drawer," Paisley barked right back.

I leaned over and pulled open her drawer, seeing a new box. I got one out and put it on, but Paisley had other ideas when I tried to get back between those legs. She pushed my shoulder.

"I need some time on top," she explained, so I let her roll me dangerously close to the side of the bed. I didn't care which way we did this. I just needed to be inside her right fuckin' now.

Paisley lifted up and grabbed my dick, putting just the tip of me inside her heat. My eyes rolled back in my head and it took everything I had not to thrust my hips upward and take what I wanted all at once. Instead, she slowly eased down, taking me one inch at a time until I thought I might just lose my mind.

When her hands landed on my shoulders and her hair tickled the sides of my face, I managed to open my eyes again. "Little more, baby."

"Just give me a second," she panted.

The thing was, I'd normally be polite and give a woman time to adjust. You didn't get to be my size and not worry about hurting a lady, but Paisley wasn't a fragile woman.

"You can take all of me." I let go of the bedspread and put my hands on her hips, right as I thrust upward. The last few inches wedged inside, and Paisley whimpered. She gripped me hard, and I stayed still, letting her adjust. "Told you."

Her eyes opened, and she was practically spitting fire. She flexed her legs to come up, and for a split second, I thought she was pissed enough to stop what we were doing. Instead, she slammed back down hard and fast enough I was the one groaning. She leaned back and grabbed my balls, still riding me like she had an end goal in mind and she was going to get there sooner rather than later. Sadly, if she kept up this pace, I'd be there before her.

Gripping her hips tighter, I pushed off the bed with my foot and we rolled again, this time right off the damn bed. I took the brunt of the fall, and while I'd be feeling that tomorrow, all I cared about was rutting deeper into Paisley's body.

"That can't..." She quit talking to groan and pant. "...be comfortable."

She was referring to the fact that my neck was bent, as the wall wasn't giving me much room. I didn't care. I'd deal with the neck brace and physical therapy later.

Apparently she did care, because with the next flex of her legs, she lifted completely off me, scrambling to her feet and holding her hand out to me. I groaned at the loss of her heat. Picking myself off the floor, I grabbed her and put her back against the wall.

"Legs up, baby."

Paisley jumped and wrapped her legs around my hips. My dick was inside of her before she even got her hands to my shoulders. Her pussy was heaven, a tight fit that had me seeing stars and forgetting about anything in the world except for thrusting my hips and making more of this pleasure.

"Fuck, Paisley, you feel so good."

My hand, the one that had been gripping her shoulder to keep her in place, drifted to her neck. She rolled her head to the side and let out a pretty little groan each time I thrust inside of her. My thumb got around her chin and rolled her head back in my direction so I could kiss her. My tongue took her mouth in the same tempo as my cock took her pussy.

Paisley's legs tightened around me and her mewling intensified. She ripped her mouth away from mine and thrashed her head back and forth against the wall.

"That's it, baby," I crooned, rutting faster and harder. "Come for me."

"Don't...fucking...tell me...what to do," she panted.

I grinned against her neck. That was such a Paisley response. Wanting her to do exactly what I told her anyway, I moved my hand from her hip to find her clit, strumming across that bundle of nerves just twice before I felt her tighten around my dick and let out a scream that sounded vaguely like my name.

"That's it, baby. Give it to me. Fuck, I love you all sweaty and greedy." I could feel her pulsing, and I was officially lost. I thrust into her hard enough to leave bruises where her body met the wall. "I could ruin this pussy all night long."

And then a wave crashed over me and I was trembling, spurting into her body and clenching her tight. Goddamn, she was everything right and perfect in this world. The one thought that stayed with me until the last ripple of pleasure finally subsided was that Paisley was the one who had ruined me. Inside and outside of the bedroom.

I pulled her away from the wall on shaky legs, getting us over to the bed before I pulled out of her and laid her down. I took care of the condom and came back to bed, pulling her back into my front and brushing the hair away from her face and neck. She was remarkably quiet, which had worry creeping in.

"Did I hurt you, baby?"

Paisley finally stirred, her hands stroking across my forearms where they were banded around her body. "If that's hurting me, I want you to hurt me every day."

I groaned and buried my head in her hair. We had eight hours until I had to pick up Elise. There was so much I could still do to this woman and she'd just given me the green light. I grabbed her hand that was stroking me and moved it to her knee.

"Hold your leg up for me."

She didn't argue, and I wondered if perhaps this was the way to keep her smart mouth from eviscerating me. Keep her so drugged on orgasms she didn't remember to argue. I was willing to give that theory a shot.

I stroked the insides of her thighs and massaged her muscles. When she began to press her gorgeous ass against me, I narrowed in my stroking, finding her clit still engorged and achy. I circled it gently, dipping below every now and again to feel her clench my finger. Paisley let out a low moan, and I knew she was ready for more. I focused in on her clit, not giving her a second of reprieve until she was keening out my name and shaking in my arms once again. Her thighs slammed together and I kept my hand inside of her while she rode out orgasm number two.

"Two-to-one ratio, baby," I whispered in her ear.

She huffed out a breathy laugh. "I thought you were shooting for three to one?"

I pushed up on an elbow to take in her tinged cheeks and sweaty neck. Fuck, I loved her like this. Not, like, loved her, but loved how she looked drunk on orgasms. Pushing away that scary train of thought, I rolled her onto her back and settled between her legs, my mouth even with her stomach.

"I haven't even started using my mouth, baby."

Paisley looked down at me with one eye open. "I might not survive three."

I shrugged and shot her a cocky grin. "Let's try it out and see."

Spoiler alert: she survived number three.

Barely.

CHAPTER EIGHTEEN

aisley

EVERY MUSCLE in my body ached in the most delicious way. I pulled my arms out from under Gannon's heavy biceps, a sheen of sweat on my upper lip. Who would have guessed the grumpy single dad next door was a snuggler? And that he pumped out heat like a space heater?

He groaned softly at the movement and banded his arm tighter around my waist. "You ruined my ratio," he whispered, sounding half asleep still.

I tried to twist to see him, but he grunted and held me still. "Too early."

I rolled my eyes and gave in to it. He wasn't going to let me go anytime soon, so I might as well rub up against that impressive morning erection.

"Wow. Grumpy right from the moment you wake up. That's admirable dedication to the grump persona."

"Shh," he muttered, burrowing his face into my hair and then thrusting his steel length against my ass.

I bit back a moan. The man was a machine. All that talk about an injured leg and he'd barely let me get any sleep last night. I'd paid him back in the wee hours of the morning by diving below the covers and waking him up from a dead sleep with the kind of blowjob that takes no prisoners. He'd nearly bucked me off the bed when he came in my mouth.

"Don't we have to get Elise soon?" I whispered instead. While I wouldn't mind going for another round, I was pretty sure there wasn't a square inch of my body that didn't feel the effects of last night in the form of aching muscles or bruised skin. Sex with Gannon was like playing a game of rugby.

"What are you going to do about this?" Gannon growled into my hair as he thrust against my ass again.

"That's what lotion is for, buddy." I bit back a laugh.

Gannon moved so fast I didn't have a chance to defend myself. I was on my back in the blink of an eye and he was wedging himself between my legs, his face a sleepy, grumpy grin that made my inside melt all over again. I lifted a hand to run my fingers through his messy hair. He was always wearing a hat, and it gave me great pleasure to see those eyes of his clearly.

"Please?" He grabbed his dick and ran the tip over my folds, feeling how slick and ready for him I already was.

"You begging, cowboy?" I couldn't help myself. I liked how he lost control when I gave him shit. I lowered my knee, giving him better access, and he didn't wait. He shoved inside with one long, powerful stroke and we both grunted, stilling and panting.

"Shit, shit, shit." Gannon pulled out, and I opened my mouth to ask what was wrong, but then he reached for the drawer next to my bed and I understood.

I squeezed my eyes shut and scolded myself. I needed to be more levelheaded around him. I needed to remember important things like condoms. I'd never forgotten before, so why was I putting myself in danger of wrecking my career over a guy who'd already proven to have oops babies?

"Sorry, I forgot," I mumbled, watching him sheath himself.

He came back over me, and shook his head. "My fault, not yours." And then he was sliding into me again, filling me and pushing away all those thoughts that were far too serious for this rushed, messy lovemaking.

Gannon dropped his head and open-mouthed kissed whatever skin of mine he could reach. I reached around to grab his ass and pull him into me tighter. So tight I would remember this moment when Elise was with us and I was back at work and these moments were few and far between. Gannon's arms trembled so much he barely held himself up. Most of his weight was on me, sliding back and forth with small, urgent thrusts that had me mewling for more.

"Why do you feel so fuckin' good, Paisley?" Gannon slid his tongue up my neck and bit my earlobe with his teeth. "I can't get enough of you."

And that was all it took to set off my orgasm. Just one heartfelt confession from Gannon and I was spiraling up to a heaven where a guy like him could be everything I needed in my life. Possibilities exploded into happy shots of light behind my eyes that made me feel better than I ever had.

"Gannon," I cried, head tossed back against the pillows.

"Yes, baby. I feel you. So fuckin' good." And then he was grunting into my neck, his huge body shuddering over me, his thrusts continuing but getting more shallow with each movement.

We lay there until the sweat had dried and I couldn't feel my legs. When I poked Gannon in the shoulder, he grunted awake and lifted his head, looking half asleep again.

"Did you seriously fall asleep?"

He blinked a few times and then pushed off of me, sliding out and flopping back on the bed. "I'm old, woman. You've worn me out."

I snorted, checking out his amazing body, not the least bit marred by the scars on his right leg. Gingerly, I rolled to the side of the bed and stood up, testing out my limbs for functionality. "If I'm walking funny today, I blame you."

Gannon rolled his head, a cocky grin transforming his handsome face. "Am I an asshole for saying I'd like to see you limping?"

I nodded, face dead serious. "Yes."

Gannon wasn't fazed as he sat up. "Then it's true. I'm an asshole."

"Make me some breakfast while I shower, and I might just keep you. Asshole and all."

Gannon stood up and took care of the condom. "Damn. Not even twenty-four hours into being my girlfriend and you're demanding breakfast."

That stopped me short. I turned and fell into his chest. "Girlfriend, huh?"

Gannon wrapped his arms around my waist and kissed my cheek. "You said you wanted follow-through. I'm giving you follow through."

My face couldn't contain the happiness filling my chest. "Yeah, cowboy, you are."

Then I slapped him hard on the bare ass and ran away as he threatened to return the favor. I made it into the shower before he could make good on his threat. We only had time for a half a bagel before we had to pick up Elise, but I wasn't really hungry. Who needed food when you had a hot man keeping you fed on steamy sex and sweet nothings?

"Daddy!" Elise ran out the front door when we pulled up, Roxy hot on her heels. "Look it!" And then she proceeded to attempt cartwheels on the Sutters' front lawn. They weren't great, but they were a start.

Gannon's jaw dropped. I clapped my hands and Roxy gave her pointers. Lucy and Bain came out, looking like they hadn't gotten much sleep either, but for an entirely different reason.

"Elise!" Gannon ran over to her, his sharp tone of voice pulling me up short. He grabbed her and hefted her into his arms. She tried to get down, but he wasn't having it. "No. No cartwheels. It's too dangerous."

Bain stepped in, obviously sensing that Gannon wasn't happy. "Sorry, man. We kept a close eye on her. I promise she wasn't in any danger."

Gannon gave him a curt nod. "I know. Thank you. Really."

I gave Lucy a hug, the two of us having a whole silent conversation with just looks.

What's his deal?

Not sure, but I'll find out.

Hope he's not mad at us.

He's not. Thank you for taking Elise.

We left, Elise babbling away in her car seat about all the things they did. Gannon's jaw was clenched tight, and he didn't reach over to put his hand on my thigh like he'd started doing lately.

"Daddy, they cawtwheels. I love them!"

"They're not safe, E-bug. Let's find something else fun to do." He kept flicking glances in the rearview mirror, as if making sure she was truly not harmed.

"Maybe some gymnastics lessons might be good? They could show her how to do them properly and safely?"

Gannon's gaze cut in my direction and I knew instantly I'd overstepped. "Not now, Pearse."

If he didn't want my opinion, then he shouldn't have hired me to watch his daughter for the last few weeks. "So that's it? You just don't trust her?"

Gannon turned into his driveway, bouncing hard over the curb before slamming it into park. "I said not now."

He hopped out of the truck and worked on getting Elise out of the back while I got out and tried to decide if I was pissed enough to stomp home and ignore him for the rest of the day. Sadly, I started work tomorrow, so if I didn't spend today with them, I wouldn't see them much this week.

Gannon got Elise playing with a new sprinkler set for kids

he'd gotten, the whips of water making her giggle as she ran through and got wet. I made my way over to his side, not sure what his deal was with the cartwheels.

"You okay?" I asked, trying to tamp down my own anger at him for speaking so abruptly to me. He'd had a point. I shouldn't bring stuff up in front of Elise.

Gannon huffed and dropped his arms from where they'd been folded across his chest. "I'm fine. I just don't want my kid doing dangerous things. Five is way too young to be doing cartwheels."

I'd thought Gannon telling me what to do these last few weeks was just him pushing my buttons, but it looked to me like he had an issue with everyone around him doing anything he deemed dangerous.

"I was doing gymnastics classes at five. Then soccer, tennis, basketball, and then volleyball. Hell, I think my first time at the batting cages was when I could barely hold a bat, let alone swing it."

Gannon side-eyed me. "I need Elise safe."

"And Elise needs to be able to play like a normal kid."

Gannon folded his arms across his chest again. "And I need you to trust my judgement as her father."

I mirrored his pose. "And I think you should show her you trust her enough to do a damn cartwheel."

"I think you're reading too much into this on account of your own shitty parents."

"Takes a shitty parent to know one."

We both stood there, steaming, huffing like bulls from our noses. Why was he being such a stubborn ass? Saying I was talking from a place of baggage? Well, yeah, that's what humans did. We formed opinions based on prior experience. Which was exactly what he was doing. Deciding everything was too dangerous for his little girl because he'd been burned. Literally.

That thought sobered me quickly. He had been burned. Badly. And not that long ago. He just loved Elise and wanted her safe. I let my arms relax at my side.

"It's none of my business, not really. Are we going to stay mad all day or should we do something fun on my last day?"

I must have gotten to him because Gannon also dropped his arms and pushed my hair behind my shoulder. "Why don't we get in swimsuits and jump sprinklers with Elise?"

I was walking away from this fight, but I would still seek revenge with one of my skimpiest swimsuits just to torture the man. "Done. See you in a few."

We both walked off to get changed, but my phone buzzed several times while I was in my bedroom, studiously ignoring the rumpled bed that had seen some major action last night.

Joe: Hey, Paisley. I need a favor. Adam is out for the next two months. Can you take his day shifts?

I did a little shimmy and answered the guy who did all the scheduling as quickly as my thumbs could type. Being given day shift wasn't technically a promotion, but everybody knew it was. Once you got off night shift, you went to day shift, and from there, you got promoted to foreman. Adam was only out for two months, but I knew I could impress my bosses in that given time. Enough that I'd at least be in the conversations about becoming a foreman.

Me: Most definitely. I'll see you tomorrow.

Today was looking good, despite Gannon being a grumpy ass about Elise's cartwheels. Working day shift also meant I'd be on the same schedule as Gannon and Elise, which meant I'd be able to see them more during the week and wouldn't spend my off days trying to fight my sleep/wake schedule. I tied my bikini top behind my back and grabbed a towel before going outside and joining Elise.

Gannon stepped out of the trailer, a pair of board shorts on his body. On anyone else, this would have been standard attire for jumping through the sprinklers, but I knew how much he hid his scars.

Elise pointed to Gannon. "Daddy has an ouchie."

I left her side, walked straight up to the grump and threw my arms around his neck. I gave him a loud smacking kiss on the lips and whispered in his ear, "You look good enough to eat, cowboy."

He growled, but I was already gone, running through the sprinklers and shrieking in fake surprise as the spray got me across the face. Elise giggled and followed me, also getting water shot in her face. Gannon let out a roar and came running through the worst of it, becoming soaking wet as he chased us both. By the time we turned off the water and sat down to eat lunch in the shade, we were all exhausted and wet and smiling.

I popped a grape in my mouth and watched Gannon cut the crust off Elise's peanut butter and jelly sandwich. For the first time, my plans weren't centered around getting that promotion at work. Somehow, these two perfect strangers had wormed their way into my vision of the future.

And I liked that new vision very much.

 annon

"MEATBALL, NO!"

I looked over to my left at Elise's cry, seeing that the dog had jumped into the makeshift wading pool I'd made for Elise. Who knew four picnic benches on the ground, a thick plastic tarp draped over, and plenty of zip ties would somehow make a pool? Poor Meatball was so excited his tail whipped the water and splashed her right in the face. I let out a sharp whistle and he jumped back out, racing over to my side to sit on my boot and made a muddy mess of the spot next to me.

"Abby didn't like that!" Elise cried, waving around an angry, soaked doll.

"Meatball says he's sorry!" I shouted back, trying to tamp down irritation at being interrupted for the five thousandth time in the last hour.

"Meatball can't talk, Daddy!" she shouted back. I bit back a smile and shook my head.

I loved my daughter, I really did, but it was impossible to get anything done when I was the one watching her. Two trailers had been delivered yesterday, and if I could just get the horseshoe pit done, I could move on to getting the trailers rented out. The money I'd scraped together for this project was running out and I desperately needed to focus on finishing the first phase of this glamping ground.

Missing Paisley wasn't just about having coverage for Elise, though. I missed seeing her prance around in her short shorts. I missed her smart mouth giving me hell. I especially missed how she made every day seem a little sunnier with her optimism and get-it-done attitude. Sure, I'd seen her yesterday after her shift, but she'd been exhausted and not her usual fireplug self. She assured me she'd adjust quickly to being back at work, but I hated to see her so worn out.

In the meantime, I was trying to get this business up and running while feeling like I was failing at parenting. I'd taken Elise to sign up for kindergarten first thing this morning and they'd said I should have signed her up last year. I'd gotten quite the stare when I explained that I hadn't known she existed last year, so that was impossible. I tried Paisley's approach and complimented the beastly administration woman instead of griping at her. She sure had grumbled a lot, but somehow Elise was now registered for the coming school year.

"Back it up, Meatball, or you'll lose a paw."

Meatball whined and backed up a few feet. I swear, that dog knew what I was saying. He seemed so dumb one second, and in the next, he acted like he understood me. I jammed the auger in the dirt and gave it a good twist, making the hole as deep as I could. I didn't want the first horseshoe thrown to topple my stake and end the game.

"Cartwheel, Daddy!" Elise yelled.

I whipped my head over in alarm, but it was just Abby doing a cartwheel along the rim of the wading pool. I shook my head and got back to securing this stake. All this time digging and building gave me time to reflect on Paisley's suggestion of gymnastics classes. We hadn't exactly had an argument, but there'd been a few heated moments the other day.

Paisley had not-so-subtly implied I was a shitty parent. I'd accused her of her own parental bullshit clouding her vision, but I also knew my own accident had clouded mine. If I was being honest, before the accident, I wouldn't have thought twice about a five-year-old taking a gymnastics course. It's just...I knew now that bad shit happened and becoming a dad had made me realize how precious life really was. And if I was diligent, maybe I could save Elise from most of the shit that life had to offer. I wasn't there for her the first five years of her life, but I could make up for it now by being the best dad I could possibly be.

It was also possible that I may have gone a little overboard.

"Hey, Elise." I looked over to see Bain in full uniform, crouching by Elise's pool. His work-issued SUV was out on the street but I'd been so lost in thought I hadn't heard him.

I put down the shovel and came over. I needed to apologize to the guy who'd been nothing but nice to me.

"Bain. I wanted to thank you again for having Elise over." He stood, and we shook hands after I pulled my gloves off. "I, uh, left your house in a bit of a mood. I wanted to apologize for that."

Bain shrugged. "It's all good. I get in moods pretty much every other day."

We both smirked, clearly cut from the same cloth. "Well, please extend my apology to Lucy, then."

"Will do. How are things going around here?"

I looked out on my property, seeing my dream begin to take shape. "It's getting there. Got two trailers installed, walkways done, the mini stage and dance floor are in, and the county just mailed me the liquor license. Now just working on the horseshoe pits and decided on a sand volleyball court by the stage. Should be close to a soft opening."

Bain lifted an eyebrow. "You got a web designer set up?"

I put my hands on my hips, trying not to feel overwhelmed.

"Nope. That's my next hurdle. Find tech help and then start marketing."

"Did you meet Andi Hellman at the wedding? Tall, brown hair, glasses?"

I nodded, remembering her well because Paisley had pointed out Andi's husband, Ethan, and told me she'd dated him back in high school. I'd disliked him instantly.

"She could whip you up a website in a day or two and do it on the cheap. And most of the Hellmans run their own businesses. I'm sure they could help with the marketing plan."

Thinking about my bank account had me swallowing my pride. "Do you mind giving my number to Andi?"

"Sure thing." Bain nodded and then paused. "Hey, could I ask you a favor?"

"Sure, man. Anything."

"When you get this place open and start to need help, would you consider hiring my buddy Lincoln? I tried to get him to move to Hell a few years back, but he was too young to see the opportunity here. He's run into some trouble and reached back out. I think he'd be just the kind of help you need around here. Jack-of-all-trades kind of thing."

I took my hat off and scratched my head. "I don't mind at all, but I might be a bit far out from being able to hire help."

Bain smiled. "I don't think you understand the power of my wife. She's already talking this place up. You just get the website going and I promise you we'll keep those trailers full."

I didn't know about all that, but I'd take any help I could get. "It's much appreciated. Speaking of, I gotta get back out there."

Bain clapped me on the back and turned to go. "Good to see you."

A thought pricked at my brain. "Hey, does Lucy know of a kids' gymnastics class around here?"

Bain's head whipped around and he smiled like he was proud of me. "Yeah, man. I'll have her send you the info."

I nodded my thanks and watched Elise play with her dolls

while Bain drove away. Wouldn't hurt to have the information. For later. Like, maybe sixth grade. I had to let my little girl go sometime, but I felt like I just got her. She was five already, but I'd only had a few months with her. To me, she was still a newborn and I couldn't quite let her go just yet.

***

"UGHHH!" Paisley sank into one of the camp chairs outside the trailer and closed her eyes, head tipped back. Her hair was in a professional low bun that somehow looked sexy as hell, but the dirt smudged across her uniform shirt told me today had not been a good day.

"Can I get you a beer?" I'd popped my head out the second I heard the loud engine on her tank of a truck pull into the driveway.

"Got two hands, don't I?" she asked the back of her eyelids.

I raised my eyebrows. "Two beers it is." I stepped back inside the trailer and got the beers out of the mini fridge.

"Come on, E-bug. Paisley's home."

Elise jumped up and ditched her dolls. My little girl's squeal warmed my heart. I kinda felt the same way about Paisley being home from work. We stepped out of the trailer and Elise immediately climbed on her lap to tell her about her day. God bless the woman, Paisley acted intrigued by every excruciating detail, though I could see the fatigue in her eyes.

By the time Elise climbed off her lap to hunt down a new imaginary adventure with the dollhouse I'd bought her and put up on the picnic table, Paisley had drained one of the long-necked beers. I handed her the next one, trying not to be a total dirtbag by watching her lips wrap around the end of it as she tipped it up to her mouth. She caught my gaze, and I saw the hint of a smile there when she saw how I was looking at her.

"I hate to tell you this, but I have some people coming over tonight."

She groaned, tipping her head back and closing her eyes again. "I'll stay here and sleep, okay?"

I did not like seeing my woman knocked off her feet like this. Every protective instinct in me was clanging out a warning. "They're working you too hard."

"Don't start, cowboy," she replied with enough steel behind her tone, I felt a little bit of relief. If she had enough energy to give me sass, she was doing just fine.

"It's, uh, it's your ex-boyfriend."

That got her head back up and her eyes showing some life. "Who?"

"Ethan and Andi Hellman. Andi's going to build my website for me."

Paisley smiled, and I hoped it wasn't because she was looking forward to seeing her ex. "Good. Andi's a website genius and barely charges. She says it's fun." Paisley shuttered. "Does this mean you're about to open Glamper's Paradise?"

I nodded, taking a pull from my own beer. "Yeah, not too far off."

"I'm sorry, Gannon."

I looked at her sharply. "For what?"

She smiled softly, reaching forward to hold my hand. "I've been so focused on getting back to my own job, I haven't been as attentive about your progress."

I opened my mouth to tell her I didn't need that kind of support from her but was cut off from telling that whopper of a lie by another truck pulling up to the curb.

Ethan waved from the driver's side. He and Andi came over and introduced themselves formally, though I was pretty sure we'd met at the wedding. Andi snagged my attention immediately by asking questions about my business and what I had envisioned. We sat at the other end of the picnic table from Elise. I tried to answer all her questions, but I kept seeing Paisley and Ethan out of the corner of my eye, laughing and talking like old friends. I mean, they were, but did they have to get along so damn well?

"So, camping, but with a glam fun side, right?" Andi was asking, blinking up from yellow-tinted glasses. She already had her laptop out, fingers clacking across the screen as she talked.

"Exactly. Would you excuse me for a moment?" I stood before she answered, making my way over to Paisley.

"Can I ask you something privately?" I interrupted their conversation but couldn't muster up an attempt at an apology.

Paisley looked at me funny, but set down her beer and hefted herself out of the chair to follow me into her house. As soon as the door closed, I spun her into the wall and pressed up against her so tight neither of us could breathe.

"What the hell is this?" Paisley asked, her cheeks turning pink as I stared down at her.

Fuck me, she was pretty. Prim and proper in that damn bun, dirt smudged across her masculine uniform, and licking her lips like she wanted me as much as I wanted her.

"Give me three minutes?" I asked, dipping my head to ghost my lips across hers.

"For what?" she asked on a long exhale.

"Just promise." I kissed a trail down her neck, tasting a hint of salt and just straight Paisley.

"Okay."

I grinned against her skin, letting go of her hips to unzip her stiff work pants.

"What are you—"

"Shh," I muttered, backing up just enough to hold her gaze and let my hands get into her pants. I pushed aside her underwear and slid between her lips. "Fuck, baby, you already wet for me?"

Paisley sighed and rested her head against the wall. "You know I am. Now hurry up and make my day."

"Yes, ma'am." I dipped a finger into her heat, loving how responsive she was.

A second finger slid home, and I pumped in and out of her, making sure to brush against that bundle of nerves that did her in every time. I didn't have the luxury of a long hour or so to tease her and make it good. This one would be quick, and when I went back out again to deal with her ex and his wife, I'd have the scent of her on my skin, grounding me.

Paisley's breaths came faster and faster until she was grabbing my forearm with both hands and sighing my name on a long exhale. I kissed her again, feeling the strength drain out of her body as she clenched around my fingers.

"So fuckin' beautiful," I murmured against her lips. "And all mine."

Her eyes opened softly, her lashes sweeping up and down with each lazy blink. "Mmm."

"Say it, baby."

That support I was thinking I didn't need from her? I was a fucking liar. I needed it more than I needed air. And when she smiled up at me, I could see she knew exactly what I needed from her.

"All yours, cowboy."

***

Me: Missing you...

Pain-in-the-ass neighbor: You just saw me this morning before work!

Me: Not nearly enough time for all the things I want to do to you.

Pain-in-the-ass neighbor: Shit.

Me: Everything okay?

Pain-in-the-ass neighbor: I just smiled because of your text and looked up to lock eyes with my coworker. Now Gabe thinks I like him.

Me: Who the fuck is Gabe?

Pain-in-the-ass neighbor: Relax, cowboy. He's like fifty.

Me: You like older men, so no, I won't relax.

Pain-in-the-ass neighbor: Seriously, we're back to this? You aren't that much older than me.

Me: Fuck yeah I am, little girl.

Pain-in-the-ass neighbor: Quit sexting with me or poor Gabe will turn bright red.

Me: What the fuck is sexting?

Pain-in-the-ass neighbor: I take it back. You are old.

aisley

I THREW MY GLOVES, boots, and hard hat in my locker, making sure to unclip all the meters hanging from my belt and put them back on their chargers. Today had been a long one. The sun had been unrelenting as I climbed pole after pole to complete inspections that were overdue already. Too many power lines in this state and not enough linemen to check them.

"Hey, Pais!"

I turned around to see Benny Campbell coming in for his night shift. I hadn't seen him since I came back to work this week. Yet another benefit of switching to day shift. He gave me a hug with a big grin on his face and I momentarily felt bad for thinking bad thoughts about him.

"You never did call me for that date," he chastised, winking.

Yep. That was why I didn't care for him. Telling him no was just the first volley in a lifetime of negotiations you didn't want to be involved in.

I rolled my eyes and launched into the one thing that actually seemed to deter men. "I've got a boyfriend, Benny. You can stop asking."

Benny jumped back, hand on his chest in horror. "No, no, no. Not my Paisley."

I grabbed my bag out of the locker and closed it with a hip check. "Never been yours, B."

He scrunched up his face. "B? I'm just B now? Reduced to a single letter?"

I shrugged. Seemed fair for calling me Pais all these years. "Be safe out there."

Benny pouted, but let me go without further bullshit. I shook my head and walked out of the building, realizing the stark contrast between Benny and Gannon. There was absolutely no spark there with Benny. He held down a physical job that many would consider masculine, but he was whiny. Gannon, on the other hand, also did a physical job, but was as masculine as they came. By the time I climbed in my truck in the parking lot, I was grinning, remembering the time Gannon had thrown me up against the wall in my bedroom. There was nothing whiny and weak about Gannon.

And maybe that's why my prior boyfriends had never worked out. I preferred a strong male who dominated in the bedroom and handled me roughly. In that small way, Gannon showed me that he trusted me to handle whatever he threw at me. I'd steamrolled my ex-boyfriends. Gannon though? He was un-steamrollable.

I drove home, cataloguing the day's aches and pains. My ankle had been in a state of dull throbbing since I started back. I'd taped the hell out of it and muscled my way through. There was no way I'd be wasting this opportunity to show the bosses how capable I was. "Foreman" would look damn good next to my name.

My boyfriend and his mini sidekick were already outside when I came home, chasing each other with water guns. Elise hit Gannon in the chest with a stream of water and he dropped to the ground, acting as if he'd really been hurt. Elise dropped her water gun and ran over to him, climbing on top of his chest and grabbing his face between her chubby little hands.

I could practically feel the peace fall over my body. My shoulders fell away from my ears. My lungs were able to breathe deeper. Even my ankle gave up the constant pulsing of pain. These were my people.

And if I wasn't mistaken, I was pretty sure I'd fallen in love with them both.

I climbed out of the truck, needing to join them. Both heads popped up and then Elise was scrambling off her dad to rush toward me. She nearly bowled me over when she hugged the hell out of my legs. I laughed and swung her up in my arms.

"I saw you take down your daddy." I fist-bumped her.

Elise giggled and then whispered so loud the whole neighborhood could have heard her. "He's faking, don't wowwy. Come play!"

Elise kicked her legs, and I set her down. She ran off to get me a water gun, screaming over her shoulder that they were in a time-out. Gannon picked himself off the ground and came over, cupping my face and studying me.

"You doing okay?" he asked, eyebrows coming together under the bill of his hat.

His thumb stroked across my cheek and I could feel myself melting against him. I was a tough mother trucker all week long at work, but the second Gannon held me, I could let all that go and be vulnerable. I hadn't known that I needed that until he gave me the space to admit weakness.

"I'm tired and my ankle is too."

He nodded once, then dipped his head to ghost his lips across mine. I needed more, but he wasn't responding to my grabby hands that had fisted his T-shirt to pull him in closer.

"I got you, Pearse," he said so firmly and yet gently, I let him have his way.

He swooped me up in his arms, dirty uniform and all,

marching to my front door. Elise came running up with Meatball hot on her heels, probably confused as to why her dad was carrying me if we were supposed to play with water guns.

"Change of plans, E-bug. Paisley is injured and needs a doctor. Are you a doctor?"

"No..." she answered, obviously confused.

Gannon spun to face her. "What do you mean? Isn't your name Doctor Elise?"

Elise looked at me, then back to her dad, finally catching on. "Um, yes! Yes I am! Doctor Hot!"

My head whipped to Gannon. He grinned, whispering, "She means Doctor Hart."

I grinned too. "I kind of like Doctor Hot..."

He rolled his eyes and carried me inside my house, depositing me on the couch and propping my leg up on the coffee table. "Doctor Hart! We need ice! Stat!"

"I'm on it!" she shouted back, racing to the kitchen and nearly tripping over Meatball, who loved all the excited voices.

Gannon pressed a kiss to my forehead, then got busy taking my boots off. "You don't have to be everything to everyone, Paisley. You deserve some downtime to relax."

"But I like being with you guys," I started to protest.

"And we can be together while you rest." Gannon crossed his arms over his chest. "There will be no arguing about this."

I opened my mouth to do exactly that, but Elise came running back with an ice pack from my freezer. She placed it so carefully on my ankle, her little teeth biting down on her bottom lip in concentration, that I couldn't find it in my heart to protest any longer.

"Dinner is next, so rest your eyes while Elise plays you spa music." Gannon handed his phone to Elise, who hopped up next to me and scrolled through his music app. Meatball jumped up onto my lap and settled down immediately.

Between Elise playing with her dolls quietly next to me, the soft music playing, and the heat of Meatball on my lap like a blanket, I almost fell asleep.

"Dinner's ready!" Gannon called, coming out of my kitchen with a towel thrown over his shoulder. He had something red smeared across his shirt.

I blinked my eyes and yelped when he picked me up again and took me to the kitchen table. "What's all this?"

Gannon put me down and held out a chair for Elise. "The only thing I really know how to cook from scratch. Spaghetti."

How did he know that spaghetti was my comfort food? I literally kept all the ingredients on hand in case I had a tough week. I looked up at him and hoped he knew how much this gesture meant.

"Thank you."

He kissed my forehead again and then had a seat across from me. "You're welcome. Now eat because your work today is not done."

I opened my mouth to question him, but he sent me a grin so lecherous I knew exactly what he meant. And suddenly I wasn't so tired any longer. Dinner was incredible and so was the game of Go Fish we played in the living room while we iced my ankle again. Then Gannon declared it bedtime and Elise protested. Hearing her cry broke my heart.

"I put Wonder Woman sheets on the bed in the guest room," I said quietly over Elise's head as she clung to Gannon with big, fat tears in her eyes.

He tilted his head. "Yeah?"

"Yeah."

"If you're sure…"

"I'm sure."

Gannon stood up with Elise in his arms. "Then I'll be right back. E-bug, you want to sleep here at Paisley's house?"

Elise lifted her head and sniffed back her tears. "Only if Meatball can sleep with me."

I was already nodding before she'd finished the question.

Gannon looked down at Meatball, who was currently in my lap, fast asleep. He rolled his eyes, but leaned down to pick up Meatball in his other arm.

"Come on, you two. Time for lights out."

The look he sent me over his shoulder had me squirming on the couch. As soon as he was down the hallway, I jumped up and put things away. There was no way I was having Gannon spend the night with me when I hadn't yet showered after work. While he read Elise a story—or made one up as he said he typically did—I got in the shower and shaved everything, just in case. Funny how I'd been exhausted when I got off work, and now I was filled with energy, knowing I'd have Gannon tucking me into his side all night long.

He came into my room almost a half hour later, smiling ruefully. "Note to self: don't tell a story about flying unicorns. She was wide awake asking all kinds of questions."

I giggled and patted the bed next to me. I'd been reading while I waited, already in my pajamas. Gannon reached down and pulled off his shoes and socks. Then his hat was tossed aside. He pulled the T-shirt off of him like he'd studied the *Magic Mike* movies. I let myself enjoy the show. Wasn't often a guy who looked like Gannon was stripping for me. The button of his jeans popped, and then he swiveled his hips while he lowered the zipper. His blue eyes twinkled, and I forgot about how grumpy he'd been when I first met him.

His jeans hit the floor, but before he revealed the good stuff by pushing his boxers down, he twirled his finger in the air. "Lose the clothes and lie on your stomach, woman."

I frowned but instantly complied, knowing by now that it was futile to argue, and I probably wanted whatever Gannon had planned. The camisole was off and on the ground in the blink of an eye, the short shorts following. I rolled and tilted my head to the side to see him approach. His boxers were tented, and I wanted what was inside. I went to reach for him, but his fingers banded around my wrist and moved my arm up above my head.

"Be good or I'll have to tie you up." His gravelly voice dishing out that threat was so delicious, my whole body shivered.

The bed groaned as Gannon climbed on top of me, his knees on either side of my thighs. His hands stroked up my back and my eyes fluttered shut. I'd died and gone to heaven. That had to be it. Nothing on earth could actually feel this good, could it?

His thumbs dug in and the man found every single knot in my neck and back, rubbing them out until I felt like jelly. Then he moved to my ass and desire flooded in like never before. I gasped, and he groaned, his hands kneading my glutes by the handful.

"Fuck, Paisley," he whispered.

"Yes," I moaned right back.

His fingers dipped low in between my cheeks, finding the evidence of my desire and spreading it around before dipping inside. I lifted my hips, needing more, so much more. But Gannon pulled his fingers away. I groaned, and he slapped my ass playfully.

"Turn over, baby. I can't do it. I need to be selfish."

I rolled and Gannon reached inside my drawer, sheathing himself in record time. He parted my thighs and plunged inside in a rush, finally stilling and pressing his forehead to mine as I adjusted around him.

"I'm sorry," he whispered, breath fanning my face.

"Don't be sorry. I wanted you too."

His blue-eyed gaze drilled into me. "I can't seem to control myself around you. I don't know what's happening."

My heart soared, but I had to crack a joke in case he wasn't on the same page as me. I couldn't hear him deny there was actual love between us while he was inside of me, absolutely wrecking me. "Maybe I have a magical pussy."

Gannon squeezed his eyes shut, lifting up enough to pull almost all the way out of my body and then thrust back inside while he watched. "It is magical, but it's more than that, baby."

And then there was no talking, just slow lovemaking. Chests

heaving, fingers clenched together, limbs wound around each other, and the kind of orgasm that leaves a mark long after the aftershocks are gone.

We fell asleep with Gannon wrapped around me, and I knew for sure.

I was hopelessly in love with my grumpy neighbor.

annon

"WHAT THE HELL?"

"Daddy, no bad words!" Elise said around her mouth full of hot dog. I'd just grilled steaks and Paisley made a side salad, but Elise had not been interested in that dinner. I was learning to choose my battles.

I hopped up and pulled back the curtain to stare out the window. Something unsettling was already starting to percolate in my gut over Paisley having to go back to work tomorrow after a perfect weekend together. She loved her job, but the risks I knew she had to take out there made my stomach clench.

"What is it?" Paisley got up too, trying to wedge in beside me to see out the window. Two headlights and a beat-up silver truck had pulled onto my property.

"Shit," I grumbled.

"Daddy!"

"You know who that is?" Paisley asked quietly.

Tension had my whole body rigid, spoiling for a fight. I

scrubbed a hand over my face and let the curtain fall back in place. "Yep. That's my dad."

Paisley's mouth opened, but no words came out, which made sense. I hadn't told her much about him, just that he was difficult and not my favorite person.

"I'll finish up with Elise and get her in the bathtub if you want to go out there and see what's going on."

I cursed under my breath, this time escaping Elise's censure. "Of course, he didn't call or text to let me know he was coming."

Paisley put her hand on my arm, trying to calm me down. If I kept up the jaw clenching, I'd need extensive dental work. "Hey, it's okay. I've got Elise. Take as long as you need."

I gave Paisley a quick nod and hurried out the door before he went looking for me. He did a double take when he saw me approaching his truck from the direction of Paisley's house. He climbed out and shook my hand, looking older than the last time I'd seen him. He still wore the same shirt he had for the last thirty years, the one with the builder logo. He should retire soon, but try telling that to Mark Hart, the winner of the stubborn mule award fifty-eight years running.

"Hey, Dad. Didn't expect to see you."

Never one for catching subtlety, Dad just looked around at the three trailers, his gaze catching on every area that I had yet to finish. He always saw the mistakes and not the accomplishments.

"Figured I'd come see how you're doing. Lend a hand if you need it. Got a few days off in between builds."

"I appreciate that, but I've got my first renters coming Friday. Not much to be done until I can buy some more trailers."

Dad frowned at me. "Where the hell you staying? In that house?" He tipped his head at Paisley's place.

"No, not staying there, but I'm dating a woman."

Dad scoffed. "Sure that's a good thing? Isn't that how you got Elise dumped on your doorstep?"

Anger burned through my veins so quickly I had to clench

my hands into fists at my side to not grab my father and shove him back against his truck. I didn't want my daughter or my girlfriend's name in his mouth. Not with that mocking tone of his that he always reserved just for me.

"I think you better head on back home."

I heard Paisley's flip-flops on the pavement, and before I could prepare for the two of them to meet, Paisley was cuddled up next to me and giving my father a fake smile.

"Hey, I'm Paisley. You must be Gannon's father?"

She stuck out her hand and my father pasted on that smile of his that made the ladies fall in his lap. Hell, his flirting skills were how I'd learned to have women coming and going from my life with ease. Well, before the accident and before Paisley, that is.

He shook her hand, and I wanted to rip his arm off his body for sullying her. "Paisley. What a beautiful name for a gorgeous woman."

Paisley pulled her hand back, wrapping her fingers around my arm. "Thank you. You must be so proud of your son here. Of what he's building. The life he's making for Elise. We just love him around here."

"Is that right?" Dad looked up at me with humor sparkling in his eyes.

"Yes, that's right," Paisley said firmly. "If you can't see it, then you haven't been looking very close."

Dad lost the sparkle in his eyes and turned to Paisley. "Excuse me?"

I'd never been more proud of Paisley, or more in love with a human being than when she stood up for me. I'd felt alone and adrift for the last six months. But not now. Not since Paisley had barreled her way into my life and propped me up with her constant belief that with enough hard work, anything could be done.

Paisley smiled at my dad. I opened my mouth to intervene because I knew that look. My dad was about to have his ass handed to him. Then I snapped my mouth shut because I wanted a front-row seat for that.

"Let's be honest, huh? You didn't come here to offer support, did you?" Paisley stepped a little closer, getting in his face and letting go of my arm. "You came here to see him fail so you could gloat." She shook her head. "That's low for anyone, but for a dad? Shameful."

His face couldn't have gone any redder. I grabbed Paisley and put her behind me even as she growled at me for the man-handling. I didn't want her in the crosshairs when my father blew. He'd never hit me, but I also knew not to push him that hard. I always just walked away from his bullshit. Not Paisley though. She went straight for the jugular and fuck the consequences.

"How about we all just cool off a bit, huh?"

My dad's hand rose in the air, finger pointing to my back. "That—that—"

"Be very careful how you finish that sentence," I growled.

His gaze snapped to mine, and he dropped his hand. He took a few deep breaths, his color returning to normal. "That beautiful woman just might be right," he said softly.

I blinked, figuring I heard him wrong.

"Damn right I am," Paisley chirped from behind me. Then she pinched my ass so hard I jumped and let her go. She crossed her arms over her chest and stood by my side, staring at my father, who looked just a little bit stunned.

"That's gonna leave a bruise," I whispered to her out of the side of my mouth.

She rolled her eyes. "Payback."

My mental image went straight to all the times I threw her around in the bedroom and I decided not to push my luck by bringing it up again.

My dad cleared his throat. "Could we, uh, go inside and talk? Would that be okay?"

"Elise is playing dolls, but I could get her in the bath so you two can talk."

I nodded. "Thank you." I kissed her forehead and then steered her back into the house, hearing my father follow us. I didn't want to talk to him, but then again, he was my dad. And he'd driven three hours to be here.

"Gwampa!" Elise ditched her dolls the second we all came in the door and ran straight for my dad, wrapping her arms around his legs. He bent awkwardly and patted her back. Then he stunned me by swinging her up into his arms and walking to the couch, sitting down with her in his lap.

"Can I get you something to eat or drink? We have some steak left over from dinner."

I shook my head slowly, taking in my woman as I settled in the chair next to the couch. She was in jean shorts and a pink tank top that matched her painted toes, looking like the sweetest little thing that had ever lived, just seconds after telling my dad he was shameful. If I hadn't fallen head over ass before this moment, I certainly felt it now.

I fucking loved the hell out of this woman.

"I'm good, thank you," my father answered, letting Elise give him a middle part and try to tamp down his hair with her hands. Maybe he was softening in his old age because he never would have let me do that to him when I was little.

"Okay, well, I'll get the little one all clean." Paisley turned to Elise. "You ready for a disco bath?"

"What the hell is that?" I interjected as Elise clapped her hands and ditched my dad's hair to take Paisley's hand.

My woman shrugged. "I got a disco ball thing from a bachelorette party I went to last year. Makes for a fun bath experience."

My brain went off the rails, thinking of other fun ways to use it, but now was not the time. The two girls walked off to the bathroom and left me with the one person I didn't know how to talk to.

Dad took a deep breath and looked like he didn't know how to talk to me, either. He sat forward and put his elbows on his knees, his hands clasped together.

"I realize I've done a poor job raising you."

"Not that bad." I couldn't let him think he was terrible. I was fed, driven to school, and had a roof over my head. A lot of kids didn't even have that.

He lifted his head. "No, let's be honest. I did the basics and then failed at everything else. Paisley is right. I came by thinking you'd be up to your eyeballs in work and stress, just like I'd been when your mom died. Like maybe seeing you struggling would make me feel better about how much I struggled. But you're not. You're thriving and so is your daughter."

I sat there stunned, afraid to move or say anything that would shut down the first heart-to-heart conversation we'd ever had.

"You're a better dad than I was, Gannon. I'm proud of you and this business you're building and the man you've become. Should have told you before."

"It's okay, Dad," I said gruffly, barely able to get the words out.

He shrugged. "It's not, but maybe an old dog can learn new tricks. And if you'll have me, I really can help out this week on any of the last-minute things you need done before your first guests arrive."

"I'd love that."

I stood up, and he stood too. We stood there awkwardly. I made the first move, lifting my arms and putting them around him. I clapped him on the back and felt him do the same. We stepped back, and I got busy staring at the hardwood floor. We weren't even close to being good at this yet, but this was a damn good start. For the first time since my injury, I was starting to feel like maybe life didn't have it out for me. That maybe, just maybe, good things were finally coming my way.

"I can get you set up in my trailer if you need a place tonight."

Dad nodded. "I'd appreciate that."

I led the way to the front door, but Dad put his hand on my arm before I opened it. He pointed down the hall where we could hear Paisley and Elise singing some song about a royal girl named Sophia in the bathroom.

"Don't lose that one. She's the type you hold on to tightly." He smiled ruefully. "She reminds me of your mother, actually. God, she had a mouth on her."

I grinned, knowing exactly what he meant and also wishing I'd had the chance to get to know my own mother. "I'm doing everything I can to keep her, believe me."

 aisley

THE WHOLE WEEK was chaotic with Gannon's dad here, plus gearing up for Glamper's Paradise's first renters. Work was also particularly crazy due to a late summer heat wave that caused everyone to be cranking their air-conditioning. The electrical lines were simply too hot to do their jobs, and we were running from one power outage after another.

I spent most of the weekend with Elise while Gannon ran around making sure his guests had everything they needed. I'd never seen the man so excited. There was a look of pride on his face that hadn't been there when he'd first moved to Blueball. Strangely, as his pride increased and his renters were clearly having a good time, his grumpiness also increased. It was like he expected something bad to happen and it broke my heart that he assumed failure was in his future.

"Hey, lover boy!" I called out the front door. Gannon was outside his trailer, dumping yet another bag of ice in a cooler of beer and sodas that he would wheel over to his guests' trailer. If he served them anymore beer, they'd be too snockered to remember to check out. Gannon was definitely shooting for the hostess with the mostest. "Dinner's ready and you're going to eat it. No arguing."

He lifted his hat to wipe his forehead, sheepishly closing the cooler. "I thought it was my turn to cook."

I lifted an eyebrow. "If I waited for you to cook, it would be a midnight snack instead of dinner."

"But I planned to make spaghetti. Your favorite." He wiped his hands on his jeans and came over, pulling me into him. He was hot and sweaty and straight-up delicious.

"Just come eat, huh? Your guests are fine."

He nodded. "Yeah, okay. Let me just wash up first."

We went inside my house and I dished up the spaghetti I'd made myself while he visited the bathroom. I'd already fed Elise, and she was currently on the couch with Meatball watching a movie I'd put on for her. I'd had two days off from work while Gannon was still running full steam ahead. I lit a candle on the table and poured two glasses of iced tea.

"Thank you, baby," Gannon grumbled, sliding his arms around me from behind and nuzzling into the back of my neck.

"Congratulations on your first guests." I spun and looped my arms around his neck. "When you come up for air, I'll take you out to celebrate."

"Shouldn't that be my job? Taking you out? I feel like I've failed at that recently."

I lifted up on my toes to kiss him for the first time since he left my bed before the sun came up. I definitely missed him during the day with him working so much, but I couldn't complain. Out of everyone, I understood placing work as a top priority.

"I think you're doing a fine job of it all."

His thumbs tucked under my shirt to stroke my bare skin. "I just want more time with you. Between work and Elise, I just fall into bed exhausted and don't give you the treatment you deserve." His face brightened before I could argue with his assessment. "Speaking of...stay right there."

Then he let me go and dashed outside, the front door slamming behind him. I shook my head and actually did what he said for once, not wanting to start my dinner without him. He came running back just a few seconds later, this time with a bouquet of flowers in his hands.

"What is this?"

He handed them to me and I took them, burying my nose in the blooms and inhaling their fresh scent. "They're for you."

I looked up at him, confused. "But what for?"

He put his hands on his hips, the grin sliding off his face. "For you."

"Right, but why?"

"What do you mean, *why*? Can't I get my woman flowers?"

"Definitely, I was just wondering if it was for a special occasion that I'd forgotten about."

He pulled his hat off and tossed it on one of the kitchen chairs. "No, just...take the flowers, Pearse."

I didn't like his tone. Why was he being so Gannon-like? "Okay," I answered, voice sharp and at odds with my tone. "Thank you."

He glared at me. "You're welcome."

I put the bouquet on the table and sat down to eat. Maybe he was just hangry. The man had been running around all day for three days straight and barely remembered to eat. He sat across from me and we began to eat in silence. When I figured he'd gotten enough in his stomach to talk civilly, I figured I'd try talking again. Carefully.

"I saw your new Smokey the Bear sign out by the fire pits. It's really cute."

"Thanks. Elise helped me pick it out. Hopefully, it'll be a good warning for the guests to be responsible for their bonfires."

I smiled at him, seeing the firefighter in him still. "Always the firefighter, huh?"

He grunted and didn't respond. The conversation fell away into silence again. Which kind of pissed me off. I'd been taking care of Elise all weekend to help him out on my days off, opening my home to them both and he wanted to cop an attitude with me? He said he wanted to treat me better. Well, here was a prime example of what he could do.

"Maybe you should post a Grumpy the Bear sign to warn the renters too," I said under my breath.

Gannon's fork clanked onto the plate. He glared at me and I glared right back. We stayed in some weird non-blinking-almost-growling stare-down for a straight minute before he relented. His shoulders drooped, and he dropped his head. When it came back up again, his eyes were soft, but pinched.

"I'm sorry."

"For?" I wasn't letting him off that easily.

He spread his hands, indicating dinner and the flowers. "This isn't how I wanted today to go. I had it all planned out."

"Had what planned out?"

He scrubbed a hand across his face. "I wanted to make you dinner, give you flowers, and tell you how much I appreciate you. How much you mean to me. Instead, you made your own dinner, the flowers were so out of left field you questioned why I'd given them to you, and I've done nothing but stir up a fight. I'm just not good at this."

I put my hand over his where it was fisted on top of the table. "Hey. I don't need you to be good at anything. I just need you to talk to me. Let me in." I paused. "And maybe not so much Grumpy the Bear."

Gannon gave me a look, but his lips were tilting up.

I scraped my chair back and stood up. "Start over."

"Huh?"

I pointed at the flowers. "Start over."

Gannon looked like he'd rather play dolls for five hours straight than do what I asked, but he moved his chair back and hefted himself to standing. See? That was why I'd fallen in love with this man. He didn't do the big gestures with finesse, but he was there for those he cared about, even when he was exhausted. He was good at this, even if he didn't see it yet.

He grabbed the flowers, the cellophane crinkling as he held them in his big hand. He cleared his throat and looked like he was working hard on holding back a smile.

"Paisley."

"Gannon."

He thrust the flowers at me. "These are for you."

I put my hands on my cheeks as if I was surprised. "Oh my gosh, Gannon. I love them!" I took them and smelled them again, this time leaving off all the damn questions.

Gannon came closer, looking at me funny. He snatched the flowers back and practically threw them on the table.

"Hey!"

His hands were suddenly in my hair, cupping my face and holding me so close I could see the specks of gray in his blue eyes. "Forget the flowers."

"But—"

"Shh." The man actually shushed me.

His thumb clamped my lips together, as if shushing me wasn't bad enough. He had a death wish, apparently. Clearly I was wrong. Gannon was horrifically bad at this dating thing.

"Just...gah!" He squeezed his eyes shut and then opened them again, looking as angry as I felt. "I love you, and you're making it really hard to get the words out. I was going to give you flowers, make you spaghetti, and then tell you over dessert how I felt, but then I lost track of time and you called me Grumpy the Bear and it all got twisted."

My brain had gone completely still. I didn't hear anything beyond the three little words that I'd been feeling, but hadn't been brave enough to use out loud.

Gannon opened his mouth to yell at me further, but I jammed my whole hand against his mouth.

"Shh."

His eyes went scary, but turnabout was fair play. And right now I didn't want to hear anymore jumbled explanations that didn't matter. The only thing that mattered was making sure he knew I felt it too.

"I love you too."

His eyes went wide and then he was a blur of motion, grabbing my hips and lifting me up. My legs went around his waist and our lips had already found each other when my back hit the nearest wall. His tongue lapped at mine, desperate and giddy.

"Daddy!"

Gannon pulled back just enough to shout back, "We're fine, E-bug. Just wrestling!"

"Okay!"

I started laughing, but Gannon cut me off with another searing kiss. "You do?" he whispered against my lips just moments later.

I grabbed him by the hair and pulled until he was looking me in the eye. "Yes. I love you. I've been thinking it for at least a week now, but was too chickenshit to say it first."

He dropped his forehead to mine, eyes squeezed shut. "And I was too chickenshit to bring it up earlier, but the more I held it back, the grumpier I got."

I smoothed my fingers through his hair, massaging his scalp. "Well, thank fuck you finally said something. We couldn't take much more Grumpy the Bear."

Gannon pinned me harder against the wall, his steel length pressed between us. "I'm never getting rid of that nickname, am I?"

It wasn't even that funny, but I felt so lighthearted all I could do was giggle. "Nope."

"Daddy?"

This time, Elise's voice was right next to us. Gannon let me down, trying to adjust himself without his daughter noticing.

"Done westling?" she asked, Meatball sitting at her feet. "Time for bath!"

Gannon cleared his throat and turned back to me. "Give me thirty minutes to get her to bed?"

"Of course." I crouched down and gave Elise a hug. "Good night, lovebug."

She grinned from ear to ear. "I like lovebug better than E-bug."

I looked up at her daddy, all cocky. "I give good nicknames. What can I say?"

He rolled his eyes and picked up Elise, leaving me to clean up and feed Meatball. Even those mundane tasks couldn't dim my shine. Gannon Hart freaking loved me.

After all the chores were done, I had a seat on the couch and texted my friends. I'd been neglecting them recently with all this time with Gannon and Elise, but couldn't think of anyone I wanted to celebrate with more.

> **Me:** It's official, ladies! We said the three little words tonight.

> **Audrey:** Holy crap! That's awesome!!!

> **Marlo:** But does he make dinner for you?

> **Me:** Sometimes, yes. Is that your criteria for a boyfriend? Must be willing to cook?

> **Marlo:** It's a good starting point, don't you think?

I laughed out loud. Oh, Marlo. It would take a special man to make Marlo quit thinking with her head and start feeling with her heart.

> **Audrey:** I don't care about food. Tell me about his bedroom skills. On a scale of one to ten, with ten being so mind blowing you'd live in a cardboard box on Main Street to get more of it, how's Gannon rate?

Me: I already have a cardboard box
picked out...

Audrey: I KNEW IT! That man is walking sex on
a stick.

Marlo: That is a very odd phrase. Why would
someone want sex on a stick? Sounds painful.

Keva: Sorry! It was bath time, and I missed the
big news. That's great, Paisley.

I expected a lukewarm response from her. Keva had been burned badly before. That's how she ended up a single mom to her son.

Me: Don't get too excited, Keevs.

Keva: Sorry. It's not that I'm not excited, I just
hope you don't have blinders on. Even if he's
all kinds of wonderful right now, make sure
you're careful. The hotter they are right now,
the more it burns when they leave.

Audrey: Damn! I'm writing that shit down...

Me: I know what you're saying and I appreciate
your words of wisdom. However, I also believe
not all men are like Linc.

Keva: WE AGREED TO NEVER SAY HIS NAME

Me: Sorry! I thought there was a time limit on
that rule or something.

Audrey: I think it's a forever rule. That boy
shows his face around here, he's gonna get his
ass kicked by my five brothers. Guaranteed.

Marlo: I have a spot in the cemetery all picked
out for him.

Me: Oh shit! Marlo, I didn't know you had it in you.

Keva: Thanks for having my back, loves. In all seriousness, Paisley…I'm ecstatic for you. Gannon seems like just what you need.

Me: Thanks, ladies. Meet up soon? Just because I'm happy in love doesn't mean I'll ditch my girls.

Audrey: Ooh! Let's try out Grass, that new salad restaurant that opened up.

Marlo: Oh dear God. Salads? If they don't have a burger on the menu, I'm not going.

Me: I will call and ask, just for you, Marlo.

Audrey: Marlo needs some meat in her mouth…

Keva: bahahaha

Marlo: You're all terrible friends.

Audrey: You know you love us.

CHAPTER TWENTY-THREE

annon

THERE WAS LITERALLY nothing I liked better than waking my girlfriend up with my face between her legs. She didn't even act shocked anymore. She just grabbed my hair and whispered for me to do it harder, faster, and right there. I gave her what she needed until she was practically smothering me, her voice cracking on my name. When her fingers gave up the death grip on my hair, I climbed over her and kissed her good morning.

"What else do you want to do today? I don't pick up Elise until noon."

Paisley cracked one eye open. "You literally kept me up all night, cowboy."

I leered at her bare breasts, the right one sporting a mark from last night. Why was that so fucking hot? "So that's how I move up from Grumpy the Bear to cowboy, huh? Multiple orgasms earn me a better nickname?"

Paisley wrapped her legs around my waist and squeezed. I

grunted at the pressure, but my dick celebrated almost being home. "You catch on quick."

I sank into her heat, both of us sighing at the same time. "Fuck, I love you."

Paisley lifted her hips and wrapped her arms around my neck. "I love you too."

I pulled back and sank back in lazily, loving a free morning to take my time. With Elise and our work schedules, we usually had to rush, not that that wasn't amazing too, but this? This was the stuff I never knew I was missing. I dipped my head to circle her nipple with my tongue. It pebbled, begging for me to take it in my mouth.

"You know what we should do this morning?" An idea suddenly occurred to me, and now that it had, I couldn't get it out of my head.

Paisley let go of my neck to grab my ass. My greedy girl always wanted it harder, which I usually gave her, but not right now. "Talk later."

I grinned, pulling back and staring down at her face. She was so beautiful. Smooth, tan skin, sun-lightened hair, hazel eyes that made me want to stare at her. And right now, that pink flush to her face that I'd put there was making me crazy.

"Let's get a tattoo together."

Paisley's eyes flew open. "What?"

I thrust hard, and we both groaned. "I have tattoos all up and down my arms. I want one that's just for you, baby."

I thrust again and this time Paisley lifted her hips to meet me. "Why is that so sweet?"

Increasing my pace, I hoped to keep her just delirious enough that she'd agree. "Come on, baby. I want my mark on you."

Paisley didn't answer me. She simply arched her neck and her eyes fluttered closed. She moaned softly while she pulsed around my dick. Damn, I was wrong. She was even prettier right now, relaxed and lost in the pleasure I gave her.

"Okay," she whispered, eyes opening again to lock with mine.

And that's all I needed. A vision of Paisley forever stamped with my mark. I hurtled over the edge, her name on repeat. I didn't care about rings and recorded documents and shared last names. Paisley was mine, and I was hers. And this tattoo could be our little secret.

I made her breakfast while she got ready. I found a tattoo place two towns over that was actually open in the morning. They mostly did mastectomy tattoos, but they could fit us in for something simple.

"I'm not tattooing your name on me." Paisley hopped in my truck before I could open the door for her. I rolled my eyes and climbed in behind the driver's seat. At least she wasn't arguing with me about which truck to take.

"I wouldn't ask you to." I was totally going to suggest that.

"I do have another idea, though."

I got us onto the road and glanced at her. I would pretty much do whatever she wanted, but I'd never tell her that.

"I think we should get hearts. It's your last name and we love each other, so it just makes sense. I know it's girly, but if we put it on your fine ass, no one will ever see it but me."

"You think I have a fine ass?"

Paisley counted out loud to ten.

"What the hell was that for?"

She frowned at me. "I tell you my grand idea and all you comment on is the part about your ass?"

I shrugged and took a turn, heading out of Blueball. "I mean, I know I have a fantastic ass, I just didn't know you thought so too."

"It was the first thing about you I actually liked."

"Ouch, Pearse."

Her hand snuck onto my thigh. "So what do you say? Matching hearts?"

I slid my fingers through hers and held her hand. "Only if you get it on your fine ass, too."

It took us longer than it should for two tiny hearts, but I wanted to be in the room while Paisley got hers. The beefy tattoo guy wasn't going to get the pleasure of staring at her ass unless I was in the room, too. We were both sitting funny driving home.

"Seriously? You like getting tattoos? This is painful." Paisley was rubbing her cheek lightly.

"It's not the pain I like, it's the design and the meaning behind it."

"We're keeping this a secret, right? My parents would have a fit if they found out."

"Paisley, you're twenty-six."

She shot me a look that said I was a dumbass. "Would you have a fit if Elise got a tattoo with her boyfriend?"

I gripped the steering wheel and tried to be reasonable. And failed.

"It's a secret," I growled.

Paisley was laughing as I dropped her off. Elise had stayed the night at Lucy and Bain's again. I was meeting Bain at Tequila Mockingbird to have lunch and he'd hand off my kid then.

They had already grabbed a table when I got there. I sat down and pulled Elise onto my lap. She had to tell me all the things she and Roxy had done before Bain and I were able to get a word in. We ordered some food and Elise was finally content to go back to her own chair and play with the dolls I'd brought with me.

I shifted several times, trying to find a comfortable position that wasn't making my jeans rub up against my fresh tattoo.

"You got ants in your pants, Gannon?"

"I'm good."

He smirked at me and I made myself sit still. "You're fidgeting more than my eight-year-old during church."

Time for a subject change. "You have a dangerous job, right?" Bain was the head warden at a prison, but liked to get out from behind the desk as much as he could, which upped the risk of injury quite a bit. "How does Lucy handle that stress?"

Bain put his elbows on the table and took a sip of his iced tea. "I guess it's a combination of a lot of things. I do my best not to do anything reckless and she knows this job is my passion. I could get hit by a drunk driver heading home from lunch today and never see tomorrow. There are no guarantees, Gannon."

I sat with that for a second. "Yeah, I know. That's the part that terrifies me."

I wasn't one to open up to people, but Bain had proven to be a person I could trust. Plus, he was a bit older than me and was raising kids. If anyone could give good advice, it would be him. As much as I was preoccupied with my new business, I spent a lot of my days and nights worrying about Paisley and Elise. With love came worry, I supposed.

"I assume Paisley's job has you worried?"

I nodded. "And Elise. She's a walking injury waiting to happen."

Bain studied me for a minute, then looked over to Elise and lowered his voice. "You went through some shit, I know. The brain is a funny thing, man. Yours used that accident as proof that shit happens. Now you're wired to see potential disaster everywhere. So you have to wire it back. Every time shit goes right, you remind yourself that there's overwhelming proof that you and your loved ones are safe."

I nodded along, thinking I could do that, but Bain wasn't done.

"And if that doesn't work, you get professional help. I wish more men wouldn't shy away from therapy." He took another sip of tea. "I see a therapist at least once a month."

"You do?" I didn't know anyone in my life that saw a therapist. Or maybe they did, but they didn't talk about it.

"Hell, yeah. I see a lot of crap on the job and I want to make sure I don't take that crap home to my wife and kids." He nudged my arm. "You saw doctors after your accident, right?"

I nodded.

"You went to professionals to fix your body, but what professionals did you see to tend to your mental health?"

I scratched the side of my face, wincing. "None."

He held up his tea. "That's the problem right there. I'll send you my therapist's number. He's amazing."

I thought about that as our server delivered our food. Elise needed her cheese quesadilla pulled apart and blown on so it wouldn't burn her. When she was settled, I tucked into my own meal. This place was amazing. I'd have to take Paisley here for dinner and try out the fajitas and margaritas.

"Hey, I meant to tell you that I'm getting another trailer soon. Figured I'd offer it up to you and Lucy if you wanted to try it out for a fun weekend with the kids before school starts. No cost, of course."

"Yeah, we'd love to. I was just talking to Lucy about that, but when I checked the online calendar, you were already booked up."

A sense of pride had me sitting up taller. Things were off to a good start with Glamper's Paradise. The work my dad had helped me with had gotten me ahead of schedule and I'd hired Rita Hellman to do my social media marketing. Best money I'd ever spent. She had people booking out weekends several months out.

"Yeah, I'm almost completely booked out for a whole month. I imagine it'll slow down to just weekends after that because all the families will have kids back in school."

Bain wiped his mouth with his napkin. "You never know. Lots of retirees and young couples travel during the week to cut down on costs. If you market specifically to them and offer a deal, you might be booked solid all year long."

"I'll talk to Rita about that." I eyed another bite of my burrito but didn't think I could put down anymore food. "I was thinking I might be able to hire on help next month. Your buddy still looking for work?"

Bain grabbed his phone. "Absolutely. I'm texting his contact info to you right now."

The door to the restaurant opened, and I actually recognized who walked in. Two of Paisley's friends and one older gentleman in a suit. Keva caught my eye, and we waved hello. The group walked over and Bain and I both stood.

"Hey, Bain!" Keva gave him a hug, and he nearly dropped his phone. He muttered something, but none of us caught it. Keva looked at him strangely, but turned to me with a bright smile. "Gannon Hart, this is Fernando Balmero."

I shook the man's hand. "Nice to meet you. I'm new here in town. Just opened up Glamper's Paradise out on the east side of town."

Fernando nodded. "I've heard my daughter talk about your place." He put his hand on Marlo's back and it made sense. I could see the family resemblance with the midnight-black hair and somber expression.

"Marlo and Mr. Balmero own the funeral home here in Blueball," Keva added helpfully.

My eyes went wide before I could school my expression. Wasn't often you met a mortician. "Uh, well, I hope I don't need your services anytime soon. No offense."

Fernando dipped his head with a hint of a smile. "None taken. I hope you don't either as you look heavy to lift and my back can't take it. No offense."

I smiled at the man. He was funny. Very deadpan, like Marlo, who was standing there staring at me like I was a fly in her salad. Paisley told me that her friends supported our relationship, but it couldn't hurt to try to win them over a bit more.

"Hey, I was thinking if you ladies wanted to come over, you could bring your son, Keva. He's almost four, right? He and Elise could play together."

Elise popped her head up at the mention of her name. "Does he play dolls?"

Keva smiled at her. "He does. Sometimes he cuts their hair, so just a friendly warning."

Elise snatched her dolls off the table and stuffed them behind her back with a horrified look on her face. "I play dolls with Daddy instead."

Fernando looked at his fancy watch. "We have an embalming at two, so we have to rush. Hope to see you around town, Gannon Hart."

"Same to you." We shook hands and he, Marlo, and Keva moved to another table to sit down and have lunch.

Bain and I sat down again, pretty much done with ours. "Okay, so you sent me Li—"

"Yep!" Bain said loudly, cutting me off. "Why don't you and Elise head on out? I'll get the check."

We ended up arguing over the check and both plopped down twenty-dollar bills to cover it. Bain rushed out of the restaurant like a weirdo while Elise toddled behind me, her dolls flying through the air.

"Come on, Abby," I said in my falsetto voice when we were out on the sidewalk. "Let's go get Paisley and go to the beach!"

Elise squealed. "Can I come too?"

I swooped her up in my arms and hustled to my parked truck. I couldn't wait to get back to Paisley. "Always, E-bug. You're my ride or die."

Elise wrinkled her nose. "I don't wanna ride or die, Daddy."

I blew raspberries on her puffy cheeks until she squealed again.

"You won't, E-bug. Not on my watch."

CHAPTER TWENTY-FOUR

aisley

"Ouch!" I whisper-yelped as my left ass cheek smarted.

Gannon smirked as he passed me on his way to the bathroom, as if he hadn't just smacked my ass while I was still getting dressed. "Oh, come on, tough girl. The tattoo has healed by now."

I raised a single eyebrow. "I'll remember that."

Gannon lost the shit-eating grin and hustled to the bathroom. He was all too familiar with my retaliation. Whatever he dished out, I gave back tenfold. Like when he hit me with a water balloon before Elise had even blown her toy whistle the other day to start the next round of water balloon fights. I'd followed it up that night with a bucket of ice water over his head as soon as he stepped out of the shower. Made a hell of a mess, but it had been worth it to hear him scream like a little boy.

On a more serious note, I'd asked Gannon if I could spend some one-on-one time with Elise. They were practically living with me at this point and we both knew very little about her first five years living with her mother. Sometimes Elise acted younger than her age, while at other times, she seemed older than me. I wanted to get to know her better and perhaps be a mother figure in her life if she'd let me.

"Elise? Did you find your jellies?" She had insisted on wearing a pair of jelly sandals that were a sparkly purple, which clashed with the Snow White princess dress. Gannon had nearly lost his cool with the stylings of a five-year-old, but I got him another cup of coffee and told him to take the day off of parenting.

"I'm weady!" Elise came down the hallway at full volume, her shoes flapping about. I bent down and buckled her feet in, and then we were ready.

"Bye, Daddy!" I called into the bedroom.

Elise copied me, Gannon grunted back, and we were off. Elise held my hand and didn't put up a fight when I buckled her into the car seat in the back of Gannon's truck.

"What about Meatball? He don't get to have fun?" Elise had tears in her eyes suddenly. Kids, man. Their emotions were hard to keep up with.

"He'll have fun with your daddy."

Elise shook her head, dark curls dancing everywhere. "No, he won't. Daddy will yell at him to stop licking."

I was kind of a badass on the job, but I was learning I was a total sucker for this blue-eyed beauty. I sighed. "Okay, stay put. I'm going to get Meatball, but—" I put up my finger when she started to cheer prematurely. "He stays on the leash the whole time we're out."

"Okay, I pwomise." Elise looked at me like I'd offered her the moon.

I went back inside and scooped up Meatball, who was whining at the door. "I got Meatball!" I hollered to Gannon. He came out from the hallway with a white towel around his waist, hair wet and dripping down his gorgeous body.

"Sure about that?"

I licked my lips. "Nope, not sure at all. I'd rather take that towel off of you and let these two play outside."

Gannon smirked and grabbed his junk. "Guess you'll just have to make up for it tonight, huh?"

Meatball licked me in the face and I pointed at Gannon. "I'll hold you to that." And then I was gone, putting Meatball in the back with Elise and trying to wipe out the mental image of Gannon, all tan and wet and mine.

"Okay, m'lady. Ice cream first with Keva and Lucas. Then we'll hit the library. Sound good?"

Elise cheered and Meatball barked. The two of them kept up a stream of conversation and barking all the way into town. I grabbed a parking space on the curb outside of You Got Served, the one and only place for ice cream in town. I shot off a text to Gannon, so he knew we got here safely. Keva was right next to me, getting Lucas out of his car seat.

"Did you know they started offering boozy ice cream?" Keva asked with a grin that spelled trouble.

I got Elise and Meatball up on the sidewalk. If Keva was looking to drink at one in the afternoon with her son at her side, there must be something very wrong. "That good of a morning, huh?"

She let Lucas jump up on the sidewalk to play with Meatball with Elise. I loved how kids could meet for the first time and instantly get along like introductions weren't necessary. Keva blew out a breath and I noticed she'd only put mascara on one eye. Now I was officially worried.

"Keevs?"

She looked at me, stress radiating from her pretty brown eyes. "Boston is officially being discharged."

"Oh, well, that's great, right?" Boston was her older brother. He'd been in the military for so long I wasn't sure he'd ever retire.

She shrugged. "Yeah, it's awesome."

"But?"

She looked at our kids playing. "He's gonna take one look at Lucas and know who his father is."

I winced. "Maybe it's time to come clean on all that, Keevs." I said it as gently as I could. All of us had been trying to tell her some version of this advice ever since that test came back with two little lines.

Keva straightened her spine and corralled the kids into the ice cream shop like the stubborn best friend she'd always been. She was done talking about it and that was that. I had to respect her wishes, but I had a feeling all the secrets she'd been trying to keep about her son were about to come crashing down.

She kept up a steady stream of conversation while we fed the little ones a boatload of sugar—and had some ourselves. Meatball was an absolute terror, having found some ice cream that had been spilled on the floor. He tried to zoom about the shop and terrorize the family that had come in behind us. Lucas and Elise were laughing hysterically over his antics, so at least that was a plus.

When our playdate was over, Keva gave me a hard hug. "I'll call you later, okay?" she whispered in my ear.

I pulled back and nodded, knowing I needed to give her time. Maybe I could call Audrey and Marlo too. Lord knew I needed backup to handle this forthcoming conversation with Keva.

Keeping Meatball in my oversized purse while we walked down the sidewalk, Elise and I dodged from shade spot to shade spot in a little game of don't-get-burned-by-the-lava-hot-sun until we made it to the library. They didn't technically allow dogs, but he was in my bag and would probably snooze the whole time now that he'd run off all the sugar in his system. Plus, I knew Hattie, the librarian. She was older than me and friendly with everyone in town, no matter how annoying or rude they were. You just couldn't look into her sweet face and hopeful eyes behind her big glasses and be mean to her.

The air-conditioning hit us in the face, and even Elise sighed in relief. I loved this little library with all my heart. Auburn Hill wasn't quite big enough to have a library, so Mom had always taken me here growing up. There was a little koi pond and water fountain inside, which younger me found fascinating. Older me just wondered about keeping that kind of indoor plumbing going without ruining all the books.

"Well, hello there, intrepid explorer." Hattie was already there, crouched down and holding her arms out to Elise. Elise looked up at me but decided Hattie looked like a good person and let her wrap her in a hug. "I haven't met you yet. You must be Elise Hart, the newest, most fun girl to arrive in Blueball. Do you like platypuses?"

God, I loved small towns. Everyone knew everything about everyone else, and while that was annoying during my teenage years, it really did make you feel warm and welcome.

"Party-pluses?" Elise giggled.

Hattie stood and took Elise's hand. "No, silly. Platypuses. They're a really cool animal and I've got just the book to show you what they look like." She shot me a wink over her shoulder and I grinned back.

I followed behind them, happy to have a librarian who exposed our youth to nature instead of cartoon books. Nothing wrong with cartoons, but there was so much more for young minds to explore while they were still open and curious. I also noted she hadn't called Elise beautiful or commented on her princess dress like most people would. Hattie was one of a kind.

"I practically introduced them."

"No, you didn't!"

I turned at the entrance to the children's section of the library to see my mother and Muriel in each other's faces just past the magazine racks, voices raised above the hushed whisper of polite library conversation.

"Mom?"

Both of them startled, instantly stepping back and pasting on smiles. "Honey? What are you doing here?"

I hooked a thumb over my shoulder. "I brought Elise to get some books. What are you doing?"

Mom and Muriel walked over, but I couldn't help but catch the murderous glance Mom shot Muriel. "Just doing some research for my next article." She put her hands on her hips, smile fading faster than Meatball licked up that ice cream spill. "Muriel is trying to tell me that she fixed you and Gannon up on a date. Is that true?"

Muriel cut in. "That's not what I said, Paige."

"Yes, you did."

"No, I said I *practically* introduced them! They were at the barbecue place acting like they hated each other, and I pulled them onto the dance floor. Nature took over, and the rest is history." Muriel did a little hip shimmy and eyebrow waggle that made my face flush.

Mom dropped the argument and grinned. "They are pretty cute together, aren't they?"

As if I wasn't standing right there.

"So cute!" Muriel gushed.

"Nothing's cute about you two harpies making so much noise a man can't read his damn paper!"

We all craned our necks to see Joseph—or was it John—Walter sitting in a club chair and glaring at us over his reading glasses. Those geriatric twins were the grumpiest men in town. Give Gannon another forty years and he'd give them both a run for their money.

"Oh, shut it, Walter," Muriel snapped.

"You don't even know if I'm Joe or John, do you? Been nipping off that flask already, Muriel?"

Mom gasped. "That is just downright rude, Joseph. And yes, I know it's you by the hair sprouting out of your ears when any self-respecting man would have trimmed it by now."

Joseph slammed his newspaper on the end table and stood up. It took him almost a whole minute, so the dramatic effect was a little lost due to his sloth-like movements. Once mostly upright, he pointed a finger at Mom. I moved closer. My mother wasn't always my favorite person, but I wouldn't let an old guy intimidate her just because he had a perpetual stick up his ass.

"You're just bitchy because you know Paisley won't be giving you grandkids anytime soon."

My face scrunched up and my ovaries protested. It was one thing for Mom to say it, but even Joseph Walter was talking about my childbearing prospects? Was nothing too private for a small town?

"You should be ashamed of yourself!" Muriel said, voice well above talking level.

"You should be ashamed of your whole life!" Joseph shouted back, swinging his bushy, eyebrowed glare on her instead of me.

"You should be ashamed of that mothball-smelling tweed jacket!"

"You should be ashamed of that rat's-nest hair!"

"I'm afraid I'm going to have to ask you all to leave," Hattie interrupted quietly from behind us. She had her librarian face on, and even Joseph shut his trap long enough to know she wasn't joking around.

A giggle escaped my mouth and Mom elbowing me in the side didn't help. I'd never been kicked out of the library before. Elise ran over and took my hand, staring up at the adults like we'd all lost our minds.

"Come on, lovebug." I started walking for the door of the library, astounded I got kicked out and not for bringing a dog in here. "Maybe don't tell your dad what happened at the library, huh?"

"A secwet?" Elise's eyes lit up.

I squeezed her hand. "Sure." There was no way she was keeping this secret. The girl had zero secret-keeping ability.

I was proven correct when the first thing she did when we got home and found Gannon cooking up hamburgers on the grill outside was to yell across the lawn about Hattie being the nicest lady ever and she told us we had to leave. Gannon looked at me with questions in his eyes. I knew he'd be questioning me later on about what happened, but for now I sat and read one of the books Hattie had checked out for Elise while Gannon made our dinner.

When he'd put Elise to bed, he came into the bedroom and collapsed on my bed. I cuddled up next to him, not wanting to go to work tomorrow. Gannon stacked his hands behind his head and looked up at the ceiling.

"I was thinking today while you two were gone."

"Uh-oh," I teased, pulling up the hem of his T-shirt and dancing my fingers along his abs.

He grabbed my fingers and stilled my hand, turning to look down at me. "I think I'm ready to have Elise start gymnastics classes."

Hope filled my chest. I knew how much it took for him to allow Elise to do something he thought might be dangerous. "Yeah?"

He nodded and sat up, pulling me with him. "Yeah. I know I need to give her some freedom to do little-girl things."

I smiled at my boyfriend, thinking he was possibly the best father I'd ever seen. For only being one for a few months now, he was killing it.

"I think this decision deserves a reward," I said quietly.

Gannon's gaze shot up and locked with mine. "Oh yeah?"

I licked my lips. "Yeah. Take off your pants."

"You telling me what to do?"

I pulled off my tank top and let my breasts spill out. He swallowed hard. "You got a problem with that?"

Gannon fumbled with his zipper but managed to get the job done, jeans bunched at his feet. "No, ma'am."

His cock was already hard, the skin hot to the touch as I wrapped my fingers around him. "Hold my hair, cowboy."

I knelt down and Gannon instantly complied, gathering my hair and holding it at the top of my head as I took him in my mouth. He grunted the second my tongue lapped at the end of him, getting the taste of him in my mouth.

"Fuck, Paisley. I love you." He slid further into my throat as I gagged around him. "I love that mouth. Shit, that feels so good, baby."

I lifted my head and made sure my hand followed, squeezing his shaft tight. I licked the head of him like I had my ice cream cone earlier today, enjoying this treat far more. There was nothing as empowering as hearing a strong man beg for more, knowing he's at your mercy.

"Give me those boobs," Gannon growled.

I felt one hand let go of my hair to squeeze my breast before moving to the other one. His cock got impossibly bigger. My jaw ached, and I was breathing almost as hard as he was, but I never did a job half-ass. I swallowed him down, forcing my throat to relax, bobbing up and down until his fingers tightened in my hair to the point of pain. Then his dick twitched, and he was filling my mouth, hot spurts coating my throat as I swallowed him down.

He finally flopped back on the bed with a groan. "I should have agreed to gymnastics earlier."

I giggled and wiped my mouth, standing up and going into the connecting bathroom to wash my hands. When I got back to the bed, he looked half asleep, dick still out and lying on his stomach, pants bunched at his feet.

"I should totally take a picture of this," I murmured, teasing him.

Gannon roared and stood up to tackle me. Unfortunately, he forgot about his pants around his ankles and ended up flopping down face-first on the bed while I laughed my ass off.

Mom was right. We really were cute together.

CHAPTER TWENTY-FIVE

 annon

Me: I'm so sorry, but the AC went out on one of the trailers. I've got to get it working before this couple gets pissed and checks out early. Is there any chance you can take Elise to her gymnastics class when you get home?

My hot sexy neighbor: Of course. She's been so excited about starting gymnastics, I'd hate to cancel.

Me: I really appreciate it.

My hot sexy neighbor: You can thank me tonight...

Me: Wear that red thong for me.

> My hot sexy neighbor: The one you stole off my clothesline?

> Me: For the last fucking time. It was Meatball.

***

AFTER PAISLEY GOT off work and picked up Elise, I got lost in the monotonous work of fixing the air-conditioning unit, getting it running just in time for the couple who rented the trailer to come back from the beach. They were all smiles and my back was all aches from being bent over for so long. I wiped my hands off and grabbed my phone. Paisley hadn't texted me when she got to the gymnastics class like she normally did when she went anywhere. She shouldn't have to text me, but she did, knowing my brain went in a bad direction when I didn't hear from her.

As it was doing right now.

I went inside Paisley's house and tried calling her. It rang and rang, but she didn't pick up. Pacing the living room, I tried to think logically when my heart rate had already picked up and my breathing was getting irregular. I called again. Same result. Now I was officially freaked out. And pissed I hadn't insisted on one of those apps where we could track each other's phones. I just needed to know she and Elise were safe.

I couldn't stay here and slide further into a full-blown panic attack. I had to do something. Without a single thought, besides finding them and reassuring myself they were unharmed, I ran to my truck and climbed in. I tore down several roads before I realized I never put the address into my navigation system. Stopping at the first stop sign I came to, I made myself breathe and punch in the address so I knew where I was going. My finger shook, but I got the job done. The engine roared as I turned the wheel and got back in the direction of the gymnasium. I pulled into the parking lot and slammed on my brakes at the curb without caring if it was a legit parking space or not.

My legs were threatening to give out as I ran into the building, eyes scanning left and right. I was aware I looked like a maniac, but I couldn't seem to stop myself. If I slowed down, I'd spiral into a dark place.

"Gannon?"

I spun to see Lucy smiling at me but looking concerned. Probably because a grown man was panting in the middle of the parent viewing area. "Have you seen Elise and Paisley?"

Lucy pointed through the clear glass. "Elise is over there learning how to stretch before class."

My gaze landed on my little girl, not one of her beautiful dark curls out of place as she copied the instructor in something resembling the splits. The air I'd been forgetting to breathe rushed out of my lungs.

"And Paisley is fixing an electrical pole."

I spun back to Lucy. "I'm sorry?"

Lucy shook her head. "There was an accident and John Walter wrapped his ridiculous Hummer around a pole. Paisley stayed to make sure no one got caught in the live wires on the ground and called her coworkers to come fix it."

I no longer saw Lucy's face or the parents around us or even my little girl taking her first class. *There was an accident.* I saw danger in front of my eyes. I *felt* danger. That familiar kick to the gut that had ended my career. My stomach revolted and I thought I might lose my lunch.

I can't do this.

It was the only thought in my head as I stumbled out of the building and spun in a circle. I couldn't keep reliving this level of panic. It clawed at my insides like a real thing, meant to take a grown man down in a matter of seconds. I couldn't take in a full breath again. I couldn't even think.

"Gannon? You okay?"

Lucy had followed me outside. I tried to rein in whatever this was that made me feel like I couldn't handle life, but there was no way to push it down. It was too big. Too consuming. She would simply have to be a witness to it, and I'd deal with the fallout later.

Her hand landed on my back. "Hey. Breathe. In for four counts, out for four counts." I felt her pushing me and my legs obeyed. I focused on my breath and somehow found myself sitting on a cement bench, Lucy right beside me. "That's it. Just breathe right now. In and out. Slow and steady."

Her calm voice pierced the fog, a lifeline I was holding on to with everything I had. The dark stars that had taken over my vision started to recede. Even the nausea was down to a level I could muster through. My stomach was still in knots, but I could handle that.

"Thank you," I finally managed to say.

Lucy just patted my back and kept talking. "I had a panic attack one time. A bull was charging me and I freaked out. Strangest sensation in the world to be brought down by your own thoughts. I froze, which was absolutely the wrong thing to do. School hadn't exactly taught me what to do when you were staring into the huge eyeballs of a pissed-off bull." She laughed, and it was a nice sound.

"Is that what this is? A panic attack?" Bain had told me Lucy was a nurse. She'd know, right?

She stood, looking into my eyes before smiling like I'd passed a test. "I think so. Have you had them before?"

I shook my head, squeezing my eyes shut. "Maybe once, but it was at the same time my leg was burning, so..."

Lucy tutted above me, her hand patting my shoulder. "Trauma can do that. It can rewire your nervous system in an instant. Have you thought about therapy?"

I opened my eyes again, happy to discover I didn't feel like I was going to pass out. "Yeah, your husband said he had a therapist for me."

The door to the building opened and kids streamed out, laughing and squealing. Elise slammed into my legs, and I stood up to swing her into my arms. I wasn't sure I'd be able to let go for quite some time.

Lucy smiled at Elise and then looked at me with sympathy. "I highly suggest you call him, okay?"

I nodded. "Thanks again."

"Anytime." Then Lucy walked off to her minivan, and I buried my nose in Elise's neck, smelling her little-girl shampoo and reassuring myself that she was fine.

By the time I got her in my truck—without a car seat because it was in the back of Paisley's truck—I was fully in control of my panic. It had been wiped clean by a streak of anger. What the hell had Paisley been thinking about abandoning Elise to stay on the job? I'd trusted Paisley with my five-year-old daughter and she'd ditched her to play with electrical lines to impress her boss? I knew she wanted that promotion, but ditching Elise was way past the line of okay. It was unacceptable.

I was in a different kind of tizzy when I got home. I got Elise playing with dolls in our trailer while I made her a hot dog for dinner. I was too pissed to think about eating. My brain was turning, kicking up more anger over the way Paisley had treated my daughter. Trust was not something I easily gave, but I'd relaxed with Paisley, extending trust maybe where I shouldn't have. She'd certainly broken it today.

I heard her truck pull into the driveway a full hour later. I wanted to race out there and yell at her. Wanted her to have some sort of explanation that would soothe the voice in my head that was chiding me for ever trusting anyone.

Up until the accident, I'd been a lone wolf, living my life the way I wanted because I'd learned early on that you couldn't trust anyone. I trusted my fellow firefighters, but even that had blown up in my face. Literally. I'd been injured so badly I had to give up my career. And then Elise had been on my doorstep with her mother. Yet another person who'd failed me. Failed Elise.

My hot sexy neighbor: You home?

I stared at my phone, tapping my fist against my leg. Now she remembered to text me? Hours after she wasn't where she was supposed to be? Pissed was a severe understatement.

"Elise? Keep an eye on Meatball. I'll be right outside."

"Okay!" I could hear Elise already giving Meatball instructions. "No barking and no licking, Meatball. And no hot dogs. Daddy said those aren't for dogs."

I stepped out of the trailer and shot Paisley a text.

Me: Outside.

Her front door opened and the smile on her face slowly slid away as she walked toward me. "Hey. Lucy brought Elise home okay?"

I lifted my head and looked at the woman I trusted more than anyone in my life. She was so pretty, even with smudges on her tank top and sweat drying along the edges of her hairline. Maybe that was the problem. I'd overlooked things because of our crazy physical chemistry.

"What were you thinking?" I said quietly, quite proud of myself for keeping my voice even when all I wanted to do was rage and scream and yell until I felt better.

She blinked, then folded her arms across her chest. "Excuse me?"

"Not excused," I snapped. "How dare you leave Elise."

Paisley's mouth opened and then closed. Then opened again. "I didn't *leave* her. I called Lucy to take her when there was an accident right in front of us."

I stepped closer, wishing I could ring her damn neck and then kiss some sense into her. "I asked *you* to take her. Then you didn't answer your phone, and I panicked. I had no idea where my child was and I couldn't get ahold of the adult I entrusted her with."

Pain flashed through Paisley's eyes and it matched what I felt in my own chest. "The adult? That's what I am now? The adult you trust for childcare?"

I scoffed. "You know you're more than that."

Paisley's crossed arms jabbed against my chest. We were so close we were breathing each other's air. "If that's the case, you should trust the decisions I make. But you don't, do you?"

"I do trust you. To a point. When it comes to impressing your boss, I think you tend to become a bit hyper-focused. Why else would you leave a five-year-old to jump in and save the day?"

Paisley's lips tilted up into the kind of smile that had my balls shrinking. "You think I would put my promotion before Elise? Is that what you're saying?"

I doubled down. "Yeah, pretty sure that's what I'm saying."

Paisley nodded and backed up. "Well, then I'd say we're at an impasse, cowboy. I can't be with a man who doesn't even trust me with the most basic aspects of his life."

Oh no. She didn't get to turn this around and make it my fault. "And I can't be with a woman who puts her job above my daughter."

Paisley damn near exploded, arms flying out to the side and the volume of her voice testing my eardrums. "I didn't do that! And you're the asshole who put me in charge of Elise because he was putting his job before his daughter! So who's the hypocrite now?"

And then, before my brain had a chance to even digest all of that, she turned on her heel and stomped back into her house, gorgeous ass bouncing. She slammed the door and locked it without a single glance back.

Goddammit, this woman! I pulled the baseball hat off my head and dropped it, kicking it with my boot. It landed softly in the dirt and didn't help at all with the frustration that had me wanting to bellow at the top of my lungs. I had guests on the property and didn't want to ruin my brand-new business with a personal squabble. Instead, I headed inside the trailer and ate a hot dog in two angry bites while Meatball sat there barking at me.

"Daddy, Meatball really wants a hot dog. I think he might like them." Elise pleaded with me, those big blue eyes being my main weakness in life.

I grabbed a hot dog off the counter and tossed it down to him. Meatball pounced, eating it faster than I did. I shouldn't have done that, but I had zero fucks left today. If the dog wanted to puke up his brains, so be it.

Sadly, at two in the morning, that's exactly what he did, and I was the one who had to clean it up. What a shitshow of a day. And I had a feeling tomorrow wouldn't be any better.

CHAPTER TWENTY-SIX

aisley

I WOKE up before my alarm, probably because there was a fire in my gut, anger and hurt mixing together to keep my adrenaline on high and my sleep scarce. Pretty sure I saw every hour on the hour as I watched my clock and went over that argument with Gannon in my head. Did he really think so little of me that he thought I'd abandon Elise to impress my boss? Even strangers I met for the first time trusted me more than my boyfriend.

That shit was messed up.

I flung off my sheet and scrambled out of bed, snatching one of his T-shirts off the floor in front of the clothes hamper. And then I saw his hat on the dresser and I was grabbing that too, which led to an angry Easter egg hunt for items of Gannon's that he'd sprinkled around my house. When my arms were full and I'd buried my nose in the pile to inhale his scent more times than I'd ever admit, I flung open the door and greeted the sunrise with the most important pitch of my life. His shit went flying across my front lawn and the immature child in me cheered. I almost felt bad that his favorite hat ended up in the puddle of muddy water around the sprinkler head that was broken and I always meant to fix, but then I remembered him accusing me of being irresponsible.

Paisley Pearse was the most responsible-ist woman in all of Blueball.

I responsibled the hell out of life and had the muscle aches to prove it. If he wanted to be pissed at me, he needed to pick a different fight, because that excuse was just bullshit. And I had a feeling he knew it yet still wouldn't back down. Because as much as I was responsible, Gannon was stubborn.

My gaze swung over to his shiny trailer. I was breathing hard and shaking from all the emotions that seemed to pummel me all at once. No lights were on inside, which meant they were all still asleep. They should have been asleep in my house, little Elise tucked in with Meatball and Gannon wrapped around me so tight I was sweating.

The first wave of tears hit me and I couldn't even look at his things strewn across my yard or I'd run out there and collect them again. I'd rather stay mad. Mad felt good. Sad felt terrible.

I went back inside my house and clicked the door shut. As much as my brain was not there, I got ready for work. I'd bury it all inside and get the job done because I was responsible. *Take that, grumpy neighbor!*

I was ready early, probably because I couldn't stomach more than a few bites of a banana for breakfast. I nearly jumped out of my work boots when I heard the door slam outside. Peeking out the window because I was too chickenshit to open the door, I saw that it was Elise taking Meatball out to pee on the grass. I hurried outside, aware that this might be my only chance to hug her before her big bad daddy came out and chased away the irresponsible lady.

"Morning, lovebug."

Elise's face transformed into a big grin, and she came running into my arms. I picked her up and held her close, breathing deep to keep the tears at bay. I wasn't just losing Gannon. I was losing the little girl I'd fallen in love with, too.

"Daddy fed Meatball a hot dog, and he puked! Ew! It was so gross! And Daddy said a lot of bad words."

I couldn't help the grin. Gannon dealing with puke overnight made me feel slightly better about my own loss of sleep. "Dogs don't eat hot dogs, silly."

Elise giggled. "Meatball does!"

"Hey, Elise. I just want you to know that you're the bestest, sweetest, kindest, funniest, smartest girl I've ever met. People are lucky to love you. Don't forget that, okay?"

Elise looked at me with all the seriousness of an adult. Then she threw her arms around my neck and held me so tight I couldn't breathe.

"I love you, Paisey."

I bit my lip, but it didn't help. Two tracks of tears streamed down my cheeks. When I felt Elise let go, I swiped at my cheeks quickly. She'd endured enough things in her five years. I didn't need to go adding to her emotional burden.

"I've got to go to work, but I'll see you later, okay?"

She grinned. "I'll have Daddy make us some water bawwoons."

I set her down on the ground, Meatball dancing at our feet, wanting attention and not looking any worse for wear after puking all night. "Sounds good. Make sure you don't feed Meatball any more hot dogs."

"Oh, I won't! Daddy said hot dogs are not dog food even with dog in the name."

I laughed sadly. "Daddy is right."

About one thing, at least.

I headed to work and got through my day without crying, but everything I loved about my job had lost its luster. I didn't want to bust my ass to be better than everyone else. I just wanted to sit on the couch and have someone play with my hair and tell me

I'm perfect just the way I am. Sadly, I didn't think any of my coworkers were up for that task.

"Hey, Pearse."

I turned, heart stuttering for some reason. Maybe because my boss's voice sounded a lot like Gannon's when he was barking out orders.

"Yeah, boss?"

"Nice job yesterday as a civilian. Heard you got everyone out and cleared the scene perfectly." He dipped his head, the gray hairs below the hard hat coming in fast and furious these days. "Work like that makes its way up to the big bosses."

Then he clapped me on the shoulder and walked off. I watched him go, feeling numb. A compliment like that would have had me walking on clouds for days, but oddly, I felt nothing. I just did what I had to when a pole went down right in front of me. It had nothing to do with impressing my bosses, or looking like a hotshot. I did what anyone would do: take care of my fellow citizens in a dangerous situation. I went home, thinking about what he'd said and why I had almost no reaction to it. Had the fight with Gannon ruined my happiness?

When I hit the Blueball town limits, I just couldn't go home. What if Gannon was out there? What if Elise was out there and I couldn't just play with her like I normally would? How could I live next to the person who'd broken my heart?

I pulled over outside Gin/Tan/Laundry and grabbed my phone out of my bag. I turned it on and waited, coming up with a plan. Maybe one of my friends could meet me for a drink. Then I could slip home once the sun went down and pretend the source of all my emotional upheaval wasn't right freaking next door. My phone dinged before I pulled up the text string with the girls.

> My hot boyfriend: Real mature, Pearse.

I bit my lip. If I wasn't hurting, that would be funny as hell.

Apparently, Gannon had found his articles of clothing. Maybe he didn't like my placement. Honestly, it was the pair of underwear hanging from my azalea bush that had done it for me. I'd have to ask him his favorite.

> Me: You know the phrase. Fuck around,
> find out…

> My hot boyfriend: Listen, last night was heated.
> Let's talk this out. You on your way home?

I frowned out the windshield, making Joey jump as he came out of the tanning salon side of Gin/Tan/Laundry in front of me. I waved that everything was okay, and he walked off.

Talk it out? Was he high on hot dogs? There was nothing to talk out. He'd accused me of being immature and selfish without even asking about what happened.

> Me: There's nothing to talk out.

> My hot boyfriend: So you're not mad at me??

I literally gasped-laughed out loud, a sound I was glad no one else heard. My thumbs practically flew over the phone screen.

> Me: Oh, I'm good and pissed.

> My hot boyfriend: Right. So let's talk it out.

> Me: We're broken up, Gannon. Nothing to
> talk out.

The little bubble hovered there for awhile while I wondered what he didn't get about this situation. He literally said he couldn't be with me. And I said I couldn't be with him. That's a breakup, genius.

> My hot boyfriend: WE ARE NOT BROKEN UP

Look who found the caps lock. Jesus. What was wrong with this man? Did he have a rock for a skull?

> Me: We most definitely are (and the lack of annoying all caps does not diminish my emphasis).

> My hot boyfriend: It takes two to break up and I'm not doing it. So, still together.

I gaped, wanting to throw the phone through my windshield.

> Me: You can't just not agree to break up. Breakups can be done by one party and the other has to agree to it.

> My hot boyfriend: Says who?

> Me: Says literally everyone who's ever been in a relationship??

> My hot boyfriend: Losers. All of them.

> Me: Okay, be serious, Gannon.

> My hot boyfriend: I've never been more serious. We ain't done, Pearse.

I threw my phone. On the passenger seat, not through the windshield.

"Ugh!" I groaned out loud a few more times and did not feel any better.

So I climbed out of my truck, walked into the Gin part of Gin/Tan/Laundry like a badass on a mission and sat my ass on one of the barstools and gestured for the bartender who I was pretty sure was the older brother of a girl I went to high school with. I was on a mission to get good and drunk. Would have been better with my friends here, but this mood simply couldn't wait for them to arrive. If Gannon thought I was irresponsible, then perhaps I'd show him what that actually looked like.

"I'd love a whiskey sour delivered every half hour."

The guy's eyes widened, but he didn't question me. When he slid the first drink my way, I tossed it back instead of sipping and relished in the burn as it made its way down. I'd feel like shit tomorrow and probably call in sick for the first time in the history working for the county, but it would be worth it to burn that man out of my brain and my heart.

I still hadn't accomplished that mission when Audrey appeared next to me like some kind of modern-day miracle, offering me a water bottle.

"Ugh, no thankth. Whithkey." My tongue felt three times too large for my mouth.

"Bar's closing, hun. Let's get you home." Audrey slung my arm over her shoulder and pulled me off the barstool, grunting like I weighed more than an elephant.

"Jeez, Aud. You need to work out."

Both of her faces glared at me. "Maybe you should try using your legs, hotshot."

I looked down and almost lurched forward into a face-plant. Which was weird because I had four legs. Surely one or two of them could help out here.

"I'm an octoputh! Look at all my legth!"

"I love you, Paisley, but if you don't shut up and walk, I'll have to call Gannon to come carry you home."

I lurched back and almost cracked Audrey in the head. "No! I broke up with him and he's being an ath."

Audrey bit back a smile. "That's what he said about you when he called me worried about you."

I frowned, wishing the sidewalk would stop spinning. Stupid sidewalks.

"He hurt me, Aud."

"I know, hun, I know."

She leaned me into the passenger seat of my truck, bending down to pick up my legs and swivel me inside, a crumpled heap of a woman. She slapped my ass and shut the door. My eyes drooped, and I shut them just to make the spinning stop. My stomach lurched as Audrey drove down the road, bitching the whole time about feeling like she was driving a big rig. When she started honking at people and cackling, I prayed for sleep.

At least then my heart would stop aching.

CHAPTER TWENTY-SEVEN

annon

I'D HAD my ass handed to me by life before, but never by a blonde bombshell of a woman with a smart mouth and a backside I wanted to turn red. Paisley had given me an earful, the words of which were still ringing in my ears three days later. I'd watched Audrey half drag Paisley into her own house, out of my mind with worry. I'd spent every minute since then looking out my trailer window for signs of life, a creepy Peeping Tom of worry. This was just me now. I was a worrywart auntie who should take up knitting and call it a life.

Paisley should have been home twenty minutes ago from work, but of course, her truck was not in the drive. I nearly got clipped in the head with a horseshoe, looking for her truck. I'd walked right into the line of fire, freaking out my guests who wondered why the owner of Glamper's Paradise was talking to himself and generally acting like a jackass.

"Daddy!" Elise called for me, her voice full of irritation.

"What's up, E-bug?" I came over to the swing set I'd set up for her. She was lying facedown on the seat, her stomach where her butt should have been. Meatball was jumping up to try to bite the hair that hung down.

I whistled, and the dog sat on his rump in the dirt like he knew he was in trouble.

"I wanna play with Paisey." Elise's sad voice cut like a knife across my heart. She'd been asking for Paisley several times a day. I was running out of excuses as to why she couldn't see her.

Imbuing my voice with enthusiasm I didn't feel, I clapped my hands. "Can't right now. We have to get you to gymnastics class!"

Elise's head popped up, but she eyed me suspiciously. "Can Paisley come to class too?"

I shook my head, locking my heart down tight. "Sorry, Elise. She's not home from work yet. Let's get you cleaned up and then we can go."

I left Meatball in the trailer with a stern warning not to chew, crap, or puke while we were gone. Only time would tell which rule he broke. The mood didn't improve much from there for either of us, even with the bribe of gymnastics. I hated to see the light dimming in Elise's eyes, but there wasn't much I could do about it. I'd already tried texting Paisley repeatedly and she wasn't answering any longer. I had a feeling that this level of mad wasn't going to just dissipate without drastic action on my part.

And I knew it had to come from me. I'd overreacted. My panic was real and so was my concern, but I'd taken it out on Paisley. The only reason I hadn't approached her already with an apology was because I was still working out in my head how to promise her that it wouldn't happen again. What was the use of apologizing when the next little thing would set me off and we found ourselves in this pattern all over again?

Elise didn't skip into the gymnastics building, which told me everything I needed to know about her emotional state. Knowing I'd hurt my daughter made my ribs ache even worse. It was like both of us were going through the breakup.

Even though I'd still argue Paisley and I weren't broken up. I refused.

Moving off to the corner of the waiting room area, I pulled out my phone and called the number Bain had given me.

"Hello?"

"Hey, Lincoln? This is Gannon Hart. I own Glamper's Paradise and am a friend of Bain Sutter."

"Hey, man. Bain told me about you. I hear you're hiring?"

I looked down, squeaking my boot against the linoleum floor. "I am. Any chance you're looking to be a jack-of-all-trades, helping me run this place?"

"Hell yeah. I almost moved to Auburn Hill a few years back, but the timing wasn't right. I like the area though and have quite a bit of variety on my resume. Whatever you need, I should be able to handle."

One tiny pebble of stress lifted off my shoulders, leaving the huge boulder that was this situation with Paisley. "Awesome. When can you come out?"

"I officially got discharged last week, but need to deal with some family things first. I could be out in three weeks? Is that too late?"

"No, that's perfect. That'll give me time to get another trailer installed. You good with living in a trailer?"

"Sure. Gotta be better than the barracks, right?"

I cringed. I wasn't military, but I had friends who were. The stories they told about living on base was the stuff of nightmares. "Most definitely. This is glamping. Upscale camping."

Lincoln chuckled. "Sounds like my kind of place. See you in a few weeks."

We hung up, and I felt like I'd mentally crossed off a huge item on my to-do list. I couldn't be a full-time dad, plus a good boyfriend, if I was working my ass off from sunup to sundown. Somehow, someway, this glamping venture was already turning a profit. If I could get one man on to help out and get a couple more trailers, I'd be fully operational a good three months before

I thought I would. I should be ecstatic, but all I could think about was how empty it felt without Paisley by my side.

"Hey, I couldn't help but overhear. You own Glamper's Paradise?"

A guy sitting in one of the chairs set up in the waiting room leaned over. Must be one of the dads waiting for his kid. He had black hair trimmed up perfectly and a hint of a beard. He was barrel chested and his thick forearms told me he frequented the gym as much as I did. I tried on a smile, but it felt weird on my face.

"Yeah, Gannon Hart." I reached out my hand and he shook it.

"I'm Diego Grass. My wife, Mandy, and I own the new restaurant in town."

I vaguely recalled Paisley and her friends talking about that place. "Is that the salad place?"

Diego grinned. "Yeah, man, but don't let that scare you. I grill all kinds of meats that go on top of the salads if you want. You should come by."

I nodded, thinking it was nice to make new friends in this town, even if the one person I wanted to talk to refused to see me. "I will."

"Those trailers of yours big enough for a family of four? I was thinking of booking one as a little staycation. With the cost of getting the business up and running, I can't take my family too far, you know?"

An idea occurred to me. I gestured to the seat next to him and he waved me over. "Absolutely. In fact, here's what I'm thinking. What if we partner up? I could use some delivery of food to the glamp-ground on a regular basis. Glampers can't live off hot dogs and s'mores for long. I'll advertise your place and you can advertise mine at your restaurant. Plus, I'll give you the 'friends and family' deal on a trailer rental."

"Dude. That's amazing! We've seen a huge upswing in delivery, so we can definitely swing by the glamp-ground on a regular basis."

We bent our heads and worked out the details right there. The gymnastics class was almost over when Diego sat up straight and put his hand on my shoulder. "Wait until I tell my wife. She worries, you know? It was her idea to open a restaurant instead of me working for other guys who don't know the first thing about food. She's also taken on the duties of stepmom and running the restaurant while I cook. It's just a lot."

"Stepmom, huh?"

Diego practically glowed talking about his wife. "Yeah, man. Mandy is the best thing that ever happened to me. After the divorce, I thought my love life was over, you know? But man, Mandy is incredible. Not easy being stepmom to two preteen girls, though. She doesn't have the authority of a full-blooded parent, but all the responsibilities of one. Sucks, but she never complains. Makes me want to work that much harder to make her business idea a success."

His simple statement hit me between the eyes. *No authority but all the responsibilities.*

That's what Paisley had taken on by dating me. She'd stepped right up and handled all the things that came with raising a five-year-old without a single peep of complaint. I'd been pissed at her parents for pushing her so hard. They were part of the reason she felt like she had to push so hard at her job. And yet I'd come sweeping in and asked her to take on the role of stepmom too, while bitching about how her parents treated her.

And then to add insult to injury, I'd judged her and declared her lacking.

Fuck, I was an idiot.

"You okay, man?" Diego was peering at me like I'd grown a second head.

I nodded quickly, seeing the kids start to file out the door and into the waiting area. "Yeah, yeah. Just thinking about what you said. Good talking to you. I'll swing by this week for dinner and try out these salads of yours."

Diego stood and shook my hand. "Definitely. You'll love them so much you'll forget you ordered a salad."

I grinned. "I'll hold you to that."

"Daddy!" Elise skipped over to hug my leg, her usual high energy finally back. Now I needed to do the things to make sure she stayed that way. For her and for me.

I swung her up into my arms and we went out to the truck. As soon as we were on the road, I hit the button on my console to call the phone number I'd already input into my phone. I had a feeling I'd have this number on speed dial if all went well.

"Daryl Hewitt. How can I help you?"

"Hey, Daryl, this is Gannon Hart. I got your name and number from Bain Sutter."

"Well, any friend of Bain's is a friend of mine. Fellow law enforcement?"

"Nope. Just a fellow jackass who needs help."

The voice on the other end of the line chuckled. "I have a cancellation tomorrow at three. Will that work?"

"I'll make it work. Thank you and I'll see you then."

I hung up and pushed down the voice that said going to therapy was a dumbass idea. Bain hadn't led me wrong so far, and I had to do something to help me manage these panic attacks. Besides, if it could help me get Paisley back and keep her, I was all in.

"Daddy, what's a jackass?" Elise asked from the backseat.

I groaned. Just when I thought I was getting my ducks in a row, they scattered like fall leaves in a breeze.

"I don't know, E-bug. I've never heard that word."

"You just said it, silly!"

"Nope. Didn't say it."

"Did too!"

"Nope."

And so it went for the rest of the day. Elise was my shadow while I got work done around the glamp-ground and Meatball decided chewing one of Elise's jelly sandals was in his best interest. When bedtime came around, Meatball found himself sleeping on the floor, not Elise's bed, so maybe that would teach him a lesson. Highly doubtful, though.

When I was sure Elise was sound asleep, I grabbed the walkie-talkie she and I used throughout the day when I was all over the glamp-ground, and headed for the makeshift stage. The glampers that were currently renting were nowhere to be found. Maybe they headed for a sunset swim on the beach. I sat on the step leading to the stage and put the walkie-talkie next to my phone. Then I swung my guitar up onto my lap and strummed out some chords.

As it usually did, a song materialized out of the chords and I played it, smoothly transitioning to the next. I'd always played the guitar growing up, but had gotten my finger callouses back when I'd been hurt and holed up at home. There was nothing like playing music to soothe whatever distress was making me feel like I wanted out of my skin. When I got to Luke Combs's "Love You Anyway" song, I put down the guitar and picked up my phone.

Me: Good night, Paisley.

I stared at the screen, but the bubble that told me she was writing back didn't pop up. I scrolled back through the messages, seeing all three nights I'd texted her the same thing with no response.

Luke had it right. Some things left a man no choice. Loving Paisley was like breathing. Even if she wasn't talking to me, I loved her anyway. Even if it took me years to win her back, I'd just keep loving her through it. When Elise showed up on my doorstep, I didn't fight it. I had no choice, so what would be the point in fighting it? Paisley was the same way. We were inevitable, so why fight it?

I just needed to get her to see that.

CHAPTER TWENTY-EIGHT

aisley

"Hey, Mom." Counting to ten commenced immediately. I didn't handle motherly phone calls well on good days, let alone days where I felt heartbroken, defeated, and dead inside. I couldn't find the joy in work. Couldn't find peace in my home. And missed that jackass of a neighbor and his daughter like a phantom limb.

"I swear. I'm the last person to know about everything to do with my own daughter!"

"Sorry, Mom. It's just been a rough few days, and I didn't feel like rehashing it." I stretched my tired legs and found a pair of clean jean shorts. Perhaps I needed to find some joy in doing laundry before I ran out of clothes.

Mom sighed. "I get it, honey. Did you know your dad and I broke up once before we got married?"

I froze with one foot in my shorts and the other raised in the air. "Huh?" The perfect couple who did everything perfectly according to plan had gone through a hiccup?

"Yes, it's true. Your father was studying for the bar exam and was taking out his stress on me. I told him to take a flying leap and went to Las Vegas with some of my girlfriends."

My ass hit the bed, shorts forgotten. "You, Paige Pearse, went to Vegas after breaking up with Dad?" This was so odd I wondered if someone was prank calling me and pretending to be my mother.

Mom laughed. "You bet I did. Made sure he knew it too. I left a copy of my flight itinerary at his apartment. He flew out to Vegas a day later and swooped me up. Then he took up golfing for those days when he was too stressed out to speak without snapping. And we lived happily ever after."

I shook my head, smiling for the first time in days. "I'm really glad you told me that. And I really hope you got in one night of clubbing before he came and got you."

Mom made a noise I'd never heard from her before. "Oh, don't you worry, honey. I sowed a few wild oats that night."

"Mom!"

She practically cackled. "I'm just saying, good things can come from heartache. If Gannon is the one for you, he'll come to his senses."

The pit of my stomach was doubtful. "And if he doesn't?"

"Well then, you just have to push him along a little."

"Push him along?"

"Mhmm. *Push* him, honey."

I heard someone pulling up outside my house. "Got it. Thanks, Mom. I gotta go put my pushing plans in motion."

"Excellent, just don't get pregnant or sully our good name."

I huffed. There it was. Annoying Mom was back. "Goodbye, Mom."

I got my other leg into my shorts and ran for the front door. Zeke was here to start putting up that fence between my property and Gannon's. I'd meant to put up a fence eventually and perhaps now was the best time to get it done.

"Hey, Zeke!" I called from the doorstep.

He waved as he got out of his truck, loaded down with white posts and vinyl fencing. Zeke had been friends with my older brother in high school. He was the quiet, intense type who got along with everyone. He also had a temper when you pushed him too far. I saw it in action one day when he'd been pitching senior year. The team they were playing was heckling our guys and being general jackasses. Zeke had taken all the comments in stride until the one batter looked right at Zeke's best friend, Rainey, in the stands and grabbed his junk lewdly. Zeke sprinted to home plate and decked the guy before the umpire blinked. He got kicked out of the game, but he refused to apologize like his coach wanted him to do.

"Come on back and I'll show you where it's going." I slipped on some flip-flops and gave him a tour of my back and side yards, pointing out the property lines.

"Shouldn't be too difficult," Zeke declared as he went back to his truck to start pulling out equipment.

I let him be for an hour or so. Once the sun got high in the sky and the temperature started to soar, I went back out with ice-cold lemonade. And the skimpiest tank top I owned. Maybe Mom was right. Maybe I shouldn't be freezing out Gannon to protect my bruised heart. *Push, Paisley*.

A door slammed the second I got to Zeke with his refreshments. Gannon stood outside his trailer, his gray eyes practically starting a wildfire along my skin. He looked good in the brief second I gave myself to look at him. His jeans fit his body like a well-worn glove, highlighting his tree trunk legs and athletic waist. The T-shirt he wore was one of my favorites, not because of the design or color, but because it was worn and washed to a level of softness that felt like heaven against my skin.

"Hey, Zeke. Here's some lemonade. You looked absolutely parched out here." I gave Zeke a wide smile, ignoring the way he darted a glance at me and took the glass, looking puzzled. Zeke wasn't loud, and you'd be an idiot to think his quiet nature somehow meant there was less going on underneath the surface.

He was especially smart when it came to people. He'd know within thirty seconds that I was flirting with him, but didn't actually mean it.

As he drank down the beverage, I scooted closer, making sure Gannon had a nice view of my ass. I hoped he envisioned the tattoo on my right cheek, knowing he'd lost my heart by being an idiot.

"Can I help you out here? Be your assistant?" I put my hand on his chest and he looked down at it. "Ohh. You've been hitting the gym quite a bit since high school, huh?"

When Zeke's head came up, he looked over at Gannon and then back at me with a smile pulling at his lips. "Sure have, darlin'. You don't mind if I take my shirt off, do you? So hot out here."

He shot me a wink, and I knew he knew what we were doing here. It wasn't a wink of flirtation, it was a wink of understanding.

"Only if I can take my shirt off too," I simpered loudly enough Gannon could hear me.

A growl and then the sound of a car door slamming came from behind me.

Zeke leaned down. "He's in his truck. I think we got him good."

I snatched my hand back. Gannon's truck engine turning over nearly drowned me out. "Thanks for playing along. I won't actually be out here. I know I'll just be in your way."

Zeke shrugged. "It's fine. Rainey always had me help her out in these weird scenarios, too." Gannon's truck roared off down the road.

I remembered how tight those two used to be. "Where's Rainey these days?"

Zeke grabbed a fence post and dropped it into the hole next to him. "Not sure. We lost track of each other after high school."

That didn't seem right at all, but it wasn't really any of my business. "Well, that's too bad. I liked her."

Zeke got busy banging things together, but I still heard him mutter, "Yeah, me, too."

I left him to his work, heading inside to pick up my house for the girls to come over. After Audrey saved my drunk self at the bar the other night, Keva had insisted on a girls' day to hash things out properly. I agreed, but only after stating it would be an alcohol-free social event. I shuddered just thinking of more alcohol.

Audrey was the first to arrive. "Please tell me that fine man in your yard is single." She shoved a covered plate at me. "Also, I brought a cheese plate for you. All cheddar and havarti, no blue cheese, just like you like it."

I gave her a hug. "Thanks, Aud. And thank you again for getting my drunk ass home."

Audrey waved her hand and had a seat on the couch. "Oh please. Like you haven't done the same for me before. Besides, I don't care about that. I want to know about the beefcake putting up your fence."

I uncovered the cheese plate and snatched up a piece of cheddar. "He's single, as far as I know, but I don't think his heart is available."

Audrey pursed her lips. "Interesting. I can work with that."

I laughed, knowing Audrey was bold enough to make a move on Zeke, no matter where his heart might be at the moment. My door opened again and Marlo and Keva came inside together, arguing over the use of raisins in baked goods. I was with Marlo on this. Raisins needed to die.

Marlo flopped on the couch beside Audrey while Keva gave me a hug and placed a batch of homemade brownies on the coffee table before having a seat on the chair opposite of me.

"We come bearing gifts and shoulders to cry on," Keva announced. "All except Marlo, who brought nothing."

Marlo glared at her. "I did too." She pulled her hands out of the pocket on the front of her sweatshirt. I didn't know how she wore sweatshirts in the summer, but I was done arguing with her over it. "The finest chocolates in the western world." She placed a small gold foil box on the coffee table.

Audrey snorted. "Leftovers from a funeral?"

"Does it matter where it came from?" Marlo snapped back.

"Thank you, Marlo. Very kind of you to think of me during a funeral."

She stuck her tongue out at me and we all laughed. Then the laughter died, and I was back to feeling like someone had dimmed the sun.

"How are you doing, really?" Keva asked quietly.

These were my best friends in the whole world, which meant I could tell them everything, and I did, telling them about the argument, the days after, and the flirting I'd attempted this morning.

Audrey snorted. "Bet that made him come unglued. Gannon doesn't strike me as a man who shares what he thinks is his."

"He hasn't contacted you since the texts arguing about your breakup status?" Keva pulled spoons out of her huge handbag and passed them out, not waiting for us as she dug into the brownies.

I leaned forward and scooped up a huge bite, too. It was still warm from the oven and exactly what I needed. "Not really."

Marlo took a bite of brownie too, knocking my spoon out of the way when I immediately came back for more. "I smell a falsehood."

I jabbed my spoon in the brownie pan and dared her to fight me on it. I was the one with the breakup and in most need of chocolate. "He's sent me a text every day saying good night."

Audrey swooned, toppling over on the couch into Marlo's lap. Marlo jabbed her with her elbow and Audrey sat back up with a glare.

"I don't know, Paisley. That sounds super sweet."

"Hey! Whose side are you on? He hasn't even attempted to apologize."

Audrey grabbed my hand as I tried to get another bite of

brownie. "He called me, worried about you. The man cares. A lot. Don't you think it's worth it to hear him out?"

Marlo answered before I could. "I don't know. If she hears him out, he'll just sweet-talk her into coming back without resolving their issues. Have you seen the ass on that man? Paisley will take one look at that stack of muscles and fall back into bed with him."

I wanted to be mad at her for her weak assessment of me, but she wasn't exactly wrong.

Keva's spoon clanked on the table as she set it down. "Can I say something?"

I eyed her warily. "Sure..."

"You know I'm the first one to tell you love ain't grand and it doesn't all end in happiness and sunshine. But...and this is a big but, so hear me out. Gannon should not have accused you of being irresponsible. However, you haven't been a parent and felt that kind of panic." Keva's eyes filled with tears.

"Remember when Lucas fell and got that cut above his eye? I lost my shit. Like, literally fell apart at all the blood and his little screams. There's something that happens when you become a parent. You suddenly have to watch your heart walk around outside of your body getting hurt left and right and somehow be okay with it. It's fucking painful and I don't know that I'll ever get over it. Gannon had a right to be panicked when he couldn't get ahold of you."

"He didn't have a right to blame you, though. That was obviously panic that made him yell and place blame, not logic," Audrey cut in.

Keva nodded. "Exactly. I'm not saying he was right, but you could have talked sense into him, Pais. But instead, you got good and mad and stormed off, essentially doing what he just did. You both let your emotions run the show."

Marlo raised her hand, and we all looked at her. "You thought he was judging you and finding you lacking, just like your parents do to you. Am I right?"

I sat back in my chair and toyed with my spoon. "I really hate when you bitches are right." As if by magic, all the anger I'd been holding for days drained from my body, leaving me weak. I leaned my head back and closed my eyes. "Ugh!"

"Dude, I get it. Parental baggage is the shits," Audrey said in the silence. And it was true. She'd been dealt a worse hand than me.

I opened my eyes and gave her an understanding smile. "Well, now I feel like an ass."

"You're not an ass, babe." Keva came over to hug me, which did not help with the tears burning in my eyes. A few spilled over and I hated each of them. "You have a fabulous ass, but you are not an ass."

"So does Gannon," I said weakly.

"He really does and I'm not one to notice asses," Marlo stated.

We all chuckled, even me. "So what do I do now?"

"I think you cry it out with us and eat all the chocolate you can stand and then we make a plan. You've got to talk to him. See what he has to say. See if there's something there worth salvaging." Audrey looked around at all of us. "Right?"

"Agreed!" Keva went back to her chair and opened the box of chocolates Marlo brought. "I'm proud of you for the clothes toss, though. That was epic. Everyone in town cheered you on for that one."

I buried my burning face in my hands. "Oh God."

Those bitches just cackled.

annon

My hot sexy neighbor: Can we talk?

I TRIPPED over Meatball and nearly clipped my face on the counter in the trailer. I hurried to type back while petting the pup's head. Thankfully, his skull was hard as a rock.

Me: Fuck yes. Now?

The bubble didn't appear, and I wondered if perhaps I already lost my chance. I'd been getting ready to send another goodnight text, not expecting Paisley to reach out to me first. I'd nearly taken off my foot chopping wood today for the glamper's bonfire. Seeing Paisley with that asshole putting up her fence had done a number on my head. I needed to talk things out with her sooner rather than later.

> My hot sexy neighbor: Shit. Boss just called me in. Some emergency near Auburn Hill. Can we talk tomorrow?

> Me: Sure. Anytime. Please be safe.

> My hot sexy neighbor: Will do.

It wasn't a declaration of love by any means, but at least she was talking to me. Or texting me, rather. I got busy bathing Elise and getting her to bed, my head filled with things I could say to make things better. My phone vibrated not long after Elise went to sleep.

> Bain Sutter: Hey, man, heard there's quite the accident on Coast Highway about ten miles south of here. Poles down and electricity out for most of Auburn Hill. Paisley out there?

Adrenaline coursed through my system. Panic followed shortly after, but I put the phone down and focused on the box breathing technique the therapist had shown me just two days ago. When I thought I had a handle on things, I picked the phone back up.

> Me: Yeah, I think so. Any chance you have Paisley's parents' phone number?

> Bain Sutter: I have both cell numbers. Want John's or Paige's?

> Me: Both, please.

He sent them to me, all the while I kept up with my box breathing. I saved both numbers in my phone and then dialed Paige. It took some convincing, but when I told Paige I had every intention of marrying her daughter and giving her more grandkids than she knew what to do with, she said she and John would be right over.

I slid my favorite baseball hat on for good luck and grabbed Meatball off Elise's bed. I tucked him under my arm like a football and gave him a stern warning to behave while I was gone. He looked at me very seriously, his little beady eyes not even blinking until I was done, which I appreciated. Then he ruined the moment by leaping up and licking me across the face.

"Jesus H. Christ, Meatball!"

I wiped my face on my shoulder and put him down.

John and Paige came quickly, saying they preferred to stay here anyway because their power was out. Part of me was worried about leaving Elise with them, but Paisley had turned out amazing, so I forced myself to leave without writing out a bullet point list of all my daughter's favorite things. I leaped in my truck and roared down the road. I put the phone on speaker and called my new friend, Diego. Thankfully, he answered right away and we put together a plan. Once his wife heard why I wanted a late-night delivery, she was all too happy to help out. Apparently, she reads a lot of romance books and said she lived for these big moments where the hero comes swooping in to win the heroine back. I didn't care why she did it. I just needed some damn food.

Almost an hour later, with the meats and salads packed in the back of my truck, I headed down Coast Highway, going right into the heart of the electrical problems. I saw flashing lights up ahead and pulled over, forcing myself not to scan the faces of the workers swarming the area to see if I could find Paisley. My heart couldn't take it if she was up high on a pole or near sparking wires.

A worker with a hard hat on approached my vehicle. "Road's closed. You'll have to turn around."

I swung open my door. "Actually, I'm here to bring food for the linemen. And women."

The guy squinted at me in the darkness. "Uh, food?"

I tried out a smile and refused to see who was up on the pole closest to me. "Y'all have to eat, right? Figured my girl would appreciate a good meal after working her ass off."

The guy started grinning, voice rising. "Hold up. You talking about Pais? You're the guy she's dating?"

I nodded, not wanting this to become a thing, but already I could see heads turning in our direction. There was only one head I wanted to turn, but I was too chickenshit to see if she was close by.

The guy put his hands up to his mouth. "Pais! Your man's here with food for all of us!" A collective cheer came from everyone gathered.

"What?"

There it was. Paisley's not-so-sweet voice hollering from up above our heads. My lungs started pumping hard, and I wasn't sure if it was nerves about seeing her or if my anxiety was picking up again.

"What's your name, man?"

Breathe in for five and hold. Breathe out for five. "Gannon Hart."

"Paisley and Gannon sitting on a pole. K-I-S-S-I-N-G." The guy was shaking his hips like an idiot and singing worse than Meatball.

"Fuck off, Benny."

I spun around to see Paisley hop off the last rung of the pole, her tool belt heavy on her waist, hard hat in place, and a weary smile. "What are you doing here, Gannon?" She dusted her hands off and pulled off the heavy-duty gloves.

Benny stood between us, a silly grin on his face. Didn't really need him using us as his nightly entertainment.

I smacked his arm with the back of my hand. "Got some steak in the back, Benny. Why don't you get it before it's gone and you're stuck with the vegetarian dinner?"

That got his attention. He ran to the bed of my truck like his life depended on it. Paisley shook her head in disgust.

"He always a handful?" I asked, easing into the first conversation I'd had with her in days.

She pulled off her hard hat. "Pretty much." Then she looked me square in the eyes and all that nervousness fled in an instant. "Why are you here, cowboy?"

My knees went weak. I hadn't realized how much I'd needed to hear that nickname again from her lips. "Brought you and the crew some food."

Paisley quirked her head to the side. "Awful nice of you." She came a step closer and I couldn't breathe. "Especially since we broke up."

"We didn't—"

And then I saw the sparkle in her eyes. The way her lips tilted up on one side. The woman was teasing me. I wanted to high-five myself. If she was teasing me, I was still in the game.

I grabbed her hands and pulled her closer, aware of some hoots and hollers from people still watching us. I didn't fucking care. Making her understand that I loved her was more important. "I brought you dinner because I believe in you and support you, no matter what. Even if what you do is dangerous, I trust you'll do your best to be safe. Least I can do is keep you fueled up on the job properly so you come home to me in one piece."

Paisley's eyes filled with tears. I watched her swallow hard, my words soaking in to a woman starved for them. Her parents had given her grief for years about her job, making her feel like she wasn't capable. And then I'd come along and played into that bullshit because of my own issues.

"You're the most responsible person I know, and I'm sorry I let my own bullshit get in the way," I added quietly. She deserved to hear the apology, too.

"Holy shit, this food is amazing!" Benny shouted with his mouth full.

Paisley ignored him. "Guess I'm glad we didn't break up over it, then."

I grinned full out. "Damn right we didn't break up. Just a little argument."

"Because you were an ass."

I dipped my head. "Total ass, but you gotta admit. You kind of expect that from me, right?"

Paisley whacked me in the stomach and I held her hand there. Anything to keep touching her. "No, actually. You're a good man, Gannon Hart."

She could have hit me with an electrical pole and I wouldn't have been more stunned. I was trying to put my life together, that was for sure. She'd met me at my lowest point, so to hear praise from her was everything I needed to hear. "I'll be a better man for you, then. Count on it."

She smiled up at me and suddenly everything around us faded. Those weren't just empty promises. I'd be a better man for her. I'd get the therapy and do the work to be what she needed.

"Now go do your pole shit and I'll see you at home, yeah?"

She reached up and kissed me quick. "I love you."

If her coworkers weren't right there, I would have dropped to my knees with relief. "I love you too, woman."

Paisley didn't actually make it home until the first rays of sunshine crept into the sky. I was already up, pacing the trailer, just waiting to hear her truck hit the driveway. When it did, I ran out and intercepted her.

"Hey." She looked dead on her feet, but still shot me a smile.

"I apologize in advance for your parents being in your house."

Her eyes nearly bugged out of her head. "My parents?"

I closed her truck door for her and guided her toward her house. "Yeah, I called them to watch Elise last night."

Paisley dug her heels in and turned to stare at me. "You called my parents?"

I shrugged. "Yeah. And Paige said they're taking Elise to the park this morning so you can get some peace and quiet to sleep."

"Paige, as in, my mother?"

The door to her house swung open and the one and only Paige stood there in a robe, holding a cup of coffee. "There you are! Did some drunk hit the electrical pole again?"

Paisley rubbed her forehead. She was cute when she was stunned. "No, actually. A squirrel bit through the wires and shocked himself. The poor thing caught on fire, which distracted a driver hauling a cattle trailer. He clipped the next pole and the back of the hauler opened up and cows were shooting out the back. Two poles fried plus cows everywhere really caused an issue. Roads are open now though, and you should have power at home."

John filled the doorway, already dressed in khakis and a pressed polo. I wondered if he slept in that getup. "You should really have those wires buried. It would solve all this ridiculousness."

I could feel Paisley's shoulders tensing up.

"Pretty sure that multimillion-dollar decision isn't hers to make, John."

He did a double take at my cheekiness. "Well, she could put in a good word, at least. If you're going to risk your life fixing those poles, you ought to get a say."

Here we go again. I opened my mouth to not-so-gently put him in his place, but Paisley put her hand on my chest, an evil grin on her face.

"I actually like working the pole, Dad."

Paige spit out her coffee all over the flowers Paisley and Elise had planted earlier this summer. I grinned like a maniac. Fuck, I loved this woman and her smart mouth. John's face turned a shade of red that couldn't possibly be healthy.

"Paisley," he reprimanded sharply.

"What, Dad? You've given me no choice. I keep telling you I like my job and I'm damn good at it, but you never listen. So I thought maybe a more direct approach would be better."

Paige started laughing, holding her cup out to the side as she bent at the waist. John shot her a glare, but she just laughed harder. John huffed and waited for his wife to calm down.

"Paisley, you're my little girl. I worry about you."

"I get it. I really do, but I'm an adult now and I've made my career choice. You can either support it or get out of my way. I highly suggest you support it."

The two of them glared at each other for a long minute or two. I could see where Paisley got her stubborn nature. I was proud of her, though, for standing her ground and demanding the respect he should have been giving her this whole time.

John finally dropped his hands from his waist. "Fine. You're right. I don't want to be at odds with each other. I don't like your job, but since you've asked me to, I'll support it. Or at least keep quiet about it."

Paisley looked relieved. And still tired. "I appreciate that more than you know."

Then she left my side to give him a hug. John held Paisley for longer than normal, his eyes closing as he held her tight. I'd bet good money I'd be in that same position one day with Elise, loving her beyond reason but not happy about some decision she'd made. I only hoped I'd have the good sense to make sure to lead with the love and not the judgement.

Paige joined them to kiss Paisley on the head. "I'm just going to get dressed and then we're taking Elise for the day. The park, lunch, and then the beach." She shot me a wink and stepped back inside. Apparently, Paige was giving me the alone time I needed with her daughter to make sure she'd forgiven me.

And while there were a thousand things I wanted to say or do with Paisley, I mostly just wanted to see her get some sleep. The woman was exhausted, and it was now my mission in life to make sure she gave herself the rest she needed to keep kicking ass.

CHAPTER THIRTY

aisley

THE DOORS SLAMMED ON MY PARENTS' very sensible Volvo sedan. Elise waved goodbye from her car seat in the back. Gannon watched as they left, then put his hand on my back and steered me into the house. I'd eaten the leftovers from the meal Gannon had given my crew while he got Elise ready for a day with my parents. Can we just talk about that for a second? Gannon called my parents, and they babysat overnight? And now they were spending the day with Elise? And my dad had in not-so-many-words apologized to me about all the grief over my career choice?

Miracles were falling from the sky here in Blueball today.

"Am I dreaming right now?" I asked out loud.

Gannon chuckled, low and deep. "No, but I hope you will be soon. Let's get you ready for bed."

I turned and slid my arms up around his thick neck. I'd had a lot of time on top of that pole to think about him coming out with food to support me and my crew. Gannon was a man of few words and not at all demonstrative, so for him to do that in front of my coworkers...well, it sucked all the wind out of my sails about being mad at him. And quite frankly, I didn't want to be mad any longer. This ray of sunshine had had enough dark days this week to last me a lifetime. Being angry at each other just sucked the life right out of me.

But I also knew I couldn't be with someone who didn't trust me. That would be setting myself up for a lifetime of hurt feelings. I didn't expect Gannon to be perfect, and our recent fight just reinforced that, but at least he was trying. I'd have to see if that was enough to make things work between us.

"Thank you for the food. That was incredibly sweet."

Gannon ducked his head. "Don't tell anyone."

I laughed. "Pretty sure my whole crew saw your romantic gesture and have spread it around town by now."

Gannon huffed. "I was hoping it would just spread a good word about Grass. Diego could use the business."

I ran my fingers through his hair, happy he'd taken off his hat. "Ahh, my man made a friend."

He grabbed my ass and pulled me into him, already hard against my hip. "Yes, I did. And I plan on making more friends here in Blueball, so thank fuck you accepted my apology."

I rubbed against him, watching the way his nostrils flared and his jaw went hard as granite. "Want to make friends with my pussy? She's missed you."

Gannon growled and then I was being lifted and tossed over his shoulder. He ran toward my bedroom and I laughed my head off as I bounced around. He didn't stop at my bed though, like I thought he would. Instead, he carried me into the bathroom and let me slide down his body.

"Strip, woman."

That deep voice had me shivering even though it was already warm outside and plenty warm right here against Gannon's chest. I raced to pull my shirt over my head while he got the bathtub running, checking the water temperature and pouring in a whole bottle of bubbles Audrey had given me but I'd never used. My clothes ended up in a heap.

"That's enough!" I giggled, watching the bubbles rise toward the ceiling.

Gannon spun around and looked me up and down with hooded eyes. "Get in," he growled, sounding as mean as the first day I met him. Except now I knew that growl was him keeping himself on a tight leash of control, not because he didn't like me.

I stepped into the bath and sank into the water like a swimsuit model dipping into the surf for her photoshoot. I loved the way Gannon's eyes traced every single movement, hunger and desire making those blue eyes burn. He sat on the edge and reached into the bathtub. White bubbles lined his arm as he pulled my feet into his lap. His jeans got wet, but he didn't seem to mind. Thumbs dug into my instep and my eyes rolled back in my head.

"Relax. You work hard and deserve some downtime."

"Hmm." I couldn't formulate words, not when the hot water relaxed every muscle in my body, the scent of the soap made me feel like I was in a field of flowers, and Gannon was massaging me like it was his mission in life to seduce my feet.

"I went to a therapist the other day."

His quiet voice pulled my eyes open. "You did?"

He nodded, gaze on the pile of bubbles. "Got issues to work through." His gaze shot up to mine. "And you're worth working through them."

As if I wasn't already about to melt into a puddle and drown, now I was relaxed and tearing up, all the emotional states I used to avoid. This man flip-flopped from Grumpy Bear to teddy bear so fast it made my heart spin.

"I love you, Gannon Hart. I know you're a package deal, so when I say I love you, I mean I love you both."

Gannon's hands froze on my feet. His eyes looked like they teared up, but mine were already full, so maybe it was just me. After a prolonged moment, he went back to massaging my feet.

"Good thing you didn't break up with me, then."

I snorted and closed my eyes. "We totally broke up."

He flicked the bottom of my foot and I yelped, sending water splashing. "No, we didn't."

We'd probably always argue, and that was okay by me. Two fiery personalities would simply have to duke it out from time to time. As long as there was love and respect, we'd be fine. I lay back again and let him drain all the tension out of my body until the water went cold. When he pulled the plug and stood up, offering me a hand out of the tub, I went willingly.

Gannon surprised me by throwing the towel at me and picking me up, wet body and all, to carry me to the bed. He dropped me, letting me bounce on the mattress with an evil grin on his handsome face. Then he stripped the T-shirt over his head and I forgot to bitch about the rough treatment. His belt was next and then his jeans. The man was built like my truck, oversized and ready to impress. He grabbed the base of his cock and stroked himself. I had a hard time swallowing.

"If you're too tired, just say so. I could use a nap myself."

I was so busy watching him work himself over I missed the cocky grin. "Sleep is overrated."

Gannon stepped right up to the foot of the bed, stroking himself and staring down at me with those hooded eyes. "Roll over, baby. Let me see my heart on your juicy ass."

I bit back a smile. "I believe the phrase is wearing your heart on your sleeve."

Gannon narrowed his eyes. "I don't care about that poetic shit. I just want to see your ass."

I snorted and rolled over. He wasn't eloquent, but I could appreciate the directness. Besides, I'd spent days teasing him with short shorts and a bikini that didn't cover what my mama gave me. I was partially responsible for creating this monster.

Gannon grabbed my ankles and pulled. I yelped, but then groaned as he hitched my hips up with his big hands and kissed my tattoo. His tongue flicked out and traced the outline of the heart.

"Does it make me an asshole to get off on seeing my mark on you?"

I pushed up onto my elbows and craned my neck to see the way he looked at me, like he'd lost all control of his feelings. Stripped raw and vulnerable, brave in the way he let me see all of him. Trust was the strongest aphrodisiac of all.

"If it does, then I'm an asshole, too. That heart on your ass is *my* mark."

Gannon ran his hand down my back, leaning over me to trace my jaw with his finger. "You're not an asshole, Paisley. You're sunshine in a gorgeous package. A badass Cinderella who can do anything she puts her mind to. You're far too good for me, but I'm selfish enough to try to keep you. I have to have you. I can't breathe if you're not speaking to me. I can't be the kind of dad Elise deserves without you reminding me of the good in this world. I need you in a way that frightens me."

I flipped over and crawled onto my knees to put my hands on his face. I wanted to plaster myself to him and never let go. "We're going to make the best team, you and me. We're going to be all the things we've each dreamed of, only because we're supporting each other. You'll see."

And then I kissed him because I needed to be closer. Needed to be entwined with him, infusing all my positivity into the man who'd been beaten down by life this last year. He'd had no one in his corner when he was at his lowest, but now he had me. I'd cheer so loud he would think he had a whole stadium at his back.

"Paisley," he murmured reverently against my lips, hands touching me absolutely everywhere.

I let him go, lying back on the bed while holding his gaze and letting my knees fall open. I lifted my arm toward him, inviting him into my body. Gannon crawled up on the bed and blanketed me.

"I can't…" he grunted, grabbing his cock and rubbing it against my center. "…go slow. I can't—"

"Shh." I put my hand over his mouth and lifted my hips, feeling his tip rub right where I needed him. The man was trembling, holding himself above me. "Don't give me slow. Give me you."

And then he did, slamming inside like he couldn't wait another second to claim me as his. My eyes fluttered shut and every nerve in my body decided to migrate south to get in on this action. How had I gone all week without this? No, not the sex, though that was heavenly. How could I have gone a week without the raw honesty of this man?

Gannon thrust faster and deeper and I took it, needing him to fill all the empty spaces in me that had been waiting for him. When my cries were swept up by his kiss and his body froze in a release so strong we were both suspended in time, I finally let myself cry.

His thumbs dried my cheeks, but he didn't try to stop the tears. There was no sadness here. This was a happiness so big and beautiful it had to spill out of my eyes. I felt myself begin to drift with Gannon's arms around me, his heart pumping against my back so smoothly and rhythmically I couldn't keep my eyes open.

EPILOGUE

 annon

PAISLEY GROANED and swiped wildly through the air. I dodged her hand like a prize-winning boxer.

"Pearse, wake up," I crooned right next to her ear.

"My day to sleep in," she muttered, squeezing her eyes shut even tighter.

I hated to do it (I actually didn't...teasing Paisley was fun as shit) but there wasn't time for sleeping. Not with the day I had planned for her. I yanked the covers off of her in one fell swoop to drop them on the floor.

"Arghh!" Paisley flung herself on her back and opened her eyes with a grimace. She was cute when she was angry. Especially when she was naked and angry. That was my personal favorite.

Elise and I had officially moved in with Paisley immediately after that big fight when she claims we broke up. We didn't break up, and I had the text messages to prove it, but I wasn't going to bring that up today.

I threw one of my T-shirts at her. "Cover up, woman. There's a child in the house."

Paisley sat up and put on the shirt, glaring at me. Only reason she was naked was because I'd stripped everything off of her last night and made her scream into her pillow.

"Is there a reason you're being a particularly rude Grumpy the Bear this morning?" she asked all snippety.

I rubbed my hands together. Elise and I had planned it all out over the last two weeks. I considered it a miracle that Elise hadn't let our secret slip.

"Today is Stepmom Day. Duh."

Paisley blinked, pushing her hair out of her face. "Stepmom Day?"

I nodded. "Yep. It's like Mother's Day but just for stepmoms."

Paisley shook her head. "That's not a thing."

"It definitely should be a thing, so I'm making it a thing." I turned toward the bedroom door. "Elise! She's up!"

We both heard a squeal and Paisley's lips hiked up in the first smile of the day. Elise entered the room biting her bottom lip, her eyes trained on the travel mug of coffee I'd poured just moments earlier and was now currently clutched between both of her hands. Meatball danced around her feet. I whistled and he came over to me for a brief second. Long enough not to trip Elise. She got it all the way to Paisley and handed it off with one of her signature eyes-nearly-shut smiles.

"Happy Stepmom Day, Paisey!"

"Oh my gosh, this is amazing!" Paisley took the coffee and reached down to hug Elise. "Come up here, lovebug."

Elise scrambled up on the bed and found a way to have most of her body lying on Paisley's. Those two had gotten so close over the last five months it almost made me jealous.

"We have toes and hot chocolate and lunch!"

Paisley sipped her coffee and stroked her fingers through Elise's dark curls. "What?"

Yep, I was definitely jealous. I wanted Paisley stroking me. I picked up Meatball as he started to bark about all the excited voices. The little guy had put on some weight, filling out to almost his full size of twenty pounds. He lay in my arms for a full three seconds and then leaped to lick me across the face.

"Jesus, Meatball!"

"He just loves you, Daddy," Elise reminded me, as she always did.

"He could love me better if he didn't crap on my shoes," I muttered. This dog had it out for me.

"Shouldn't have left them out in the backyard," Paisley said just loudly enough I could hear.

Elise giggled, and the two of them shared a look. I knew that look well. I hoped to always see them teasing me like little co-conspirators. That's what today was all about. Sure, it was to celebrate Paisley being an amazing mother figure to Elise, but there was so much more I had planned.

"Okay, E-bug, let's get to scrambling those eggs while Paisley gets ready." I put Meatball down and watched him follow Elise out the door.

I felt Paisley slide her arms around my waist from behind. "Stepmom Day?"

I stroked her arms, loving the way she felt pressed against me. I was crazy for this woman and so was my daughter. "Yep. Hallmark needs to get with the program. Stepparents get all the responsibility and none of the recognition, but not on my watch."

Paisley's hands slid to my crotch. "You're sexy when you get all fierce."

Clenching my teeth, I removed her hands and turned around. "Go get ready, woman. You have a hot chocolate pickup at Crazy Beans at nine thirty, pedicures at Nailed It at ten, and lunch at Grass at noon."

Paisley's face split into the kind of smile that made my

stomach feel all gooey like a chocolate chip cookie. "You really planned a whole day for me?"

I smacked her on the ass and pushed her toward the bedroom. "Fuck, yes, I did. Now put some underwear on or you'll make all the old men in town have heart attacks when you flash them."

I got her and Elise on the road right on time. I'd gone to all the places and paid for the services and tipped like I was made of money so Paisley wouldn't have to worry about a thing. That gave me about three hours to get my next plan in place.

***

"THIS SHIT IS THE DEVIL," I muttered under my breath. The paper streamers I'd intended to string all along the band stage either ripped or wrapped around my body. I heard a snort from behind me and nearly clotheslined myself on the string of white lights I was also trying to string across the makeshift stage.

"Probably a pretty good idea you recruited us to help," Keva drawled.

Marlo just looked around and shook her head at the mess. Audrey was the only one who shot me an encouraging smile.

I waved a hand around. "I'm thinking we get the white lights up and scratch the streamers."

Keva put her hand up. "How about you get the golf cart ready and we'll handle the rest, big guy?"

I frowned at her, but quite frankly, I needed their help. Badly. "Fine."

I walked off and got behind the wheel of the brand-new electric golf cart I'd been hiding for two days behind one of the trailers on the far end of my property. I wanted the golf cart to be part of the surprise. It zoomed like a champ over the glamp-ground and made me grin like a kid. The child seat I'd had installed on the passenger side was all kinds of rad.

Another hour of work by many hands and we'd gotten the string lights up across the dance floor and another couple of strings up in the huge oak tree next to the stage. The streamers were somehow up along the sides of the stage and looked beautiful. The place was swept and as clean as it would ever be.

"You better have some fire extinguishers ready just in case," Marlo said, looking around at all the white candles that had been placed all around the space.

"Please. I'm a firefighter. I think I got it handled."

"Alright there, Smokey, just saying." Marlo held her hands up and backed away.

The girls left and intercepted Paisley and Elise as they were leaving Grass. They took a trip to the library, where they were under strict orders to make Paisley pick out a book to read. She kept saying how she used to like to read these romance books a few years back but had given them up for more serious non-fiction books that would help her on the job and in life. While gaining knowledge like that was admirable, I also pushed her to do some light reading, too. Being able to turn your brain off and relax was important. It just wasn't something Paisley was good at.

Besides, maybe if she checked out one of those super smutty romance books, she might turn some of that sexual tension on me. Double benefit, you know?

Keva's text came through right on time.

> Keva: Lucy just gave us the "bad news" about cutting your leg open. We're on our way back. Paisley is not happy you decided not to go to the emergency room.

I chuckled and put my phone in my back pocket. I'd asked Lucy to "run into" the girls as they came out of the library and let them know she'd just gotten a phone call from Bain. The story was that he'd been over here helping me with a project and I'd cut myself. I knew that would get Paisley swooping in to save the day. I also wanted her girlfriends with her to make sure she wasn't in a panic when she drove. Safety first, my friends.

I lit all the candles and checked my pocket for the hundredth time today. The first trickle of nerves set in. I wasn't at all nervous about changing my single status for life, but I was nervous she might turn me down. Talk about package deals. I was always bracing for her to realize that maybe an old guy like me with scars and a daughter—and a dog who couldn't control his bladder when belly-rubbed—wasn't quite what she envisioned for her future. Somehow, she seemed to like the chaos, so I was going to put a ring on it before she changed her mind.

I heard her truck before I saw it. That big engine was impressive, but the blonde bombshell in a pink sweater and skin-tight jeans sliding out of it without even turning off the truck was even more impressive. Elise was not with her, which made sense. I'd asked Keva to keep her in her car.

I needed a couple of minutes alone with Paisley before everyone else came.

"Gannon!" Paisley ran toward me, her hands hitting my chest and then sliding down all my extremities at once. "Where? What happened?"

I snatched her hands off of me and held them steady until her eyes quit frantically looking me up and down for injury.

"I thought I'd hit rock bottom, Paisley. I kept saying my life was over, and it was. Thank God."

Her whole body stilled. "What?"

"Moving here with Elise was a last-ditch attempt to patch together some sort of a life. And then I met you. In a towel and crutches, lighting me up for stealing your panties."

Paisley's mouth opened, then closed. Her gaze left mine for a quick second, widening as she finally took in the streamers, lights, and candles flickering all around us.

"Gannon?"

"I knew coming out here to Blueball would be the start of a new life for me, but I had no idea how perfect it would become. All because of you."

I got down on one knee, dipping into my pocket to pull out the diamond solitaire that was uncomplicated and stunning, just like my woman. I held the ring up and watched it catch the light from all the candles around us and the string lights above us.

Paisley gasped, and I wanted to freeze time. Her eyes filled with tears, but her body was stiff as if she was still in shock.

"I went through hell and came out a better man. Not because of the pain or uncertainty, but because you were standing on the other side, ready to love me, scars and all. We're gonna fight like cats and dogs some days, but I promise to always put you first, to support you in all you do. I have no idea what you want with a grumpy neighbor like me, but I'd be forever the luckiest bastard in all the county if you agreed to be my wife. Will you marry me, Pearse?"

A tear slipped down Paisley's cheek and I counted myself lucky that she felt comfortable enough to do so. Paisley only cried in front of a few trusted people, me being one of them.

"Yes, I will, cowboy," she whispered.

I stood up and spun her around, too relieved to remember to put the damn ring on her finger. I put her down on her feet, but kept my arms around her waist. Probably would never let her go again.

"No take-backsies."

Paisley threw her head back and laughed. "You don't make the rules, Hart."

"We'll see about that," I muttered.

"Shush and give me that ring." Paisley held her left hand out.

I slid the ring on her finger and something clicked into place. Everything about this felt right. As if every single one of my thirty-six years was leading me to this town, this glamp-ground, and especially this woman.

Paisley stared down at her hand, another tear falling. "It's beautiful, Gannon."

I tucked some hair behind her ear. "Not nearly as beautiful as you."

And then my lips were on hers, sealing in her answer. I didn't get enough time with her before a throat clearing had us lifting our heads. Marlo and Audrey stood there, but it was the golf cart zooming up that had Paisley's mouth dropping open again.

Keva was driving, her face beaming from behind the plexiglass shield of the golf cart. Elise was strapped into the car seat holding a poster she'd helped me color last week. The golf cart came to a stop in the dirt and Paisley slapped her hands to her mouth.

Will you be my stepmom for life?

Then my woman was running, skidding to a stop at the golf cart and crushing Elise to her in a hug that had all of us wiping our eyes. It wasn't enough that she said yes to me, I needed her to say yes to all of it.

"Daddy said you have to say yes or no," Elise said when Paisley let up on her grip.

Paisley lifted her head to find me standing right next to her. Tears were bubbling over and I knew she'd give me shit later for making her cry. Totally worth it. She looked back at my little girl and my own eyes got misty.

"Absolutely yes. I'd love to be your stepmom forever."

"Told ya, Daddy!" Elise hollered and then giggled uncontrollably as Paisley wrapped her up in a hug once again.

Meatball barked from the backseat of the golf cart. I was sure he had faces to lick, but I'd gotten a tie-down installed back there just to keep him controlled.

"Let's party!" Audrey shouted.

Paige let out a holler as she and John came out from behind a huge tree. Bain and Lucy and their crew of kids helped shove the picnic tables closer. Diego and Mandy brought out the food and got everything set up so that we could eat all night. Other people I didn't know that well were here because Paisley's friends had insisted on it. I didn't care who the hell was here. All I cared about was that Paisley was ours. Forever.

"I can't believe you planned all this," Paisley whispered, burrowing into my side with wide eyes.

"I can't believe you didn't argue with me over my proposal," I muttered back.

She pinched my ass so hard I yelped.

"Behave yourself, woman. Your parents are here."

Paisley snorted. "They know better than anyone I like riding the pole. *Your* pole, cowboy."

I gasped. "Talking dirty at your engagement party? For shame."

Paisley looked up at me, those hazel eyes looking as happy as I felt. "Is there something else you want me to do with my mouth?"

I dropped my head. "Lord have mercy. We need to mingle, woman, but you better not be making promises you can't keep."

Paisley went up on her tiptoes and kissed me. "I'll keep the most important one of all. I'll love you forever."

And then I went against my own order and did not mingle. I kissed the hell out of my woman and I wasn't even sorry.

***

Keva

I WAS FINALLY happy for those two. I'd put away all my baggage around love and seen them for what they were. But truth be told, they were so adorable it made me a little sick to my stomach. Janice, my next-door neighbor who'd become like a mother to me, handed me Lucas. She watched him so much I had to admit that she and I were both raising him.

"Hey, baby." I kissed his little head and breathed him in. "Did you get some cake?"

He shook his head and kicked his legs. He was doing that more and more these days, wanting to be running around instead of in my arms. It made my heart ache to give him space, but I knew I had to do it.

"No, Mama." He tugged on my hand, pulling me in the direction of the dessert table.

"You want anything, Janice?" I asked over my shoulder.

Janice shook her head and edged toward the quieter side of the glamp-ground. I knew where she was going. She needed to light up a cigarette and inhale that nicotine. She'd tried to quit a dozen times over the last few years, but always gave in. Thankfully, she never smoked around Lucas, which would have been a deal breaker for me.

Lucas pointed at each of the desserts he wanted to try, but as the number increased past five, I made him narrow it down so he wouldn't be up all night on a sugar high. Marlo waved me over and we went to go sit with her at a picnic table. We ate our desserts and watched everyone dancing, Paisley and Gannon in the middle of it all, softly rocking back and forth to a fast-paced song.

"Those two." I shook my head and Marlo snorted.

"I know." Marlo put her head in her hand and stared at them. Almost wistfully.

"Marlo? You okay?" Marlo was never wistful. Stoic, deadpan, and realistic to a fault, but never wistful.

"Keva!" Audrey hit the table with her hip, unable to slow down her run. She didn't even wince.

"What is the matter with—"

She cut me off. "He's here." Audrey was breathing so hard I started to get alarmed.

"Who's here?"

I could see the whites of Audrey's eyes all the way around her brown irises. She flicked a glance at my son and it was official. I was panicked. If something affected Lucas, I went into full mama bear mode. It just happened. A program of nature for mamas to protect their young. I rose from my seat and grabbed her face, pulling her attention back to me.

"Who, Audrey?"

Her fish lips, squeezed between my fingers, opened and closed. Then her eyes turned sympathetic, and the blood froze in my veins.

"Linc."

IF YOU NEED MORE of Gannon and Paisley, I don't blame you! Download their extended epilogue here.

STAY TUNED FOR BOOK #2 in the Blueball Band of Brothers...

ALSO BY MARIKA RAY

<u>All Steamy RomComs Set in Hell:</u>

Grumpy As Hell - Hellman Brothers #1

Bro Code Hell - Hellman Brothers #2

Friend Zone Hell - Hellman Brothers #3

Cougar From Hell - Hellman Brothers #4

Falling First Hell - Hellman Brothers #5

***

Ridin' Solo - Sisters From Hell #1

One Night Bride - Sisters From Hell #2

Smarty Pants - Sisters From Hell #3

Ex Best Thing - Sisters From Hell #4

***

Love Bank - Jobs From Hell #1

Uber Bossy - Jobs From Hell #2

Unfriend Me - Jobs From Hell #3

Side Hustle - Jobs From Hell #4

Man Glitter - Jobs From Hell Novella - Grab it FREE here!

***

Backroom Boy - Standalone

<u>Steamy RomComs:</u>

The Missing Ingredient - Reality of Love #1

Mom-Com - Reality of Love #2

Desperately Seeking Househusbands - Reality of Love #3

***

Happy New You - Standalone

<u>Steamy RomComs with Delancey Stewart</u>:

The Spare and the Single Mom

<u>Sweet RomComs with Delancey Stewart</u>:

Texting With the Enemy - Digital Dating #1

While You Were Texting - Digital Dating #2

Save the Last Text - Digital Dating #3

How to Lose a Girl in 10 Texts - Digital Dating #4

<u>Sweet Romances</u>:

The Marriage Sham - Standalone

***

The Widower's Girlfriend-Faking It #1

Home Run Fiancé - Faking It #2

Guarding the Princess - Faking It #3

***

Lines We Cross - Nickel Bay Brothers #1

Perfectly Imperfect Us - Nickel Bay Brothers #2

<u>Steamy Beach Romance</u>:

1) Sweet Dreams - Beach Squad #1

2) Love on the Defense - Beach Squad #2

3) Barefoot Chaos - Beach Squad #3

* Novella - Handcuffed Hussy

4) Beach Babe Billionaire- Beach Squad #4

5) Brighter Than the Boss - Beach Squad #5

* Novella - Christmas Eve Do-Over

Bookbub - https://www.bookbub.com/authors/marika-ray

TikTok - https://vm.tiktok.com/ZMJvnQ2Cv